In Spite of It All

Constance Bierkan

outskirts
press

PRAISE FOR IN SPITE OF IT ALL

"Bierkan matches the fine historical details with a bubbling plot involving Claire and Madeleine [whose] offbeat love stories generate engaging momentum.

"The mission to recover the collection of Nazi propaganda art is played out skillfully alongside the story of the famed, real-life Monuments Men,… and at the center… is a pair of German soldiers… whose lack of intelligence is used for well-timed comic relief.

"An atmospheric and often involving international tale… Bierkan appears to have done an impressive amount of historical research, as she manages to evoke both the brutality of life in post-war Germany and the heedless indolence of some Americans during wartime with dramatic effectiveness."

Kirkus Reviews

PRAISE FOR FREE TO BREATHE

Wyoming, 1907. The winters are always harsh in the Rockies but, this year, the cold is the least of Ryder Tibbs' worries. He's seventeen when he watches his mother finally pack her things and march out of his life.

An avid reader, all Ryder's ever wanted is to go to college—but now, with his father's cruel eyes fixed solely on him, that dream is slipping out of reach. "No man makes a decent wage from a pile of books," Joby insists. Ryder wants to argue, to fight—but defying his father, even over the right to choose his own future, is something he's never even considered, let alone tried.

It's only when he meets Montana, an eccentric and rough mountain woman with a fierce streak a mile long, that hope begins to sprout. If Ryder's going to make it in this grim world, she says, he's got to find the courage to stand up for himself—and she knows just how to go about it.

Free to Breathe is the latest novel by Kirkus Star-winning author Constance Bierkan. In this tender and atmospheric tale, Bierkan leads the reader into the wild heart of Wyoming, but also into the heart of every boy who yearns to be free..

"Bierkan is an adept storyteller, confident in her craft. [She] accentuates the tale's pacing with frequent and beautiful evocations of the bucolic setting, as when Ryder notes 'the scented cold before a snowfall' or when he notices the wild world around him: 'I looked to the horizon along the Sierra Madre, which was glowing pink as the early morning sun rose over the Snowy Range to shine upon the freshly fallen snow'. *"

Kirkus Reviews

PRAISE FOR ALONE IN A CROWDED ROOM
AN ADOPTION STORY

When five-year-old Lexie Saunders learns she is adopted and is told she is handpicked by Mother from a line-up of baby cribs, her life is forever changed. Instead of feeling special, Lexie becomes haunted by "Mama," the mystery lady who gave birth to her.

The disappearance of Mama leaves a hole in Lexie's heart, keeping her separate and feeling different from others. She often experiences acute loneliness even in the midst of a crowd of friends or family. Were she to learn the reason for her adoption, perhaps she would feel complete. However, searching for Mama means a possible rejection plus it might devastate the mother who has raised her.

Lexie, Mama, and Mother have each suffered greatly: one the loss of a mother, one the loss of a child, and one the loss of fertility. Together in the adoption triad, they are like the notes of a musical chord, inextricably intertwined for better or worse.

In recognition of her adopted grandparents and aunt's unconditional love, Lexie will eventually gain the courage to search for answers plaguing her over a lifetime. Will they bring closure or open old wounds? (192 words)

"**Bierkan is a powerfully evocative writer**, and the way she depicts the bond between mother and unborn child is uncanny . . . In this poignant work filled with emptiness, loss, love, and hope the prose is startlingly realistic . . . The result is a deeply affecting story that may prove a source of comfort to those with similar adoption experiences . . A masterful adoption tale: heart-rending and life-affirming in equal measure."

Kirkus Reviews

"Fear is a reaction.
Courage is a decision."
Winston Churchill

*I dedicate this to my mother, whose courage
in 1945 is an inspiration.*

*Margaret Buck Reynolds
1918-2020*

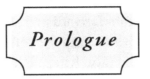

Prologue

1945

Before dawn of an April morning, thick layers of fog seeped into the village of Merkers, Germany. With this ghost-like quality hanging over the entrance to Kaiseroda Mine, two members of the Hitler Youth were provided with the perfect cover for their secret mission. They were there on orders from Nazi high command to seize a hidden stockpile of Hitler's commissioned and much coveted propaganda art. This stash, created by a stable of artists Hitler had personally selected as early as the mid-1930s, currently lay sequestered hundreds of feet below the earth's surface. Until recently it had been free from detection by the Allies.

General Eisenhower's army, however, had discovered the mine along with hordes of other artifacts and treasures from all over Europe. Generals Eisenhower, Bradley, and Patton unanimously determined to confiscate the propaganda art as soon as it could be arranged. As for the art stolen from museums and private collections, that was for the Monuments Men to return to their rightful owners.

Ernst and Klaus, two of Hitler's last conscripts, and young men who were still wet behind the ears, were tasked with taking control of the propaganda before the Americans could secure it for all time.

A pair of growling Rottweilers confronted Ernst as he hopped down from the truck. He stood stock still, staring at them. As they glared back, quivering, ears forward and showing their teeth, Ernst reached back into the cab and extracted a fresh hunk of bloody deer meat. The dogs looked hungry. After he lobbed it at their feet, the dogs pounced on it. While they tore at their windfall, Ernst tossed his still-glowing cigarette butt to the ground and entered the mine unimpeded. Before he even pushed the "down" button on the shaft elevator, the dogs were dead.

Ernst, skinny as a reed, heart pounding in his scrawny throat, struggled into the hidden chamber. It was pitch dark, damp, and musty. But soon enough, he found a switch on the wall and dared to bring up some light from a single bulb dangling from the ceiling. Levering the door to Room 5 open with his backside, he entered, wheeling a dolly with him. Haphazardly, Ernst began to load multiple crates of all shapes and sizes. Each time he was ready to send up the cargo in the tiny four-by-four-foot elevator, he shouted to Klaus for an all clear. The racket of their voices echoing and ricocheting off the cave walls made both cringe in fear. Never mind that the mine's elevator whined like a banshee each of the nine times it went up and down the shaft until Room Five was completely emptied of its contents. If Ernst and Klaus were discovered, they'd be shot on the spot.

"I counted roughly four hundred pieces," Klaus complained, batting away a cloud of cigarette smoke.

"Yeah, well, be glad it wasn't five hundred," Ernst countered.

Klaus wasn't mollified. "What is this junk? And why do the Americans care about it?" He lit another cigarette. Blowing out the smoke in a long stream through his nose, he added. "This goddamn war is making our guys think up some pretty crazy ideas. Let the

Americans keep it. I couldn't care less!"

Ernst wagged a finger at Klaus. "You call it *junk*? This is price-less art, considering our people might want to see a Fourth Reich someday." He pulled the door closed. "Start the truck. I'll be right back."

Suddenly, a pair of low-flying B-17's screamed overhead. Bombs began exploding near enough to shake the ground these boys were standing on. And the answering salvo of gunfire from their own side forced Ernst and Klaus to dive for cover. Anti-aircraft shells flew over their heads. The whole business was over before Ernst realized he'd pissed himself while Klaus had heaved up his breakfast. Not too far away, dogs began barking. Men were shouting. They held their breath and craned their heads to listen.

"Fuck, we gotta get outta here!" Klaus hissed.

"No shit! Wait a sec, though." Ernst ran back to the entrance of the mine.

"Hey, come back here! We gotta skedaddle."

Picking up a chunk of salt, Ernst drew an image on the rock face. It was a facsimile of an American cartoon, a taunt left by the advanc-ing Allied troops to infuriate the Germans by bragging about their capturing a town or redoubt first. Ernst thought it hilarious to turn the tables on those damned Yanks.

Kilroy was here!

When the truck's stubborn engine finally roared to life and gath-ered a modicum of speed, only a silvery half moon threw any light on the road. At Klaus' urging, they did not use their headlights. Neither man chose to speak, each lost in his own thoughts about the mission ahead.

"It's a good thing we have this much light," Ernst said, striking a positive chord. "Let's be glad the Americans haven't spotted us."

"I s'pose. But until the sun comes up, travel west is gonna be real slow." Klaus leaned over the steering wheel to better discern the dirt track ahead. "What's our ultimate destination, do you know?"

"Nope. Instructions for each layover, however many those might be, will be available at each of our stops."

"What's our first stop?"

"Larochette."

"Never heard of it. Where's that?"

"Luxembourg."

Thirteen hundred and sixty-three kilometers away, a member of the Resistance, co-ordinating with the American government, known only as *Le Petit Oiseau* or Little Bird, received a telegram. It read:

OPERATION PROTECT PROP ART
IS NOW IN PLAY STOP

Claire

September - December 1944

Chapter One

When the first light of dawn pinked the sky over New York City's skyscrapers, the city was instantly awash in a rosy cast of promise. It was September 10, 1944. Claire Fitzgerald's wedding day.

In her shabby studio on State Street, one block east of the Battery, Claire sat up in bed, arched her back, and stretched mannequin arms high and wide above her head. She faced the single ray of sunshine streaming through her window and smiled. Outside, the persistent jackhammering on the Brooklyn–Battery Tunnel had already begun, while the far-off bellow of the seven o'clock Staten Island Ferry announced its arrival into Whitehall Terminal.

Claire's rose-petal complexion, which rarely required any makeup, glowed. And why wouldn't it? The prospect of walking down the aisle and into the arms of William Wentworth Campbell III filled her with a radiance no cosmetics could ever replicate. Furthermore, the tides of Hitler's rampage across Europe were finally turning. In June, the Allies had stormed the beaches of Normandy and gotten a foothold on German-occupied soil. The subsequent liberation of Paris, Florence, Brussels, and Antwerp were all very good reasons to feel reassured that World War II would be over by year's end. Everyone predicted it, and she, an America Firster, would gladly be done with it. When she'd first met Billy, she had been a card-carrying member of an organization opposed to America's entry into World War II. She and her friends from the fashion world ardently believed the interests of the United States should always take precedence over those of foreign countries. Why expend life and coin abroad when there were needs still unmet at home? As passionately as she had felt, she nevertheless hid her official membership in the America Firster organization from Billy, knowing neither he nor his family would approve of such an affiliation.

Claire smiled. Not only had she succeeded in luring Billy off New York's bachelor roster, she had also managed to secure a marriage proposal everyone had warned her would never come. Many pretty girls from prominent families had tried and failed, because William Wentworth Campbell III had doggedly clung to his bachelorhood. Flopping back against the pillows, Claire raised her hand to the sunlight to admire the brilliant four-carat diamond perched on her ring finger. A kaleidoscope of color danced on the opposite wall. She'd won!

Becoming a Campbell meant Claire would be part of a most distinguished family, ranked just beneath the Vanderbilts or the DuPonts. Not bad for an Irish girl from the Bronx whose German-born widower father was a custodian at the Plaza Hotel and could barely speak English at an eighth-grade level. While Claire couldn't help reveling in her personal coup, she did love Billy for his bon vivant spirit. The man enjoyed every benefit his social standing provided, but he didn't seem to care a whit about any of the luxuries. Billy didn't look down his nose at others. He rather liked to lift up the morale of those who were less fortunate than he, but not necessarily because it was the kind thing to do for others as much as it was because it made him feel needed. Claire didn't see it at first. All she knew was that he made her feel comfortable, especially while learning to navigate his social circle. Claire counted on her marriage to William Campbell to bring her a happier and better life than the one marking her formative years. After today, she would no longer be bound by her difficult past.

Claire was born in 1918, the year of the Spanish influenza. An estimated fifty million people were killed worldwide. Claire's mother, severely weakened by a flu-infected pregnancy and protracted labor, never fully recovered after childbirth. When she fell victim to the flu again in 1925, she never did recover. Claire was but a little girl of seven, old enough to remember her mum, too young to understand why she was taken from her. Shortly afterward, Claire's father shipped her off to Staten Island to live with his sister, Elsa. He had had no idea how to raise a child, and even less a girl. So for ten years, Claire lived in a house where there was no affection, a lot of emotional harassment, and only one bed to share with her two female cousins. In the same room were her two male cousins, whose crude talk and unwanted glances kept her vigilant most nights. By the time she was seventeen, she was so deeply resentful of her father's abandonment that she dropped all contact with him.

Claire's one outlet from the drudgery under Aunt Elsa's roof was school. There she could thrive, engage with peers, and be recognized for the academic excellence she achieved. In fact, her studies came so easily to her that she won a full scholarship to Barnard College, Columbia University's sister school on Manhattan's Upper West Side. Unable to afford the books or the daily commute from Staten Island, Claire was forced to turn down the invitation to join Barnard's Class of 1940. Devastated, Claire chose to go to work instead. Soon enough, Claire's aunt had begun to grouse about how many mouths she had to feed, so she demanded Claire pay her for room and board. Rather than pay her aunt money for so little in exchange, Claire moved to lower Manhattan and found work there—first with the Bell Telephone Company, then as a dental hygienist. Though both these jobs provided reliable sources of income, Claire was bored. She wanted excitement. After much encouragement from her friends and co-workers, Claire decided to pursue a model-ing career and soon she was recognized as the "Runaway Runway Belle" of New York's fashion industry. Always in demand by both Bloomingdale's and Bergdorf Goodman, she was the star of both stores' spring/summer and fall/winter fashion shows. She usually led the parade of girls and was almost always selected to wear the wedding gown at the show's grand finale.

It was at one such show back in February, a mere nine months earlier, when she'd met Billy. He'd accompanied his mother to the Bryant Park gala event and Claire had felt his eyes on her the entire time. When she asked her boss who the handsome fellow was, she'd already hatched a plan to make his acquaintance. Later at the recep-tion, she managed to linger near enough to Billy's entourage for him to palm his calling card into her hand. When his mother noticed the mutual attraction with some displeasure, she whisked him from the venue and into their chauffeur-driven Cadillac. Billy had winked and shot Claire a roguish grin. Claire called him a tasteful three days later.

Lifting the studio portrait of Billy from her bedside table, Claire said aloud to his smiling face, "How different you are from me, Billy Campbell." Billy's easy confidence was something she'd nev-er been able to achieve. She tended toward being self-conscious, which made her awkward. Usually, it made others uncomfortable, too. So, while she loved the theatrics of modeling and the attention it brought in terms of celebrity, she struggled to rise above the fear that she might be judged as superficial. After all, Claire was a good student with many academic accolades. She was hardly vacuous. Hanging out with other models was often difficult, though, as she felt the need to hide her intellect and simply go along. These girls were hard-working and certainly well-intentioned. They didn't de-serve her scorn. Besides, many of them had great senses of humor despite their personal hardships, and that levity was an inspiration.

The one thing on which they all agreed was their desire to marry and to marry well.

Claire touched Billy's image. "I'm counting on you, Billy Campbell. Make me whole, won't you?" Instantly, however, Claire dropped that plea. Billy didn't like it when she became too needy. He wanted her to feel secure enough to stand on her own two feet and not rely on him for her well-being. Claire swung her legs to the floor. Folding her hands in her lap and bowing her head to pray to a God she'd formally renounced a year prior, Claire whispered, "Dear God, thank you for bringing me Billy. I promise to make him a happy man." She stood up, satisfied with herself for showing gratitude instead of just pleading for something. But when an afterthought struck, she plopped back down again and squeezed her eyes shut. "PS, I think I deserve a little happiness after all I've been through, don't you?"

At precisely five o'clock, Claire stood at the entrance to the Grand Ballroom of the Plaza Hotel. *Show time*, she thought. A cello–guitar duo began to play Pachelbel's Canon in D and the congregation, turning as one, let go a collective sigh of approval. Claire was the epitome of elegance as she made her solo approach to the altar. Wearing a satin dress with a high round neckline, long sleeves of lace, and full ball gown skirt, Claire glided gracefully down the aisle, hips thrown forward, her model's pace proud. Her only adornment was a pair of pearl earrings given to her by Billy's father, Commodore Randall Campbell. Claire approached Billy with all the aplomb she had acquired during her years on the catwalk. No one could see that underneath the bouquet of pink and white peonies with cascading greenery, her hands were trembling. She could feel all the eyes of New York's upper crust boring into her, and she feared they were judging her, coming to unkind conclusions. *She's terribly pretty; no wonder Billy fell so hard* or more likely, *She must be preggers and Billy's just doing right by her.* Better yet, *Wouldn't be at all surprised if she's marrying him for his money.* And finally, *It won't last, you know . . .*

Claire handed her bouquet to one of the little flower girls whose crown of Shasta daisies was slipping over her ear. Billy, ever the charmer, stepped off the altar to straighten the child's headdress. After he kissed the little girl's flushed cheek, an aggregate of *aw*'s wafted from the rows of gold Chiavari chairs behind them. As usual, Billy had captured the hearts of everyone in the room.

Billy reached for Claire's hand, his robin's-egg-blue eyes sparkling. He glanced at her red lips and said softly enough that only she could hear, "Hey, gorgeous, you ready to do this?"

Claire looked up into his face and saw that the dimple she found so delightful was forming in his suntanned cheek. It reminded her of the first time she'd laid eyes on him nine months earlier and had hoped this irresistible man was single. She placed her hand over his starched piqué shirt and murmured, "If you'll still have me."

Billy turned to the minister. "The lady says 'Let's go,' Reverend."

As soon as Reverend Reynolds said "You may kiss the bride," Billy cupped Claire's cheeks in both hands and whispered, "I loves ya, Fitzie." His kiss was deep and slow and unabashed. When he pulled away, his arms were still around her. "Look outside," he said, nodding toward the window. "A rainbow. It's God's promise."

Claire was so touched by the hoarseness of emotion in his voice, a tear slid down her cheek. She shook her head, as she was wont to do when discomfited. "All our dreams are painted on that sky."

Flashbulbs erupted in strobes of white and blue once the wedded couple turned to walk down the aisle. Cameras clicked and whirred while the paparazzi surged against the red and gold rope barely keeping them constrained at the back of the ballroom.

"Oh, my goodness," Claire exclaimed. "I didn't know they'd be here."

"I'm so sorry," Billy muttered. "Mother must have commandeered them for the society pages. Shall I send them away?"

"It's fine. Let them riot," Claire said through her teeth as she smiled into the lenses thrust in front of her. "I'm used to it."

"Well, I hate it." Billy had always avoided the paparazzi while Claire, who never wanted to let on that she secretly loved it, welcomed the attention. It meant she had "arrived."

It pleased Claire to no end that her new husband was such a stunner in his white tie tuxedo, the coat cut well back at his slim waist and a double-breasted v-shaped waistcoat highlighting his broad shoulders. From his wide-winged collar all the way down to his patent- leather pumps, Claire couldn't help basking in their combined bride-and-groom *Vogue Magazine* glamor. Appearances mattered.

To Claire, the receiving line was an endless parade of shallow greetings and inconsequential remarks, all of it exhausting though necessary for its traditional courtesy. Both Claire and Billy, bored to sobs, were relieved when the last to extend their blessings shuffled off. While white-gloved butlers passed hors d'oeuvres and poured Veuve Clicquot into crystal flutes, a cacophony of voices, mostly male, were haranguing about the war.

"The Nazi Party's dream of a thousand-year reign is the fantasy of a lunatic," offered one fellow within earshot. "But methinks it's doomed."

"No question," said his elderly companion, whose skin was wrinkled like a rumpled bedsheet. "That damned Third Reich was built on nothing more than sand. Now that our boys are there, it's about to be washed out to sea."

"I still say something should be done to stop that madman," interrupted another, joining the group. "Do you suppose Hitler's military might turn on him?"

"The Führer ought to be shot," exclaimed the first fellow.

"Wouldn't that be grand? We'd have victory in Europe a lot sooner."

Billy, whose back had been to this lot of old codgers, now turned to join them. Claire was obliged to turn as well, as she was on Billy's arm, but she didn't like what she was hearing. Not because she supported Hitler, but because she hated the topic of war and saw no end to it. "You fellas do realize," she interrupted, "America's next enemy will be Russia, don't you?"

The gentlemen, most of them Billy's father's friends from the Yacht Club, seemed startled by Claire's suggestion the war might not end so quickly. She continued, "I read that Stalin will force the Nazi-occupied countries liberated by his armies into becoming Russian satellites. It won't matter one whit if Herr Hitler is gone." For someone who hated war as much as she did, she was nevertheless well informed. "Eastern Europe will merely exchange one yoke of tyranny for another." What she didn't dare say was that that's what always happened with war- mongering. Who could wield the biggest stick, lob the heaviest bomb, or have the last word? As far as she knew, peace was never given a chance.

"No, dammit!" bellowed the mustachioed man. "FDR and Churchill will never let that happen."

Claire felt Billy looking at her. She couldn't tell whether he was proud of her for speaking up or dismayed by her pessimism. Hopefully, the former, as he hadn't added anything to the discussion.

"We'll have to see, now won't we?" said Billy. "Of course there's the Pacific theater, too. Who knows how long those Nips will hold out." Claire shook her head at his offensive language.

"Quite right," the men agreed.

"Let's go," Billy said into Claire's ear.

"You mean just slip away?"

Billy pulled Claire into a dark alcove and rubbed the back of her neck. He kissed the top of her head. She stood there with her eyes closed, forgetting for a moment where she was.

Billy suddenly grabbed her hand and led her across the dance floor as if on a mission. Bypassing all the conventions — first dance, best man's toast, dinner, and even the carving of their three-tiered chocolate raspberry truffle cake bedecked with pearls, ruffles, and plump roses of ganache — he was making his escape.

At the exit, he stopped abruptly. "I should ask you if you mind?"

She did a little, but his rebelliousness was so contagious, she said, "Whisk me away, good knight!"

"Billy?" called his mother, rushing after them. "You mustn't leave yet." She clung to Billy's sleeve. "Whatever will everyone say?"

"Have pity, Mama," Billy cajoled. "This gala is indeed lovely, and Claire and I thank you for this incredible party . . ."

"Why do I hear a 'but' coming?"

"Because you do. This extravaganza is more for you and Father. Not us." His mother's sharp intake of breath could be heard at the table nearest the door where they were standing. Those guests craned to listen.

"There is too much talk of war," Billy hissed. "It upsets Claire and I find it entirely unsuitable for our wedding day. So, I must ask for yours and Father's forgiveness with permission to be excused."

Not waiting for his mother's answer, Billy snatched a silver plateful of petit fours sitting on a side table and stuffed them in his pocket. "These are delicious, by the way." Then he strode from the ballroom. Claire shrugged her apology, seeming to say *I must do as my husband wishes* and pitter-pattered after him, her kid leather heels clicking across the black and white marble floor to where he waited.

Chapter Two

At the double-door entrance to the bridal suite, Billy swept Claire into his arms and cradled her close to his chest. Butting the door open with his hip and stepping inside, he paused to look into his bride's eyes.

"Here we are, Mrs. Campbell. Are you ready for some serious lovin'?"

Claire, a shy virgin who had insisted they wait until they were married, dropped her head on his shoulder in a bashful gesture of submission.

A canopy bed strewn with rose petals awaited with the satin sheets already turned down. Claire trembled and her liquid brown eyes were round with apprehension.

"May I undress you?" Billy asked as his gaze roved up and down her petite figure. She hesitated. "Please tell me you're not planning on making me wait any longer than I already have?"

What was that supposed to mean, Claire wondered. But when Billy winked at her mischievously, Claire chose to not take his comment as a complaint, but rather a tease. Billy, recognizing his gaffe, covered for his tactlessness. "Wait, what I meant was are you going to make your grand entrance adorned in something ultra-fine and tantalizing."

She had spent almost a month's wages on a negligée set, but

it seemed silly at that moment to be setting the stage for the inevitable disrobing. Maybe, Billy was feeling as awkward as she. Claire looked up at the ceiling, then down at the floor. She opened her mouth to speak, but was at a loss for words.

"Come here," he whispered. When his lips touched hers in a slow and sultry kiss and his hand cupped her breast, all her senses began to hum.

Fluttering out of his embrace, Claire said in a higher voice than was her norm, "I don't know why I'm so nervous. I feel like I've known you all my life, so I shouldn't be—."

"Hush," Billy said. "How am I supposed to get you out of this dress if you're going to fidget?" But then Billy fell across the bed, pulling her down on top of him. "I want you now!" he cried, his excitement pressing hard against Claire's hips. Then in one fluid move, Billy pushed clouds of wedding satin out of his way and had his way. It seemed as though he didn't even realize what he was doing. Had he forgotten this was her first time?

Claire tensed and bit her lower lip so hard it bled. She cried out upon his final selfish thrust.

Falling back onto his back, spent and breathing hard, he gushed. "I'm so sorry! But please understand I've wanted you since the day I first laid eyes on you."

"I'll be all right," she soothed, none too sincerely. "You got me through the painful part fast." What she didn't say was that she'd wished there had been more romance.

"I'll be more gentle next time." He pulled the sheet over their naked bodies and promptly fell asleep. At some point between rounds two and three—or was it four—they had discarded their clothes in order to explore each other's bodies. She had delighted in his feather-light touch. When it was her turn to pleasure Billy, he guided her hand and showed her what he liked.

Past midnight, both were staring up at the coffered ceiling, too

17

dazed to sleep and a little drunk from the Meursault Billy had opened earlier. Far below on Fifth Avenue, honking traffic and shouts for taxis reverberated up and down the cement canyons of Manhattan's Upper East Side.

"A penny for your thoughts," Billy murmured.

"I was thinking how when I left home, I tried to erase every bit of my past. Losing Mummy, being cast out by my father and sent to live with my aunt, not having enough money to accept the scholarship from Barnard, which is an oxymoron when you think about it, my selfish aunt expecting me to pay for my own keep, and then finding out..." Claire stopped mid-sentence.

"Finding out what?" Billy sat up and leaned on one elbow. "Tell me."

Claire rolled away. "It doesn't matter. I've come to learn that one's past cannot be expunged. That, unfortunately, it seems to travel with you."

"Okay," he drawled, "but what does 'expunge' mean?"

Claire rose, took a sip of wine from her glass by the side of the bed, and remained pensive. Billy folded his arms behind his head and crossed his ankles. Claire could tell that he was eager to know what was on her mind, but she couldn't bring herself to expose her darkest secret; not yet. Especially not on their wedding night. It would have to wait. All she did say, however, was something very opaque. "I guess it's a matter of whether I run from my past or learn from it."

"Yeah, okay. I suppose I agree with that, but what were you going to tell me?"

Claire wrapped herself in a cashmere throw blanket, downed the last of her wine, then padded into the bathroom and locked the door.

Chapter Three

Even though Claire was mightily disappointed when she found out what Billy had planned for their honeymoon, she smiled and held her tongue. In all honesty, a ten-day stay at Thunderbird Hill, a dude ranch in Arizona, was not her idea of anything romantic or glamorous. In fact, it was downright thoughtless, given that she was not the outdoorsy type. Billy knew that. Niagara Falls, as corny as that was, would have been a good deal better. To make matters worse, Billy's wedding present to her was a pair of custom-made Lucchese cowgirl boots. She'd have preferred a roasting pan from Bloomingdale's.

"I know it's new for you, but you'll love it," Billy said.

At that moment, as if on cue, Billy's old cat, Sneakers, entered the library and wound his way around Claire's ankles. She shuddered. Didn't this darn feline know she wasn't fond of cats? "What in the world do you do on a dude ranch?" Claire asked, already nervous about the answer.

"There's horseback riding, skeet shooting, hiking, you name it. And at night, there are campfires with sing-alongs, moonlight rides, and square dancing."

"Sounds like a lot of snakes and bugs," Claire said as she watched Sneakers hop onto the sofa and deliberately park himself next to her. She sidled away, but he merely tucked his paws and tail under himself and gazed up at her unblinking. Claire sighed and changed tacks. "I take it you're familiar with this place?"

"I've been going there since I was a kid."

"Oh. I didn't know." There was still a lot she didn't know about Billy. With a sweep of her hand, Claire dislodged Sneakers from the chintz. He growled in protest and left in a huff.

Billy took the seat his cat had vacated and pulled Claire into his lap. Wrapping his arms around her slender waist, he said, "Mother and Father began taking me there in '25 or'26." Claire smiled at Billy's formal appellations for his parents, which were so unlike hers of *Mummy* and *Daddy*. "I was hooked on horses from the very first day I ran into the barn." Claire smiled again. She could just picture eight-year-old Billy windmilling his arms and kicking up clouds of gritty dirt in his brand-new Western boots.

"Years later, I had the pleasure of meeting Satin Baby, the new girl in town. That palomino filly was an Amazon. At seventeen hands, she was a vision in gold, the belle of the barn." Billy's expression was so wistful Claire thought he was recalling his first sweetheart . . . which in some respects, he was. "Anyway, it wasn't hard to get why Satin Baby was at the hitching post and not in the enclosure with the others, because she was stamping her creamy front leg and restlessly tossing her platinum head."

"You always did like flamboyant blondes . . ."

"Hey! What's that supposed to mean?" "Billy asked with mock sore feelings. "I married you, didn't I?" He poked her in the ribs.

"I was just kidding," Claire said. "You know the expression 'Blondes have more fun,' right?"

"I do. And the rest of that expression goes 'But brunettes get married.'"

The morning after they'd arrived at Thunderbird Hill, Billy took Claire to the barn for their ten o'clock ride. Frank, a grouchy old ranch farrier who'd worked there for years, hobbled around the corner as Billy led Claire into the barn. He was carrying his farrier's box of horseshoes, nails, hammers, anvil, nippers, and picks. As this cacophony of metal jangled against his blue-jeaned hip, his limp was plain to see. So was the angry scowl etched across his wizened face. He wagged a nicotine-stained finger in their direction.

"That damn bitch bit me!" he yelled, gesticulating toward Satin Baby. She was twenty-eight now, and apparently as cranky as old Frank. "I ain't ever shoein' that shrew agin!" He hurled the shoeing box to the floor. "In fact, goddammit, I quit!"

With no warning at all, nine hundred and thirty-five pounds of equine vengeance, powered by a backward kick from Satin Baby, struck Frank as he stomped by. The man went down howling, and as Satin Baby turned her focus to Claire, the uninvited stranger in her domain, Billy jumped in front of his wife. Both Claire and Billy backed up against the tack room wall with nowhere farther to retreat. Claire bleated and began to shake like a leaf.

The ranch hands out in the corral and up in the hay loft came running when they heard the commotion. They formed a semicircle in front of Satin Baby. Waving their hats and spreading a web of arms wide only made matters worse, because Satin Baby threw her head back in terror. With nostrils flaring, she whinnied a piercing scream and lifted off the ground in one upward sweep to stand on rear legs. She ripped away from the ring to which her halter rope was attached. She was both frightful and stupendous as thick tendrils of spun-gold mane made a fan in a shaft of morning sun. It was as if she just hung there, fore hooves menacingly pawing the air. Ears laid flat back against her neck, looking as mean as ever and intent on doing harm, she wheeled, still standing, to face

21

Claire again. Those big round eyes turned into oily black pools revealing her whites.

Claire slid to the floor behind Billy with a scream. Billy sprang forward, crossed his arms, and made himself taller. Employing an ominous yet somehow reassuring silence, he signaled a force of will Claire had never seen before. Billy staked a claim to ground he had no intention of surrendering. He did not move and neither did anyone else. Defeated, Satin Baby crashed to the ground all a-quiver and foaming at the mouth. Billy took one step forward and held out his flattened hand. She waited for what seemed like forever, glaring. Nobody dared to blink or breathe. The only sounds to be heard were the bluebottle flies hovering over the muck truck.

"Hey, old girl, remember me? Your best buddy?" Billy reached up to caress her neck. "You and me go way back." Satin Baby snorted and tossed her head. "I've brought someone I'd like you to meet." Billy reached for the rope dangling from her halter. "Her name is Claire and she's my wife." The men chuckled. "You gonna apologize to my wife for scaring the bejesus out of her?"

Satin Baby flicked her tail and let her head hang low as if contrite. She was no longer breathing hard or wild-eyed. Billy cradled her massive head against his shoulder "There, there, baby-doll," he crooned, gently tickling her whiskery chin.

The honeymooners did not ride that morning. Instead, Claire dragged Billy into the bar and ordered Bloody Marys. As for the rest of their vacation, Claire did not go near the barn. She tried to hike, but after encountering a rattlesnake on the trail, she opted for the indoors where she could read, presumably safe from the vagaries of the great outdoors.

"You ride, Billy," Claire had urged. "I wouldn't dream of depriving you of your favorite pastime."

"But, sweetheart, the whole point of being on a dude ranch is to be outside, enjoying all the things you can't do in a city. Plus, the whole point of a honeymoon is to do stuff together." He thought for a second. "'Course, we can do that every night, right?" He wiggled his eyebrows suggestively.

Claire ignored the innuendo. Instead she thought about Satin Baby, whom she'd watched from the patio one afternoon while Billy was fishing with the guys. That mare had been in full flight all afternoon long. She galloped from one end of the paddock to the other, coming to such sudden stops at the fence. With her forelegs locked in front of her, she practically sat on her rump in a cloud of dirt. Whatever for? She whinnied at nothing and no one, but then wheeled around to charge in the opposite direction as if being chased by a goblin. It was then Claire made up her mind that horses were too dangerous for her to try and ride. Their size, their strength, and their sheer madness was not for her to trust.

Once back home, Billy stated, "A dude ranch wasn't your thing, was it?"

"I'm afraid not." She sniffed and reached up her sleeve for a Kleenex.

"It would have been more fun if we'd been able to play together. I never saw you between breakfast and dinner."

"I'm sorry."

"Seriously, Claire, what would be your ideal vacation?"

"A trip to Europe," she answered quickly. "I've never been."

"Aside from the fact there's a war on and that's impossible, what would we do in Europe?" Billy rolled his eyes. "Don't tell me we'd read history books!"

"Well, since that's not your thing, I'd do the reading and then we'd go see the sights and I'd explain everything."

"Sounds like being back in school."

"All right. So let's try something else. Just nothing west of the Mississippi."

Billy tilted her chin upward with his finger. He was going to kiss her, she just knew it. With his lips slightly parted and his eyes drifting closed, his tongue began searching for hers.

Why did he always seem to think a kiss fixed everything? Claire laid a splay-fingered hand against his chest. "Not now, Billy."

Chapter Four

"Give it a chance, honey. In a few more weeks you'll be so used to Sneakers there won't be any more jitters."

Billy's cat gracefully jumped up and took up residence in Claire's lap. She sneezed and blew her nose. "Does that apply to an itchy throat and watery eyes too?"

Sneakers was a sweet-natured black cat with four white paws and a blaze across his nose. Gazing up at her with his inscrutable green eyes, he butted her chest with his silky-soft head.

"See? He loves you," Billy cajoled.

"Fine," Claire replied from behind her newspaper.

"'Fine,'" Billy repeated flatly. "When a woman says 'fine' it usually means it isn't."

Claire slapped her coffee cup into its saucer. "What do you want me to say, Billy?"

"Oh, I don't know. That you think Sneakers is a cute name, you know, given the white feet."

"It's hardly original." Claire immediately regretted her acerbic comment. So she decided to play along. "He looks like an Arthur. Or a Henry."

"You can't be serious."

"Okay." But for Claire it was not okay. Since when had they discussed the fact that she'd be sharing Billy's home with a cat? And why hadn't Billy remembered her telling him that whenever she was around one, she would dissolve into an unsightly puddle of mucus?

Sneakers squirmed, landed on the floor with a heavy thump, and sauntered across the sunroom as if he owned the place. On his way, he rubbed himself against the upholstered armchairs, the ottomans, and a table skirt, leaving in his wake long black hairs at every one of his rest stops. In front of the picture window, he hopped onto the sofa and sprawled across the cushions in a ray of sunlight. Claire watched in disgust. He seemed to be sleeping, but every now and then his ear twitched as if what he were really doing was eavesdropping on their conversation.

"How are you spending your day?"

"Tennis on the indoor court with the guys this morning, and if the weather holds I'll probably paint on the beach after lunch." He studied her. "You? What's on your agenda?"

"I'll probably read. I've only got a hundred pages or so left, and . . ."

"Oh, for the love of Pete, that's all you ever do is read!" Sneakers appeared out of nowhere and jumped back into Claire's lap. He began to knead her legs, nails partially out.

Claire leapt from her chair. "Dammit!" she cried, dumping the cat to the floor. Sneakers shuddered his contempt, arched his back and skittered away, skidding on the tile as he disappeared around the corner.

"Be nice to Sneakers. He loves you."

"That cat needs to be de-clawed."

Billy, ignoring that last statement, looked at Claire, his brilliant blue eyes beseeching. "Won't you please pick up a tennis racket?"

"I've already told you I don't know how."

"I'll sign you up for lessons with Jack Brewster, the pro."

"No thanks."

"Why not?"

"I'm not an athlete, Billy. I've already told you that," Claire considered her next remark. "A million times."

"I think anyone can learn a sport if they want to," Billy said. "You just don't want to."

"No doubt, you're right." Claire resisted sarcasm this time. "Honey, I don't want for us to argue."

"In other words, drop it?"

"Please." Claire folded the newspaper, placed it on the table with a pat and left the sunroom.

Claire was growing more and more frustrated with how much Billy complained about her reading. Instead of her reading less, she had always hoped that after their wedding and once they'd settled down, Billy would read more. For most of her life, books had been the escape hatch through which she could disappear after her mother had died. During those years growing up wondering why her father thought she'd be better off with an aunt who resented her, fiction had lifted her spirits. Novels were her friends who never let her down or challenged her for being different. Books meant good grades, which in turn meant college. Maybe even a career, though a profession other than teaching was not expected of women in the forties. *Oh, dear,* she thought. *What am I to do with a non-reader?*

Claire curled up on her chaise longue and opened Margery Sharp's best seller, *Cluny Brown*. Sneakers, much to Claire's dismay, helped himself to her lap again and settled in for a snooze.

Madeleine

October - December 1945

Chapter Five

Gull music filled the air while baby waves skated back and forth across the sand. Their rhythm was as melodic as a lullaby, which was why Madeleine came to Petite Plage, Little Beach, almost every afternoon. Here in this intimate Breton inlet of soft sand, Madeleine could forget about the German occupation of her beloved France. She hurried to her favorite spot above the algae-covered rocks hemming the cove. Slipping off her espadrilles, Madeleine dangled her bronzed legs over the edge.

Gazing across the English Channel, Madeleine watched white clouds stitch a satiny chain against a horizon of gray water. These temperamental waters had a tendency to match Madeleine's moods—gray as granite for when she was irked, otherwise azure when cheerful.

After the United States had entered the war, Madeleine, like every patriotic Frenchwoman, had begun praying for an Allied invasion. Living under a cloud of false normalcy yet restrained in every way by Nazi rule was driving her crazy. While there had been the daring and heroic evacuations from Dunkirk, the bombings of St. Nazaire, and the nightly air bombardment of nearby Saint-Malo, rationing for her had been the worst hardship. And, of course, her mother's tight restraints on her movements.

After the Armistice in June of 1940, the year Madeleine had

turned eighteen, a menacing calm descended over Kersaint. That is, until one afternoon when an armada of Nazi lorries rolled into town. At first, the German soldiers were polite and well-behaved, even jolly—singing and marching as the villagers looked on. After Hitler declared war on America, however, the Germans started acting like the occupiers they were, moving into the vacated holiday homes, taking advantage of all the contents. Not long after that, the officers actually demanded billets for their troops. The de Beaulieus' house, *grâce à dieu*, was too small, but by '43, a sentry had been installed on their roof, replete with siren and machine gun. German watch-men had eyes on the sea day and night, expecting the Allies to show up—just like Madeleine and her fellow villagers, but no one dared admit that to the occupiers.

The waves were rolling bigger now, lifting dinghies and sail-boats from the muck where they had lain lopsided for most of the day. Like sleeping dogs anchored by gravity, the boats were all pointing in the same direction by the tilt of the planet. A gust of wind lifted Madeleine's long blonde hair and whipped sharp ten-drils across her face, lashing her shamrock-green eyes. She gathered her hair into a knot at the nape of her neck while she contemplated Portsall, Kersaint's dilapidated sister village across the bay. A trail of screeching gulls shadowed a group of shrimp boats surfing the tide back into port. They were coasting because petrol was scarce and taking advantage of the tides was a means to stretch a fisher-man's monthly ration. The setting sun's rays refracted the reds, yel-lows, and greens of the moored craft bobbing from their buoys. Just an hour earlier, had Madeleine wanted to purchase a snack from Madame Benoit's crêperie, she could have walked across the bay's spongy bottom instead of all the way around. Brooding, as it turned out, had been preferable to fetching a flourless crêpe.

Madeleine tucked her knees to her chest and wrapped her arms around them, remaining in this posture until the sun slipped into the sea. She was more maudlin than usual today and for once she wasn't focusing on her own sorrows alone. For over a hundred and fifty years, harsh salty winds had weathered Portsall's buildings to the color of sand. The Breton blue shutters and window frames were cracked and flaking. In Kersaint it was no different. None of that had ever mattered before. The wear and tear lent the towns their charm. But ever since France had been occupied, Kersaint and her sister village looked as though they were not only tired of fighting the elements but sagging in submission to the occupation. She could see Nazi patrols loitering on the quay, smoking and talking, ogling the women as they walked by.

A chilly mist engulfed Madeleine in a veil of gray. It was time to go back home. Sunset was her curfew, and she was already late. She took one last look at the broad horizon where sea and sky made it possible to envision distant and exotic lands. She sighed deeply. Maybe I'll take off for Morocco, become a Bedouin femme fatale. She smiled to herself, a bemused grin as this thought took root. She began to skip, her heels kicking up small clouds of sand in her wake. *Je pense que oui.* Morocco here I come.

Along the dirt path that wound between hedgerows of wild roses, now a heavy jumble of drooping rose-hips, Madeleine heard a lorry, its engine coughing as it lumbered slowly into town. No one had fuel, so the sound of an engine usually meant trouble—Nazi trouble. She peered through a break in the pine trees. Usually, the only vehicles coming into town were Gestapo, their black and white swastikas flying ominously from their front fenders. Only once had she seen a Red Cross jeep come into town. Its red and white flag had seemed like a bastion of hope, but in the end it was there only to take away a woman found dead, lying face-down in a tide pool a mere three inches deep. Madeleine watched as an unmarked truck pulled up to the back of the village chapel. Père Gilles, Notre Dame Chapelle de Kersaint's chaplain, waited at the back of the church, one hand holding on to his skullcap and the other waving the truck into the yard. This was the second time Madeleine had witnessed such a delivery. What was in those crates disappearing into the chapel basement? New Bibles, hymnals, perhaps, or wafers and wine for the sacrament? These would be welcome, if in fact that was what they were, as the parishioners had gone without any consecrated elements of the Eucharist since the invasion in '40. Four years of doing without had thrown a good number of Catholics into a state of abject fear for their souls.

Madeleine lingered long enough to observe Père Gilles look all around to see if anyone was watching before peeling back a curtain of purple clematis from the chapel wall. Behind it was a heavy steel door. It took all his body weight leaning backward to pull it open. Rusty hinges squealed and cobwebs, now disturbed, fluttered in the breeze. Père Gilles and the other fellow, a burly-looking German in battle fatigues, began unloading crates from the truck and lugging them inside.

Annabelle was waiting at the door for Madeleine when she finally got home. It was after dark and past curfew. Clutching a strand of pearls in one fist, and a monogramed handkerchief pressed to her lips in the other, she demanded, "Where in heaven's name have you been all afternoon?"

"Not 'all afternoon,' Maman." She kissed her mother on each cheek. "I was doing what you always suggest."

"I suggest many things. To which are you referring?"

Madeleine rolled her eyes and slid past Annabelle to head upstairs to change for dinner. Knowing it annoyed her mother to see her gambol like an untamed animal, she took the steps in twos, her long, coltish limbs her thunderous engine. At the landing, she hung over the banister and answered impishly, "Staring at the ocean, Maman, becoming one with the sea."

Chapter Six

Madeleine banged the table, making the silverware jump. "Maman, I've got to get out of here!"

"Have you forgotten there's a war on?"

"Of course not! But it's absolutely dreadful here and I'm bored to sobs!" She pushed her chair back. "The war is almost over anyway. I highly doubt Herr Schitler cares what we do."

Annabelle cringed. Ever a patient woman, she folded her linen napkin and placed it to the left of her dinner plate. She sighed. Surely this was another of Madeleine's youthful outbursts, designed to shock for the sake of her own amusement. "And where might you go, dear?"

"Morocco."

"Are you mad?" Annabelle rang a little bell to summon Sophie, their housekeeper and cook. "Go to Morocco? You'll do no such thing!"

Much as Madeleine loved her mother, she loathed her mother's imperial manner of speaking to her as if she were an underling. The elegant Annabelle de Beaulieu, née Walpole, acted as though she were still a lady-in-waiting to Queen Mary. She was all about decorum. Annabelle was not about to permit her daughter to travel alone.

Sophie lumbered in from the kitchen, stoop-shouldered. She was a thickset woman with pendulous breasts who had nursed three

35

children of her own as well as several others during the first world war. Her watery eyes were as black as olives, and she glared at Madeleine. Evidently, she had been eavesdropping again. Despite her limited understanding of English, she understood enough to know that Madeleine was upsetting her mother. With much clatter, huffing and puffing, she cleared the dishes.

"There'll be no further discussion, darling. Understood?"

Madeleine blew her blonde bangs upward and stomped from the room without asking to be excused.

Madeleine was fed up with doing and saying what others expected. How could she be her true self if she always held herself in check, never said what was on her mind or did what felt right? If her mother wanted to live within the confines of protocol and respectability, let her. But why should she?

Up until now, Madeleine's daily existence had been an endless salvo of infuriating do's and don'ts. Her mother's maddening insistence on conforming to conventions harked back to the days of Victoria and Albert. It was 1944, for heaven's sake! And a war was on. Who was there to impress, anyway? Certainly not the bloody Krauts. For too long Annabelle had held Madeleine's spirit captive like a songbird in a cage. She was tired of perching demurely for others to admire.

Annabelle was descended from Vice-Admiral Charles Beckworth, 1st Viscount, 1st Duke of Hillsborough, Bedminstershire. As a member of the aristocracy, Annabelle had always had an image to uphold, regardless of her title having been watered down over the generations. Sadly, Annabelle's place within the English peerage system as a baroness became a disgraced one when she fell in love with a French naval officer and had the audacity to elope. It was such an outrage, King George expelled her from his and the queen's service. How ironic that Annabelle, having moved to the Breton shores with her beloved and having no desire to ever return to England as lady-in-waiting, nevertheless behaved as if she were still there.

Annabelle's extensive wardrobe of Empire-waist gowns and velvet chokers still hung in two oversized armoires. Pendants and brooches boasting cabochon-cut rubies and emeralds, heirlooms dating as far back as King George III, were nested among her silk chemises and camisoles. Her furs and worsted woolen manteaux were neatly packed in trunks in the attic. Sachets of lavender and rose hips rested among her lace handkerchiefs, hosiery, and corsets.

Despite the fact mother and daughter lived in a modest stone cottage in a rugged seaside village, Annabelle insisted on dressing for dinner, a habit Madeleine found annoying for its misplaced formality. Every night she donned a costume of silk or satin; gowns sprouting trains flouncy bows cinched tightly at the small of her back, or tiers of ruffles. As for the jewelry, she kept that well hidden, knowing a Nazi could show up at the door at any given moment. Madeleine thought the charade bizarre, but allowed her mother these small pleasures, given the times.

For this dinner, Madeleine had reluctantly exchanged her pedal-pushers for a sundress and white cardigan. While they dined in the dining room-cum-kitchen, Annabelle held her silver fork and knife like an aristocrat while her daughter sulked and pretended to not be there. The table had been set with crisply ironed linens, Spode china, and a vase of wispy larch branches in the center. The meal consisted of a meager helping of puréed carrots and a tranche of stale baguette with a morsel of black-market Comté. Underneath the table linens, the table was pockmarked and singed from abuse. Sophie used the dining table to fillet any fish she was lucky enough to catch after curfew or to knead dough, flour rations permitting. Who could ever guess that what lay beneath Annabelle's carefully constructed façade was so utilitarian?

Facing her mother squarely, Madeleine carefully weighed what she was about to say. Part of her wanted to forgive her mum as opposed to constantly finding fault with her. But rationalizing the whys and wherefores of her mother's behavior wouldn't get Madeleine where she wanted to go. After all, one shouldn't live for others. Even if Madeleine's baroness mother was deliberately maintaining a façade of superiority as her way of refusing to acknowledge the impact of the Nazi presence in her town, it didn't mean Madeleine must do the same. She might even have agreed it was better to ignore or look down on the bloody Germans than surrender, but couldn't one drop the social pretenses behind closed doors? Annabelle apparently knew no other manner of coping. And unfortunately for Madeleine, she was expected to do the same as her mother. *Quel* bore!

Billy

January - March 1945

Chapter Seven

The basin between the peaks at the top of Cannon Mountain was vast, steep, and covered with swirls of crusted icy tips. Billy looked down, then across the expanse to the other side. Clean and glistening, the mountains were blindingly white as far as the eye could see. A sudden gust of wind whipped around him, causing even him at one hundred and ninety pounds to wobble. He looked over at Claire who had actually lost her footing and was white with fright.

"This is going to require a serious commitment to maximum speed if you want to get to the other side," Billy shouted.

"I don't like speed," Claire whimpered. Billy looked over at her again. Claire's lips were blue and quivering, her teeth chattering.

"It's the only way to make it up to the ridgeline on the other side." Claire edged away from the lip of the piste. "You can do it if you believe you can."

"You expect me to schuss down that?"

"Piece of cake," Billy quipped, though in truth he knew it was no such thing.

Snapping on his skis and wrapping safety straps around his ankles, Billy planted his poles in the snow and leaned back against them to wait for Claire. Trouble was, she was still frozen in terror.

Another sixty-mile-an-hour gust roared up the saddle, this time almost knocking them both down. An icy spray smacked them in their faces.

"Please don't make me do this."

Billy poled to the edge of the rim. "Fine," he yelled over his shoulder. "But I'm going. You can take the cable car back, I don't care." And he was gone.

Claire waited for Billy at the base of the mountain. A picturesque chalet nestled beneath a canopy of thick pines was where she wanted to take Billy for lunch. He had thought to go back up for another run, but thinking better of it, agreed to go in. Smoke curled from the chimney and mouth-watering aromas of *pommes frites* and charcoal-grilled bratwurst filled the air.

Billy stomped the snow from his boots, withdrew his gloves and then tucked them under his arm. "You shoulda been there," he crowed, cupping his hands and blowing into them.

"I just couldn't, I'm sorry. That mountain was too big for me."

As they entered the restaurant, a shelf of snow fell from the lintel with a soft whump. "Dammit," Claire bleated, swiping the wetness from her neck.

"Let's get that table over there," Billy said coldly and led her to a table in front of a crackling fire on a stone hearth. He could feel Claire's gaze drift over his face.

"You're mad at me, aren't you?" Claire stated once they were seated.

"It's just that I didn't expect you to be such a coward." It was hard for Billy to look at her.

On the one hand he desired her with a passion, but on the other she had a knack for really disappointing him.

"I know."

"How are we to ever have any fun together if you won't do the things I love?"

Claire stared into the fire. "I could say the same to you, you

42

know." She looked up to see how her words had landed.

"It makes me mad."

"It's sad, I agree." She thought for a minute. "Why don't you describe your ski down. I want to see it through your eyes."

"That's dumb." Billy scraped his chair back, annoyed. "You know I'm not good with words."

Claire reached across the table and clasped Billy's arm. "Just try, okay?"

"Okay," he acquiesced. "Let's see, um… Once I got across that big bowl, I traversed some pretty frozen pistes, carved tight turns down another steep part and then stopped by an old barn."

"There was a barn way up there?"

"Yup. Farmers send their cattle or sheep up there in the summer. They keep supplies and even a bed for themselves for whenever they might stay a while. There's fencing up there, too, but they lay it down for the skiers come wintertime."

She smiled. "Continue."

"At this point, I was in powdery snowfields. You would have loved it for the easy gliding." He smiled ruefully. "However, at the tree line, I encountered ice thanks to the shade of a poplar grove. That you wouldn't have cared for."

"Oh dear. I fear you're right," Claire agreed. "I am a ninny."

Billy nodded. "You said it. Not me."

The drive back to New York City was long. Claire slept most of the way while Billy drove, clenching his teeth and ignoring the speed limit.

Chapter Eight

When Billy awakened the next morning, he rolled his head on the pillow expecting Claire to be there, but she wasn't. The muscles in his cheeks tightened, pulling his lips into a thin line.

"Good morning!" Claire chirped as she carried a breakfast tray into their bedroom. "I commandeered breakfast for you. Claire handed him a cup of coffee. "Regular, as in New York style, right?"

"No, I take it black." They'd been married for how long, and she hadn't noticed how he took his coffee? "What are we to each other?" Billy blurted.

"What in the world do you mean?"

"You're hard to read, Mrs. Campbell."

Tears sprang into Claire's eyes. She folded her arms across her chest. "Are you talking about me sleeping all the way home?"

"I am, yes. Among other things."

"Such as?"

"Well. I don't really know you as well as I should. You don't give me that much."

"Intimacy involves sharing one's most private thoughts, which means taking risks I'm not yet ready to take."

Billy's broad shoulders slumped. "But you can trust me."

"I'm a ninny, remember?"

That did little to appease Billy, so in response he looked away

44

and stared out the window. Two plump pigeons were perched on the sill, canoodling.

"I'm terrified, okay?"

"Well, forgive me if I say I'm terrified, too." Billy threw the covers off and strode naked to the foot of the bed, where his silk robe lay in a puddle on the floor. Reaching into first one pocket and then the other, he located his Benson & Hedges and Cartier lighter. Once he snapped the silver case shut and lit his cigarette, he blew out a stream of smoke.

"*You're* terrified? Of what?" Claire demanded.

Squinting through the cigarette smoke which curled around his head, he answered slowly, "Aside from never entirely knowing your heart because you insist on holding stuff back from me, I fear never winning my father's approval."

"Oh, come now, Billy. You're a grown man."

Not to be dissuaded from his self-pity, Billy persevered. "He's a business tycoon, an Olympic silver medalist, a Yalie cum laude, and," he inhaled, "a ladies' man to boot." The exhale was long and slow.

"And you're what? A big ol' bump on a log?" Claire took Billy's cigarette from him, inhaled deeply, and then handed it back. Exhaling, she shook her head. "You are a fine artist when you bother to get out your easel and paint box, a superb dancer, and one of the most popular men in Manhattan. Plus, you're pretty sexy, ya know… though you don't need to aspire to being a ladies' man. Not anymore, anyway."

Billy stubbed out his cigarette and pulled Claire into his arms. When he kissed her, she tangled her fingers in his black hair and pressed her slim frame against his. It wasn't but a minute before Billy slipped her nightie off her shoulders and had her pinned underneath him on the rumpled sheets.

"What about our breakfast?" Claire giggled.

"I'm half-English. We like our toast cold."

Later, they sat opposite each other under the window, Claire spooning a soft-boiled egg from an egg cup and Billy buttering his cold toast and watching her. He was brooding again, but she appeared oblivious.

"I flunked out of Princeton, ya know." Claire looked up, startled. "Father got me my job at J. P. Morgan & Company through a fraternity brother of his. They gave me a corner office, if you can believe it, with a huge expense account. My sole task was to wine and dine the rich and famous."

"Nothing wrong with that," Claire said.

"I'll admit I enjoy hosting clients at Yankee Stadium or Aqueduct, but anybody can do that."

Claire put down her spoon and dabbed at the corners of her mouth with her napkin. She'd never heard Billy talk like this. She'd always thought of him as a confident man-about-town. Right now, he sounded insecure, maybe even a little depressed.

"I understand your father has big shoes to fill."

"You can say that again, tootsie-cakes." Billy leaned across the table and kissed her. "Thank you."

"Why don't you throw yourself at your painting? Take an entirely different route from the one your dad has chosen so there's no reason for comparison. Who cares what people think, if you do what you love? Besides, you're really very talented."

"I won't make any money at it."

"You don't need money, silly!"

Billy was on the verge of tears. He'd been so restless of late, yet he couldn't tell her what he really wanted to do because he knew she'd protest. Violently. What he wanted to do was serve his country: enlist in the fight for freedom and help put an end to the Axis of Evil. But there was no way Claire would ever understand. Ever

46

since December 6, 1941, Billy had wanted to avenge Japan's preposterous act of aggression on his fellow Americans at Pearl Harbor. How dare they declare war on the United States! He wanted to end the Nazi reign of terror across Europe, especially after Hitler had had the gall to declare war on the US as well. To sit out the war in safety and have his friends think him a spoiled brat—or worse, a coward—was humiliating. Billy had had a hard time defending himself when jeered. After all, he was healthy and fit, still young at twenty-seven. Okay, so one leg was an inch shorter than the other. So what? What was he doing still at home and living in the lap of luxury? Being denied a commission because of it had broken his heart. This wasn't a "handicap," as described by the recruitment officer, but an inconsequential ski injury. All it had been was a spiral leg fracture improperly set by the local veterinarian in backwoods Vermont.

"If the war persists into '44, come back and try again," the officer had suggested. "The Army will probably be running out of men at that point and take you regardless of your shorter leg."

"You're upset you can't be over there because of your stupid leg." Claire had read his thoughts. "Get over it. I'm thrilled you can't go."

Billy exploded. How many times had they argued about his privilege to serve, which had been taken away from him? That it was involuntary, not at all his choice? "Dammit, Claire, I want to fight like every other red-blooded American. It's my right to have that honor even if it gets me killed!"

"Oh, Billy, no!" she wailed.

"Don't 'oh Billy' me," he yelled. "You America Firsters have no clue what we patriots feel." He dragged his fingers through his hair. "Patriotism is apparently foreign to you!"

"That's not fair," Claire said quietly. "And I am so a patriot. Just not the same kind."

"What's not fair is that my wife has no appreciation for what I'm all about. She hates dude ranches. Won't ski or play tennis. Can't take her nose out of a book . . ." Sneakers sauntered into the room and leapt onto the bed. "She even hates my cat!"

Billy gulped back a sob. He felt depleted.

"Gadzooks, I think your father's recent non-stop badgering has done a number on you, Billy." He shook his head and groaned. Claire persisted. "Do you honestly believe a stint in the army would make him stop?"

"No, Claire. You've got it all wrong. Just because my father's valor is well-known does not make me a wannabe hero. I just want to serve my country." Billy was so exasperated he couldn't find the words to express his feelings. "Let's just drop it."

Billy appraised Claire's naked body, visible through her peignoir. Better to just have sex, he thought, than try to share his hopes and dreams or deepest fears with her.

Chapter Nine

Billy stood in front of an easel with a palette in one hand, daubing smudges of magenta and cerulean with a flat knife. He studied the saltwater lagoon, which was prettily hemmed by a small crescent of sand in front of him and a natural rock wall to the east. Despite the sunlight, an afternoon chill was blowing in, and along with it a peculiar suspicion.

Since the wedding night, he and Claire had never used or practiced any contraception. So, shouldn't she be pregnant? If it wasn't already too late, shouldn't they be pursuing some kind of birth control? Even though Billy wasn't ready to have children yet, he did want them someday. Billy packed up his supplies and marched across the ivory beach up to the house. He felt the sting of cold salt water spray on his cheeks and dreaded the conversation he needed to broach.

Billy found Claire reclining on a chaise longue in the sunroom. She looked like a doll, all one hundred pounds of her petite frame propped against the chintz cushions as if placed there by a child. Claire lay her open book across her chest when he entered.

"All you do is read," he jeered by way of a preamble.

Claire ignored the barb. It wasn't the first time she'd heard it. "It's Betty Smith's debut novel, *A Tree Grows in Brooklyn*." Claire marked her place with a pressed sprig of Japanese anemone and closed the book. "It's a best seller and I must confess I quite identify with the heroine."

"I'm glad you're enjoying it."

"You didn't come in here to talk about the book I'm reading. You seem cross. What's on your mind?"

"No, I didn't." Billy nudged her feet over and sat at the bottom of her chair.

"What's wrong?"

"Are you pregnant?"

Claire allowed a lengthy pause to hang in the air between them. She answered his question with one of her own. "Heavens to Betsy, why do you ask?"

Billy reached for Claire's hand. She looked frightened and seemed to be on the defensive. "Our lovemaking has been stupendous," he began, tickling the inside of her palm, "and frequent," he added, wiggling his eyebrows suggestively.

"But?"

"Well, it just occurred to me that it would be pretty unusual if you weren't already preggers. Considering how active, you know, we've been."

"Well, I'm not."

"Are you sure?" Billy pressed.

"Quite sure," Claire said softly.

"I just thought we should probably wait a year or two, but don't get me wrong. I want kids. Four, in fact." Billy knew he was gushing. "Two boys and two girls would be perfect, but we probably should have a plan, don't you think?" Receiving no feedback, Billy babbled on. "Or maybe not. Hell, if you are pregnant and didn't want to tell me because it's too soon, I get it. I'd be thrilled... Truly."

Claire sat stone still. The book dropped to the floor, and nonplussed, Billy bent to pick it up. He knew his wife to be uncommunicative, but he'd never seen her this tight-lipped.

With all the patience of a saint, Billy waited for the tension to subside. He stroked Claire's lower leg. "Talk to me."

Like a jack-in-the-box, Claire shot off her chaise longue. "Fine!" she cried. "I'll tell you." She pulled a hankie from her sleeve. "I can't bear children!"

The crudeness of her outburst made Billy recoil. "You hate kids?"

"No! I'm saying I can't make babies because I'm . . . I'm . . . oh, I so despise the word . . . I'm barren!" Tears streamed down her face.

"As in infertile?" Billy was incredulous.

"When I was seventeen, I developed growths on my ovaries. The doctor thought he could excise the cysts, but they were too large. In order to save my life, he said he had to remove them both."

Outside, a sea bird shrieked and then there was a terrible elongated silence.

Claire fell back against the cushions on the chaise and watched as her husband stared at the floor with an empty-eyed expression. He was very still.

Claire fingered the string of pearls around her neck. "I should have told you, but I just couldn't find the right words or the right time."

After a frighteningly longer moment still, Billy sighed heavily, slapped his hands on his knees and slowly stood up. Looking down at her, he said stonily, "You sure as hell should've."

Within fifteen minutes Billy had summoned his chauffeur, Boots, packed an overnight bag, and was headed back into the city to stay at his pied-à-terre on East 68th and Madison. From the darkened comfort of his Pierce-Arrow, he stared glumly out the window, periodically unleashing a blizzard of swear words.

Boots glanced in the rearview mirror. "Everything all right, sir?" Boots had been in the Campbell family's employ since Billy was four years old. He had formed a bond with the boy, giving him attention and buoying him up whenever his father, the senior Campbell, could or would not.

"I forgot my cigarettes. Can we stop to pick some up?"

"Check the compartment under your elbow, sir."

Billy lifted the lid of the center console, and sure enough, an unopened pack of Benson & Hedges was there along with a book of matches. "You're a godsend, Boots." Billy lit his cigarette and shook out the flame. "The missus doing well?" Boots' wife, Isabel, who was the household's cook, had been known to threaten Billy when he was a child with pigs' knuckles and sauerkraut if he asked her what was for dinner too many times.

"Fit as a fiddle she be." Boots looked over his shoulder as he joined the traffic on Flushing Avenue. "She'll make sure Miss Claire is comfortable while you're gone."

"So you know about our little row?" Billy didn't know whether he was upset or not about the domestic help being privy to his private life, but he had come to accept that there were rarely any secrets in a house with servants. The joke had always been one couldn't even change one's mind inside a locked closet without everyone knowing it within the hour.

Boots took a leap and said, "Not so little, I'm afraid." He checked his boss's expression again, fearing perhaps he'd overstepped.

"I know I should sympathize with Claire, but I can't help thinking about where that leaves me."

"Quite the conundrum, sir." They were crossing the Brooklyn Bridge over the East River, and the end-of-the-weekend congestion back into the city was heavy. He welcomed having Boots in his corner.

"The thing is, Boots, she didn't tell me she couldn't have kids.

She should have told me before we got married." He chain-lit another cigarette and exhaled.

"Of course, sir," Boots agreed. "But might I suggest you consider adopting?"

"Wouldn't be the same."

"Yes sir, I understand."

"Would *you* want to adopt someone else's kid?"

"Never thought about it, Mr. Campbell. Me and Isabel didn't want kids back when we could have had 'em. It's too hard to imagine."

Billy leaned his head against the rear passenger window and craned his neck to look up at the Empire State Building. "I'm always amazed."

"Remarkable piece of ingenuity, that," Boots commented.

"Well, yes, it is, but I was remarking on my wife."

They laughed and then for the few blocks more that it took to reach the apartment, the two men rode in amicable quiet.

"Here we are, sir," Boots announced, sliding up to the curb. Billy didn't wait for Boots to open his door but hopped out on his own. "Early to bed will do you a world of good, Mr. Campbell."

In the front hall, Boots handed Billy his suitcase. "Thank you, Boots." Billy patted him on the upper arm. "You're too good to me. I'll ring for you if I need the car tomorrow. I'll probably go into the park and get some exercise. Maybe go to the Claremont Academy and see if I can lease a horse from the stables."

Boots touched the brim of his cap with a nod. "That should be just the ticket, sir."

Billy had no idea he'd taken a left turn in the opposite direction from the park until he found himself heading down the Avenue of the Americas to where he knew there was a recruitment office on Seventh and 49th. The place was swarming with men of all ages and modes of dress queuing outside and around the block. Evidently, there was no end to the desire to take a gun against any hostile, be he German or Japanese. No amount of December cold could dissuade these fellas, either. After two hours, Billy was able to take a seat inside. It was ten thirty-five. A little after one o'clock, he was finally called into the recruiting office of the congenial-looking Captain Allen.

Although there was an ongoing draft in effect and almost anyone who wasn't a criminal was enlisted, the screening process for officers was more involved. In less than two minutes, Billy had Captain Allen convinced he wanted to serve as an officer. He was presented with a packet and told, "Go home, son, and fill out these forms. Come back when you're done, and we'll take it from here." Billy, showing no desire to leave the office, took his leave only when the captain shouted, "Next!"

Not to be deterred, Billy found a table in the corner of the outer office and went to work on the forms right away. He answered medical questions such as how many surgeries he'd had or bones he'd broken, whether he'd ever seen a psychiatrist. Did he wear eyeglasses or a hearing aid? Have any dentures? There was a section on crimes or felonies he might have committed, the level of education he'd attained, his past addresses going back ten years, marital status, number of offspring, a list of his hobbies. He was required to list the names and addresses of five family members, which he was reluctant to do because he had no intention of informing his family of his plans until he was already ensconced at Officer Candidate School. Nevertheless, Billy was not going to botch his chances, so he filled in all the boxes.

"Back already?" the bespectacled secretary asked.

"That I am," Billy replied. "Will the captain see me?"

Captain Allen came to the door and looked Billy up and down. "You sure are one determined fella." He turned and waved Billy in. While the captain studied the pages to make sure everything was complete, Billy twirled his gold wedding band around and around on his ring finger.

The captain liked what he read and smiled broadly. "So you're Commodore Campbell's son, eh? Well, if you're half the sailor he was, the army will be mighty beholden. I'm recommending you go straight to OCS."

"Really?"

"Can you get yourself to Fort Benning by next Tuesday?"

"I sure can, but there could be one glitch. You see there was a medical evaluation… er, I wanted to talk to you about."

"Yeah, I know. I see from the paperwork from a couple of years ago it says your shorter leg precluded us from taking you. Well, barring any new irregularities that might show up on your next physical; we don't care about that anymore. You can walk, right? Swim? Hell, we might even teach ya how to fly."

Billy shot out of his chair as if at attention, ready to salute. "That would be fantastic! Sir."Captain Allen laughed and walked around his desk to extend his hand to Billy. "Welcome to the finest fighting force on the face of this earth, William!"

When Billy got back to his house in the Hamptons, he took the stairs by twos and burst into the bedroom suite of rooms he shared with Claire. "I just joined the army!"

Claire lowered her magazine. Her eyes glittered with disapproval and his with a mix of pride and defiance.

"I am not having anyone think I'm one of those cowards who finagles exemptions by entering the priesthood or enrolling in divinity schools, or so-called labor forces 'necessary to the war effort.' Godammit, I'm someone who's gonna defend this country! You can't stop me, Claire. My mind's made up."

"So I see," she said calmly.

"I report next Tuesday."

"All right then." She remained calm, if not aloof. It was this kind of reaction which always got Billy's goat.

"Claire, say something!"

"What should I say when all I can think of is the prospect of you dying?" She looked daggers at him. You want me to bless your damn decision?" She tossed her head back as if to shake out the ugliness that was happening. "I can't tell you what you want to hear. I simply cannot do it, Billy."

"But it means so much to me."

"You are driven to prove your worth by killing an enemy I do not see. Just because other guys are signing up willy-nilly, that does not make you a coward. It is they who are fools. And now you're just like them."

"That's uncalled for!"

"Can't you be a conscientious objector?"

Billy began stepping out of his clothes, leaving them on the floor. "Absolutely not!"

"Why ever not?"

"I hate those goose-stepping Krauts for rounding up all the world's Jews. And I hate the Nips for what they did to my country. They all need to be stopped."

"Well, I hate all the death and destruction, too, but shooting back at people is no way to solve disagreements."

"Disagreements?" Billy raked his hand through his hair. "Are you kidding me? Freedom is at stake! If we roll over and play dead, you can bet you'll be speaking German and shopping at Bergdorf's with Deutschmarks within the year."

"For pity's sake, what a ridiculous exaggeration!"

"You think so?"

"Let's face it, Billy, this isn't really about you championing liberty. It's about you paying me back."

Billy opened his mouth to protest, then thought better of it. He picked up the bundle of clothes he'd discarded on the floor and dumped them on the nearest chair.

"I can't dignify that accusation with a response," Billy said.

"Why not? You know it's true. I didn't tell you sooner that I couldn't have babies, so now you're going to retaliate by doing the one thing I begged you not to do."

Billy disappeared into the dressing room and re-emerged securing the sash of his silk paisley robe. He dropped into a chair and covered his face. Then looking up, he said, "I'll be honest with you. When you told me there would never be any children, it occurred to me I had nothing to live for. Not that I want to die, of course, but there'll be no little ones counting on me to raise and protect them."

"Billy, what about me?"

"Let me finish." He took a deep breath and said, "You've set me free, Claire. Now I can do what I was meant to do. Oh, I'll come home when the war is done, and we'll figure out what kind of life we want to have then. Okay?"

"You're not going to let me have a say?"

"You've already had your say."

Madeleine

February -March 1945

Chapter Ten

It had been too long a winter and Madeleine had had just about enough.

"If you forbid me to go to Morocco," Madeleine warned, "I'll put on a beret and join the Maquis!" Folding her arms across her chest, her pout was as melodramatic as any five-year-old's.

Annabelle gazed at her daughter unimpressed. "There'll be no working with the Maquis."

"Why ever not?" Madeleine stomped her foot. "I can't think of anything more exciting—or patriotic, for that matter—than working for the Resistance and harassing our captors."

"That may be, but joining the Resistance is unbecoming to a lady."

"Plenty of young women are in the Resistance, Maman," Madeleine flicked her blonde braid behind her shoulder. "It would be jolly good fun to blow up bridges and railroad tracks."

"Enough." Madeleine rolled her eyes. "It's much too dangerous."

Madeleine was not to be deterred. "I hear the Maquis help downed RAF pilots escape by guiding them over the Pyrenées. It's frightfully noble."

"Darling, you are familiar with the Milice, are you not?" Madeleine shrugged. "They're a paramilitary organization created by the Vichy regime, with German aid, to combat French Resistance.

The Milice participate in executions and assassinations; they round up Jews and résistants for deportation. They are a particularly brutal arm of the German occupation."

"I know, this, Maman . . ."

"They will kill you, darling. Without remorse."

"But the Maquis are fighters, too. In spite of the potential for torture or death!" Madeleine glowered at her mother while Annabelle scowled right back. "You know, I could sign up and start spying right here."

"Whatever do you mean?"

"Something very peculiar is happening at the church." Madeleine had her mother's full attention now. "I saw a shipment of crates arrive at the chapel. What do you s'pose Père Gilles is storing in the crypt?"

"I have no idea." Madeleine noticed that her mother seemed agitated. She was patting her pockets as if looking for something.

"Did you lose something?" Wanting to goad her mother, Madeleine said, "Bodies, perhaps?"

"Oh, for God's sake, Madeleine, you're incorrigible." She sagged in her chair. "On second thought, go to Morocco, if you must. Never mind that you'll suffer terribly from the heat. I'll even bet you my mother's pearls you'll be horrified by their culture. Arabs live very differently than we do. Women are chattel."

"You're such a xenophobe," Madeleine responded. "I find the Moors quite exotic."

"See for yourself." Annabelle glided out of the room.

As the day of Madeleine's departure for Marrakesh grew closer, Annabelle became increasingly frantic. She couldn't bear to enter Madeleine's room where she was packing her trunk and assorted valises. "Please don't go, *ma petite*!" Her cheeks were tear-streaked. Madeleine, seeing her mother with no shred of her habitual reserve, almost capitulated.

"I'll be perfectly fine. You yourself approved my accommodations."

"How utterly foolish of me."

"I'll be back before you know it." She handed her mother her hankie. "The war will probably be over by then. Won't that be grand?"

Two days later, with the help of the driver, Madeleine loaded several valises onto a Citroën bus at the cottage gate, its back end spewing a plume of black exhaust. Annabelle, standing at the roadside, choked on the smoke while upstairs, Sophie pressed her forehead against the cold windowpane, mouthing the word *adieu*. When the driver released the brakes and set off, spraying Baroness de Beaulieu in the shins with a blast of sand and gravel, it was tantamount to a gross insult, for which Madeleine felt so great a regret, she dared not turn around in her seat.

Soon enough, Madeleine was on board the Douglas DC-4, barely perched on the edge of her seat. She held her breath as the plane charged down the runway. In minutes, the seaside village of Kersaint was but a speck on a quilted landscape far below.

February - March 1945

Chapter Eleven

Claire wanted to believe she and Billy had come to some sort of a truce. Having resigned herself to Billy's enlisting, she presumed by virtue of the silence that hung between them that he was getting used to the idea of their not having any children. After all, there'd been no more angry words and they'd resumed relations— she dutifully acquiescing to preserve the peace, and he ever the hungry male. That there was no intellectual intimacy between them didn't seem to bother Billy. She, on the other hand, silently railed against the lack of it. As a result, Claire could not have been more wrong about their ceasefire. Nevertheless, when found standing on a platform with a husband who was preparing to go to off to war, she could not help but be caught up in the drama of their farewell. It very well could be their last, and she was scared.

Claire and Billy stood on the platform next to the *Champion*, the Atlantic Coast Line Railroad's newest addition to its fleet of trains. The locomotive was brand new, built in the Art Deco style which was all the rage in the Thirties and Forties. Its sleek, streamlined engine was painted in geometric blocks of metallic burgundy and navy blue, and notwithstanding the drama of the moment, there was a sense of fun and adventure with this quirky-looking train.

A shrill, mournful whistle pierced the air, signaling the time for goodbyes had run out. Claire looked up into Billy's face. He looked sad. Would he change his mind? Not likely. The train coughed up clouds of steam and whistled again. Claire gripped Billy's lapels. How could she let him go off to war? Bitter and angry to boot?Billy crooked his finger under Claire's chin, gently raising her face to meet his. A darkness gathering in his light-blue eyes turned them into pools of gray. Claire hiccuped a sob.

Pushing back a strand of hair from her face and tucking it behind her ear, Billy murmured, "I'll be fine. When I get back, we'll figure stuff out." He pulled her closer. She gulped when her husband's lips trembled against her own. They were soft but not urgent. It was as if Billy were performing a kiss because at times like this it was expected. She could feel how he was already pulling away from her.

There was a rumble, then a squeal of the brakes as the wheels began to rotate. Claire clasped Billy's cheeks in her soft hands. Her voice wavered, though it was fierce. "Tell me, is all forgotten?" She forced a smile as she looked into his solemn, deep-set eyes. Billy nodded, yet his stillness and the way his eyes darted away from hers betrayed his lie. She was losing him and now there was no more time to repair the damage.

Billy gave Claire one last squeeze and then bounded down the platform. Jumping aboard the departing train just before the platform ran out from under his feet, he waved to Claire. But she had already turned toward the exit and 33rd Street.

An unnatural silence descended as the last car of the *Champion* snaked its way from the station, its caboose lights flashing in a Manhattan blur of freezing rain. And while Billy rolled toward Fort Benning, a sharp emptiness settled in Claire's heart. The vacuum, the sudden absence of her husband, was more debilitating than anything she had ever experienced. Once again, she was bereft of love. Not so much in the physical sense; rather, she felt cut off from a spiritual connection. She had no special person—no ally who understood her and accepted her, foibles and all. Almost instantly, she felt abject loneliness, and it hurt terribly.

While Claire had decided it best to drop her objections to Billy's going to war, privately, she had not changed her mind about the war. To her, there was no valor to be had in joining this or any other battle. Violence only begot more violence, and despite what political leaders might have claimed at victory parties, no one was ever really the winner. How could they be? Blood was shed, lives snuffed out, family members and friends left behind to live the rest of their days grieving. War seized that which was most precious and could never be restored—property, limb, one's very existence. At twenty-seven, Billy had no business joining those fresh-faced, foolish boys—babies, really—lined up on every other city block eager to get themselves killed. That Billy had been lured away from Claire by a bigger sense of duty than that which he had vowed to her at the altar was hard to comprehend. But since there would be no children, his duty to country had obviously taken precedence. It was an amorphous, invisible calling which brooked no protest, not even from his wife.

At first, Claire tried to keep up with her social and charity commitments—reading to the blind, volunteering at the 49th Street soup kitchen, her bridge group, and Mondays-with-the Ladies Lunch at the Colony Club. But by March, she'd run out of gas. The winter blahs threw her into a depression so deadening she couldn't be bothered to dress or even brush her teeth. All she could manage each day were a few pages of a book whose title and author she was incapable of recalling, and much more wine than was befitting to a lady. This inertia, compounded by the dark, short days, left her numb. Weeks of night seemed to swallow her whole, there being little reason to leave her Madison Avenue flat or head to the Hamptons merely to flounder there.

Claire eventually summoned enough energy to leave the city and seek the fresh air on Long Island. Boots and Isabelle went with her, per the Campbells' instructions.

Prompted by the kindly Isabelle, Claire folded her newspaper and bundled up to take a walk. She entered the woods behind the house, immediately comforted by the cushion-y feel of the moss-covered trail underfoot. She inhaled the smell of rain and pine trees in the air. Hard as she tried to resist, thoughts of the war invaded her mind. She doubted very much that the German Reich would ever fall. Hitler's forces were too mighty. The drive for world domination was already too deeply rooted in every German's heart, and much ground had been won by them thus far. As for the rumors of Hitler's campaign against the Jews, she didn't believe them, they being too preposterous and hideous. Yellow news, she surmised, designed to drive up newspaper sales or recruit more fools.

Claire was prepared to accept any new world order for the sake of peace and the return of her husband. It was that simple. Equally so, she hoped Billy would reconsider adoption upon his return. Especially if it meant stitching together their frayed marriage. Claire turned back toward the house, the wind now at her back propelling her to a future which lay like the storm clouds hanging over her head. Damn if her life wasn't on hold. She resented feeling suspended like a marionette on a string, the handler uncertain of where to place her on the stage. Life was coming at her too fast, rendering her out of control. Shouldn't it be the other way around? That she should be the driver, determining her course?

Claire lifted her face to the sky, the sun's rays warm on her cheeks. It had been five weeks since Billy had left. Every morning since then, she had awakened with a fleeting sense that he was lying there beside her. And every time, the stark reality of his absence hit hard. Claire would start her day like every day before it. In tears.

Billy had telephoned while she was out, and Boots had taken the message. "He's stationed at Dutch Harbor, Miss Claire." When she looked perplexed, Boots filled her in. "Alaska, ma'am."

"There's no war there."

"No, Miss Claire, not anymore. That's the good news. But apparently, there is a lot of rebuilding going on. You know, since the Alaskan campaign to rid those Japs from our islands."

"Sounds like you two had quite the conversation," she said, unable to hide her bitterness.

"Not a long one, Miss Claire. Long distance, after all."

Claire was devastated. How she had longed to hear his voice, his laugh, his news. How she had hoped to be reassured that he missed her, and more importantly, had forgiven her. Now Billy was four thousand miles away. In the middle of nowhere. Out of reach until the next phone call—if there would be another phone call.

Claire ran upstairs to her bedroom, closed the door, and turned on the radio to full volume. Boots and Isabelle did not need to witness her anguish.

Billy

March - 1945

Chapter Twelve

All Billy had ever wanted when he was growing up was for his father to accept him for the artistic and gentle soul that he was. Not pigeonhole him into a place where he didn't belong. As a result, Billy and his father had spent the former's youth as if they were two ragged pieces of broken glass each looking for a fit. The father wanted his son to swim the butterfly, Billy wanted to dive. The commodore preferred Billy to sculpt, but he wanted to paint. They never did find that fit. Maybe the risk of permanent breakage was too great, so father and son had lived in a state of tenuous accord, each rankling the other but keeping the peace for the sake of Billy's mother, Caroline.

At least both men agreed on America's involvement in the war. When Billy had unexpectedly phoned his father from Fort Benning to tell him he was about to become a 2nd lieutenant in the army, his father fairly bellowed, "Well it's about time, son!" This backhanded approval was short lived, though. After Billy graduated from the accelerated officer candidate program, he reported for advanced training with the Army Corps of Engineers, having been selected for this occupational specialty due to his artistic proclivity. The commodore, of course, had hoped his son would be detailed to something more Hollywood like the 10th Mountain Division, or any of the Airborne Divisions. Be that as it may, by early March of '45,

Billy had received orders to ship out to Dutch Harbor, Alaska. This was the largest American military installation, set in the middle of the Aleutian Islands running southwest across the Bering Sea, in order to facilitate the shortest possible route between the United States and Japan.

Billy was late to the party. He had hoped to at least blow up underwater obstacles or clear undefended ports, but the Aleutian Islands Campaign had begun in 1942 and was quelled by August of '43. After heavy bombardment and hand-to-hand combat, the Japanese had been driven off the tiny islands of Adak, Kiska, and Attu. Now in 1945, Billy was there to simply monitor the rebuilding of roads, runways, bridges, and barracks.

Billy hated his duty and wanted a transfer almost the day he arrived. In a letter home to Claire, he wrote:

Dearest,
How I miss your voice, your smile. Believe me, there's not much smiling going on around here.

I've landed in one godforsaken place and while I'm happy my country saw fit to purchase the territory of Alaska as a buffer against Russian or Japanese aggression, it is the most rugged of frontiers. Rainfall is nonstop and the damn wind never quits. The sun rarely shines for more than a few hours a day and it's usually obscured by fog anyway. The land is devoid of trees. There is little color unless you want to call white a color. Rather, it is gray, wet, and very dreary.

I'm told that the work in the Aleutians is the most arduous ever undertaken by the Army Corps of Engineers. Do I see any valor in that? Not really. From here to Anchorage or Seward by boat is 1,600 miles and we are expected to maintain airfields, garrisons, and all of the operating facilities. The vast distance of project sites from sources of supply, the lack of adequate transportation, and the extremely cold and stormy weather have served to make this really difficult. Also, the isolation of the bases, the shortage of an experienced workforce, and the lack of equipment slow our progress. Since there are no recreational facilities available at our remote camps, it's really hard to keep up the morale of the guys. What these boys need is a visit by Rita Hayworth or the Andrews Sisters. That'd be a real good shot in the arm!

What I need, my darling, is you. I can't wait to be in your arms again. I know no day or heartbeat can ever be promised, but rest assured that here in Alaska I'm relatively safe compared to our boys in the Pacific or crossing into Germany. You might be thinking, So war is not all it's cracked up to be, after all, huh? but let me just say this: I'm here to win this fight, whether it's with a gun or a hammer, so you and I can live in a free world.

Yours always,
Billy

PS I and a few others are getting furloughed some time in February. Want to meet me in Fairbanks if I can arrange it? It'll only be for a long weekend, but that's better than nothing.

Chapter Thirteen

The army's report stated that the C-47 carrying nineteen men on furlough bound for Fairbanks was flying at an altitude of twelve thousand feet when it encountered a severe downdraft, forcing the pilot to go on instruments into a heavy bank of clouds. The plane slammed into the mountain peak belly-first, instantly splitting the fuselage open. Then it slid down a precipitous slope, finally coming to rest a third of a mile down from the point of impact.

The army's rescue mission, the first of its kind to ever be mounted in such steep topography, engaged tractors, trucks, cans of gasoline, tents, radios, stoves, food provisions, and climbing gear, all of which had to be hauled in or parachuted from the air. For over eight days, a team of twenty expert climbers slogged through blinding blizzards in arctic temperatures to reach the crash site. The bulk of the wreckage was finally dug out from under fifteen feet of snow. The fuselage was ripped wide open, its mangled edges sharp and curled where the metal was shorn. All around the wreckage, the expedition team excavated as deep as the ice would permit. Sixteen bodies were found in the vicinity of the crash site and three, Billy being one of them, were classified as "missing." The commodore gave the formerly unnamed granite tower lurking behind Mount McKinley a fitting name: Mount Deception.

Claire

March - April 1945

Chapter Fourteen

Billy's funeral was an ostentatious affair held at St. Patrick's Cathedral on 5th Avenue with Archbishop Spellman presiding. His Eminence happened to be a close confidant of President Roosevelt and was acting as the president's agent and military vicar at the time of Billy's demise. The commodore and Caroline were honored to have him officiating alongside Reverend Reynolds. Every who's-who on the New York City social register was in attendance, and what a spectacle.

Consuelo Vanderbilt, attired in a black silk knee-length dress with puffed shoulders, a waterfall of pearls around her neck, and a black snood cradling a mass of dark curls, sat in the third pew. Consuelo's husband, the dashing WWI flying ace Frenchman Jacques Balsan, stood in the aisle to survey the congregation before taking his seat beside his wife. Jakie Astor, son of John Jacob Astor who had gone down with the *Titanic*, arrived with his new bride, Gertrude Gretsch, a glamor puss with movie-star blonde waves and perfect teeth. The disgraced divorcée Wallis Simpson, who according to the tabloids had forced the abdication of England's King Edward VIII, happened to be in America at the time and apparently slipped into the church unnoticed. Once the musical prelude had finished and Archbishop Spellman's scriptures began to drone, Wallis took a seat in the back row.

Claire hardly paid any attention to the memorial. Sitting in the front pew, flanked by her mother and father-in-law, she clutched Billy's cap in her lap. Tuning out the archbishop, she recalled the long-distance telephone call she'd received after the commodore's private expedition of search and retrieve had returned.

It had been a bad connection. "What did you say?" The voice at the other end of the line sounded as though the caller were underwater.

"This is Michael Parson, ma'am." He had bellowed into the phone so loudly Claire drew the receiver away from her ear. "I have more news about your husband's plane crash."

Claire had squeezed her eyes shut. "Go on." She'd flopped onto her sofa and wrapped herself in an afghan, sensing the need to cocoon herself against whatever new news was about to hit.

Mr. Parson cleared his throat. "The Land and Sea Rescue Team has just completed one of the most elaborate and daring rescue expeditions ever undertaken. They—."

Claire sighed, exasperated. "Mr. Parson, forgive me, but I already know this. My father-in-law has filled me in on all the gory details. My husband is dead. In fact, his memorial is slated for a week from next Saturday."

Claire didn't want to hear the details again. The army had recounted the particulars of their rescue mission during which they reported retrieving sixteen bodies and now Land and Sea, as personally hired by the commodore, had gone back up Mount Deception to do what the army had failed to do. She knew all too intimately how it had taken days of arduous trekking. She knew it had been undertaken in some of the worst winter conditions ever recorded and that it had been the first of its kind to ever be mounted. But while Claire knew she should feel grateful for the efforts made by these brave men, it was impossible for her to truly empathize with their hardship. These guys had come back. Billy was never coming home.

"Get to the point, please."

"The main part of the wreckage was discovered under a ten-foot snow avalanche which was initiated by the collision. The fuselage was ripped open and the wings torn off. One of the engines was found embedded in ice near the peak. Most of the wreckage slid fifteen hundred feet down the mountainside."

Claire gulped. "Was there evidence of a fire?"

"No, ma'am, no fire despite the fuel still being in the tanks."

"I don't know why I ask; the crash was devastating enough."

"They did find an unbroken bottle of whiskey outside the cabin, though."

"How odd." Claire was prompted to ask, "Anything else?"

"They found the pilot's flight bag. Undamaged——."

"Just like the whiskey," Claire interrupted.

"Uh-huh. And nearby, they found a Dopp kit, playing cards scattered in the snow, some of the soldiers' furlough papers, chewing gum, and a pack of cigarettes."

Claire sat up straight. "Benson & Hedges?"

"Yes, ma'am, and there's more." He paused, causing Claire to hold her breath, fearful of what he'd say next. Could it be Billy's body had been found? Tears were already filling her eyes as she imagined cradling Billy's broken body in her arms.

"Mrs. Campbell, are you still there?"

"I'm here," Claire choked.

"One of the men found your husband's officer's cap." By virtue of the silence echoing down the line, Mr. Parson correctly assumed Claire didn't believe him, so he added. "A photograph of you is tucked inside, ma'am. Across the top of the snapshot is the name 'Fitzie' scribbled in red lipstick."

"That's my maiden name. Billy has called me that since our first date . . ."

"We'll have this delivered to you, ma'am, as soon as the next transport leaves for the East Coast." He hesitated. "Please know on behalf of the entire team at Land & Sea we send our deepest condolences for your loss." He hesitated as if to say something more but did not. It was clear that he presumed Billy was dead like the others. No way any of them could have survived the frigid conditions, let alone walked off that precipice.

"Goodbye, ma'am."

Claire staggered over to her bed and crawled under the covers. She stared blankly at the plaster ceiling with its network of cracks. How was it possible, Claire wondered, there were bodies missing, yet things as small as a bottle of bourbon, playing cards, or an army cap were easily retrieved?

When the memorial was over, Caroline and Randall Campbell escorted their daughter-in-law from the church back to their house on 68th and Park. They thought it best Claire be tucked into bed with a sedative upstairs while they hosted the reception in their drawing room.

They say that when your soul is wounded, it is a more profound pain than anything a body might sustain, and Claire recognized the truth of it as she felt she'd been abandoned by everyone, not just Billy. Even God, though she'd already abandoned him long before he had had the nerve to leave her hanging. An injured body heals itself, scars and all. But an injured spirit? How does anyone close that hole? Prayer may console, but it doesn't bring anyone back.

Alone again at twenty-two, Claire was adrift. Her world was a vast empty stage. Lower Manhattan's snow-covered streets made for a blank sheet of white nothingness. From her bed in the Campbells' six-story brownstone, Claire's mahogany-brown eyes followed lacy white flakes of snow as they fell past the window, clinging to telephone wires and balcony railings on their descent to the street below. She wondered if she ought not follow the pretty little crystals. Would her landing be as gentle or silent?

This dire thought lasted but briefly. She knew Billy would be ashamed of her cowardice were she to take her own life. Furious, in fact, for her being so utterly weak, thinking jumping from a sixth-floor window was any way to reach oblivion. As a result, while the snow muted her surroundings, bringing a seeming peacefulness to the otherwise rambunctious city that never slept, Claire began to accept her clamoring grief for what it should be—temporary. She wanted her coming days and years to have purpose. But what exactly did that mean? From early childhood, life had sped at her, almost like an attack. She'd had to play defense. It was high time she go on the offense. But how?

As Claire became accustomed to the loss of Billy, she began to eat again. A few crackers and cheese washed down with half bottles of Burgundian reds. It was sustenance enough. As for Caroline, who had long since embraced Claire as her own, she had never given up inviting Claire to lunch or suggesting they take in a Broadway matinée.

Chapter Fifteen

"What if he's still alive?" Claire blurted. She was heading south down Sixth Avenue to the Theatre District with Billy's mother, who had decided that taking in a matinée would do Claire some good. They had tickets for the much-anticipated Tennessee Williams play, *The Glass Menagerie.*

It was Easter time, but a biting cold still held New York in its grip. That afternoon, charcoal clouds were muscling their way across the sky over Midtown Manhattan. To Claire, it seemed spring would never come, the atmosphere hanging over New York still gloomy. It didn't help that Claire's persistent suspicions that Billy might still be alive were growing stronger.

Caroline stopped abruptly and turned to face her grieving daughter-in-law. "Sweetheart, that's impossible."

Claire's brown eyes shone with tears. She fumbled for a hankie, but Caroline, seeing her trembling hand come up empty, pulled one of her own from her purse and handed it to her.

"I feel his presence. I see him at every turn. Bloomies, on 5th, even over there. Look!" Claire cried, pointing.

"It's completely natural for you to react this way," soothed Caroline. "His death is too fresh, the funeral only a few weeks ago. Your mind is just not yet capable of embracing this horrible reality," Caroline counseled.

"So it's just wishful thinking?"

"Come," Caroline coaxed. "Curtain goes up in twenty minutes. We don't want to miss the first act." She fastened Claire's coat tightly under her chin just as a mother might for her small child, and looking up into her face, she admitted, "I see him too, sometimes. Especially in crowds. It's normal."

Arm in arm, they covered the last three blocks in silence. Claire bit her lower lip as hard as she could bear, so as to not break down. Damn this war, she thought. Lives have been shattered. Loved ones torn apart. I lost my husband, Caroline and the commodore their son. Billy's spirit is everywhere, but the military, by virtue of its silence, asserts he's dead.

The lights dimmed and the chattering audience immediately hushed. As the curtain slid open in the darkness Claire felt Caroline's hand reach for hers and hold it in her lap. Glancing over at her mother-in-law, she saw an expression in her eyes she could not read. Was it commiseration over their shared grief? Or concern that Claire might not ever heal?

Caroline leaned close to Claire's ear and whispered the translation. "Don't cling to the past, honey. You'll miss your chance for a future."

Claire squeezed Billy's mother's hand. That was truly big, coming from someone as bereaved as she must be.

Madeleine

March 1945

Chapter Sixteen

It was easily one hundred degrees Fahrenheit outside when Madeleine disembarked from the DC-4. Almost immediately, she melted like butter. But by sunset, when the temperature dropped fifteen degrees, she no longer needed to dab at her forehead and the nape of her neck with a hankie. When she stepped into the inner sanctum of L'Auberge Marrakech, she was stunned by the simple beauty and refreshing air greeting her. Madeleine stopped in her tracks.

The inn was intimate and inviting. Built in the style of a *riad*, this was a traditional Moroccan house, with several stories encircling an Andalusian courtyard and a fountain in the center. Pattern upon pattern of hand-painted tiles graced the floors in splashes of burgundy, cerulean, gold, and green. It looked as though Arabian rugs had been unfurled. Within the atrium, orange and lemon trees grew in jumbo wooden crates placed between small dining tables and chairs to create a semblance of privacy. The effect was charming, all the more so for the sweet perfume of mimosas permeating the air. Along three sides of the courtyard, tall arches, with cozy alcoves hidden beyond flowing diaphanous draperies, spoke of secrets sensual in nature. The sight of a couple embracing in the semi-darkness of one hideaway teased a shiver from Madeleine.

She approached the innkeeper's desk, where an imposing man in a crisp white *thobe* greeted her with a generous smile. Instantly,

Madeleine became tongue-tied.

"Bonjour, Mademoiselle de Beaulieu. My name is Aboud Aziz." Blue, almond-shaped eyes brazenly appraised her. "Welcome to Marrakesh."

The electricity passing between them caused Madeleine's brain to short circuit. Instead of meeting this handsome man's gaze, she directed her eyes toward his *iqal*, the thick black rope haloing his headdress.

"I am pleased to make your acquaintance." He reached for her hand and gently turned it over. First looking into her green sea glass eyes as if for permission, he then grazed her palm with the softest kiss.

Madeleine giggled. This man was so daring, she had no idea how to respond.

"Your suite is on the second floor." He reached behind him to a bank of numbered cubbies and lifted a brass key dangling from a hook. "Please, come."

The following morning, Madeleine awoke to the aroma of freshly brewed coffee wafting up the stairs. There came a knock on her door and before she could even say *entrez,* or rise to throw a robe over her shoulders, Aboud swept into her bedroom.

"Bonjour, ma belle." Aboud was carrying a breakfast tray, the contents of which he proceeded to set up on a little round table on the balcony. A pewter coffee service replete with creamer and sugar bowl, a hand-woven basket piled to overflowing with croissants, mini baguettes, and *pain au chocolat,* small pats of butter, and assorted miniature pots of jam.

"Have a seat." Aboud pulled a chair out for her.

She hesitated. Her night shift was sheer. Were Madeleine to approach the window where the sunlight was pouring in, he'd get quite a view. Did she dare? Yes, why not? So, on slender bare feet, Madeleine crossed the room, straight down a single ray of sunshine stretching across the floorboards. She moved slowly, locking eyes with Aboud's. She had no intention of being the first to pull away her gaze. And he, realizing she was ripe for the picking, held hers.

When Aboud handed her a napkin and their fingers brushed lightly, a pulsing heat rose in her.

Aboud sat down beside her. "It so happens that I have the morning free. Allow me to show you our city."

Acutely aware of his proximity and the citrus fragrance of his eau-de-cologne, a flush crept over Madeleine's chest and throat. Blooms of arousal reddened her cheeks.

Aboud's face settled into an expression of artificial concern as he placed the back of his hand on Madeleine's forehead. "Perhaps, you ought to go back to bed," he teased. "Skip the walk." He eyed her rumpled bed.

Madeleine smiled faintly at the wickedness of his suggestion, took a sip of coffee, and then began to butter a crusty portion of baguette. She spotted a pair of Moussier's redstarts loitering on the railing of her balcony. Their ebony heads and wings slashed with white sharply contrasted with their orange-red breasts. Aboud waited for her reply, a roguish grin tugging at his lips. Finally, she turned to study his face. He was all male, commanding: perfect teeth, alabaster-white against his dark complexion, square jawline, and brilliant blue eyes, the shade of lapis lazuli. He was a strikingly beautiful man. Irresistible.

Madeleine's smile was demure, a contrivance she'd practiced in front of the mirror ever since she was fourteen. But her heart was racing. "A walk into town would be lovely."

"A walk it is." On his way out, he flipped the bed covers back up over the pillows, leaving no misunderstanding as to what he would have preferred they do.

Chapter Seventeen

Aboud was waiting for Madeleine at the bottom of the stairs. When she appeared in a white blouse and a pair of loose-fitting men's white trousers cinched at the waist with a thin red leather belt, he nodded his approval.

Bowing at the waist, he swept his lips across the back of her hand, and said, *"Comme tu es belle, mademoiselle.* Très chic."

"Your French accent is perfect." Madeleine slipped her hand from his.

"I am half French, on my mother's side," Aboud replied. "It explains why my skin and my eyes are not as dark as a full-blooded Moroccan."

"I like your shade of brown." She looked into his face. "The contrast with your eyes is striking."

"And I am enthralled with your shade of yellow," he murmured, taking a strand of her gleaming hair in between his fingers. "It's like spun gold," he whispered in awe. A shiver ran down Madeleine's spine.

The two seemed to have forgotten they were standing in the lobby. Once again, they couldn't pull their eyes away from each other. Madeleine replied, "I'm half French too. On my father's side. I was raised in Brittany among the Celts."

"Ah, a pagan," Aboud mused. "I think the world of pagan

women. So free and uninhibited." His eyes scanned the length of her body.

The direction of their conversation, so unexpectedly suggestive, was startling. Madeleine, inexperienced with flirting yet eager to try her hand at it, wasn't sure how to handle the intensity she felt radiating from Aboud's taut body. She had never encountered so sexually alluring a man, and the fact that the chase was already underway threw her off balance. She was used to being in the lead, teasing the boys who didn't know how to respond. This fellow was no boy, and he very much did know what he was after.

Flicking her hair behind her shoulder, Madeleine sashayed across the foyer. Aboud did not follow, still rooted to the tiles at the foot of the staircase. She stopped and turned back to face him.

"Are you coming?"

It was already eighty-five degrees Fahrenheit and while Madeleine felt uncomfortably warm, Aboud seemed impervious to the heat. As they threaded their way through the crowded *souk*, Aboud's hand was warm and sure against the small of Madeleine's back. In the sweltering heat, she might have preferred his hands be kept to himself, but she liked the chivalry and wasn't about to reject it.

They headed down a narrow aisle crowded with spices, kilim cushions, colorful plates, embroidered leather poufs, and brightly woven blankets with little pompoms sewn into the hems.

"You're staring," Aboud bent to whisper in her ear.

She pointed at three women whose eyes were the only thing visible under black abayas. "Those poor women! I'd liquify like a scoop of sorbet buried under all that robing."

Aboud said, "They're used to it."

"Why do they wear such a ridiculous costume in this heat?" Madeleine fanned herself with her straw hat. "Is it modesty? Because if that's why, it's utterly ridiculous!" She clearly didn't like what she saw, just as her mother had warned.

"If they cover up, they cannot tempt men," Aboud explained. "We Moroccans don't like to share our women." He pulled Madeleine close to his hip. "À *chacun son goût, ma belle*." To each his own.

Madeleine felt scolded. Before she could come up with a quip of her own, loudspeakers on the minarets of a nearby mosque began to broadcast the muezzin's midday call to worship. Aboud reached for a small rug rolled up in a basket like so many distributed throughout the market. Turning eastward, he unfurled it on the ground at his feet. Dropping to his knees, he bent forward until his chest practically touched the ground and then stretched his arms out as far as they would go. Like a great white egret, Madeleine was left standing among a lake of dark-skinned men and women in prayer.

Shifting her weight from one foot to the other, she looked around, not sure what to do with herself. Should she move away or remain still? Suddenly, Madeleine detected the smell of cumin. Or was it coming from the portly merchant who had suddenly dropped behind his long counter of spices and disappeared from view? Containers rich with the blended aromas of saffron and curry and bottles of argan oil had already tickled her nose, and now, seeing all these people lying on the ground flatulating, Madeleine felt a giggle rise in her throat.

Aboud, sensing her disrespect, hissed, "Find somewhere else to be."

"Easy for you to say," she scoffed. "There are bodies everywhere."

"Go!" he snapped. "You don't belong here!"

Madeleine glared at the prone Aboud cross-eyed and stuck out her tongue. Where was she supposed to go? The women in the market seemed to have vanished. Between her fingers she twirled the yellow tansy flower Aboud had given her earlier. She flung it at his back.

Madeleine tried to circumvent the men unnoticed, but every now and then she was forced to hop over someone. Navigating around arms, feet, and heads, she kept up a steady stream of *pardonnez-moi* and *je m'excuse* as she weaved through the prostrated crowd. Feeling more and more out of place, she began to scurry down the market corridors. Stalls of patterned hemp rugs and woolen blankets stacked high beneath scores of intricate metal lamps of all shapes and sizes transformed the passageways into a kaleidoscope of moving shards of color. She raced past the cheerfully painted ceramic plates and shallow wicker baskets, things which normally would have tempted her to bargain. Hot tears of frustration ran down her cheeks. Even the fresh fruit and trays of pastries couldn't make her stop. Besides, there was no one to serve her, as they were all lying face down in a trance of devotion. Finally out on the sandy street, she breathed a sigh of relief.

Aboud caught up with her and grabbed her by the arm. "You cannot walk alone."

Madeleine snatched her arm away. "You told me to go away. Rudely, I might add. I'll bloody well do as I please!"

"Not in Morocco, *ma chère*." He adjusted his *ghutra*, which had unraveled during his run to catch up with her.

Madeleine was not inclined to give in. "You told me to go away, did you not?"

"In Morocco, women must be accompanied by a man at all times."

Madeleine glared at him. "You can't have it both ways."

"These are not my rules, my little firebird. Nonetheless, you must obey them while you are here in Marrakesh."

"Or else?"

"Leave the country." He said this deadpan. Did he really mean for her to go, just like that? She saw his expression shift from cross to amused. "But I don't think you want to, do you?"

Madeleine touched her chin with her finger as if considering her options. "Hmmm. Maybe yes, maybe no."

"Come, we'll sit at that café across the street." Aboud offered her his arm and she took it. "There is much I must teach you about our customs."

At their little wrought iron table, Aboud's long legs stretched out before him in so pleasing a manner, Madeleine felt the urge to sit on his lap. Knowing this to be too preposterous an antic in any culture in those days, she instead sat slowly, crossed her legs, smoothed a crease in her trousers, and dangled a foot close enough to the inside of Aboud's calf that he could feel the air whisper against his bare skin.

No sooner had they finished their glasses of *arak* than Aboud jumped up and tossed a few dirhams on the table. He held out his hand. "Let's go."

Madeleine unfolded her legs slowly before she stood. With her slender, long limbs, yellow-blonde hair, and sun-kissed skin, she knew she was alluring.

The walk back to Auberge Marrakesh was more of a sprint. For Aboud's every stride, Madeleine was obliged to take two or three. Clouds of sand churned under his heels and when they reached the hotel grounds, Aboud yanked her behind a waterfall of purple bougainvillea and pressed his body against hers.

"You're driving me mad!" He cupped her bottom in his hands and clasped her hips against his. With a roll of spasms flooding her body, Madeleine allowed herself to be pushed backward.

Aboud was pulling at her blouse when Madeleine stopped him. "Not here."

Aboud reluctantly dropped his hands.

"Tonight?" she offered.

"I do not like your games." He ran his hand down the front of his robe. "I'm going to tell you something you should know about men."

Madeleine's ocean-green eyes stared him down. "And that is?"

"To seduce but not follow through is dangerous." Aboud strode away, every footfall laced with fury.

Larochette,
Luxembourg

May 1945

Chapter Eighteen

Destination Larochette, Luxembourg: a quaint market town, which lay sleepily in a narrow valley. Ernst and Klaus could barely see as their truck churned its way down the unpaved road, which was entirely enveloped by woods. It meant they were off the beaten track and well shielded from view. Sheets of rain cut diagonally across the windshield, making it hard to dodge the potholes. Skidding right, then left in the thick mud left by springtime's melting snow had both boys tense with frustration. At least they'd reached their first layover without detection.

Ernst approached the farmhouse while Klaus remained behind the wheel—a necessary precaution in case a quick escape was called for. As far as Klaus was concerned, no so-called safe and secure location was ever a sure thing.

Ernst was less skeptical. He took a deep breath and tapped lightly on the door. Shifting his weight from foot to foot, he waited. He thought he heard movement coming from the upper floor, but nothing. Ernst knocked again, this time a little louder. When still no one came to the door, he turned toward Klaus in the truck and shrugged. Having to wait this long didn't seem right, and Ernst's heart began to hammer so loudly, he could barely hear himself think.

To make matters worse, Allied bombs were continuing to fall to the east. They thumped dully like the faraway footfall of mastodons, which had Ernst spooked. "Do you hear that?" Ernst called, peering into the cab. Klaus nodded, convulsing a response.

At last, a light came on, but still, no one came to the door. The longer it took for their contact to show his face, the more nervous both men became. Klaus, who'd had enough, frantically waved to Ernst to return to the truck.

"It's a trap," Klaus hissed, throwing the truck into reverse. He gunned the engine, but the truck refused to move, his tires unable to gain traction in the mud. "Sonuvabitch!" he exclaimed.

Just then, the farmhouse door opened.

A grizzled old fella, naked but for his tattered robe gaping open and his bare feet shoved into unlaced Stormtrooper's boots, stood there appraising them from his stoop. Seemingly satisfied, he greeted them with a *Sieg Heil*. Ernst and Klaus climbed out of the cab and returned the salute, chuckling. This was hardly Hitler's finest specimen of a Nazi diehard, but then who were they to judge? If this farmer would hide the propaganda until it was safe to be in another transport and on the road again, so be it.

Wordlessly, the farmer, whose name had been deliberately withheld from their orders, pointed at the truck, the barn and then panto-mimed the locking of a door. Klaus understood the instructions and returned to his vehicle. Ernst, leaning sideways, looked longingly inside the house. If that body language weren't enough of a hint, he scuffed the mud from his Wellingtons on the metal boot scraper af-fixed to the threshold and gave the old geezer a look suggesting he be invited in.

"*Hereinkommen*," the farmer said when Klaus was back on the doorstep. Inside the dark kitchen, smoke from a wood-burning fire hung in the air, the embers in the fireplace still aglow. Reaching into an icebox and extracting three bottles of home brew, never mind it was only ten o'clock in the morning, the farmer handed one to each of his guests. He popped the cap off his and raising it, cried,

"*Prost!*" Without even bothering to savor it, he chugged the entire thing down.

Ernst wiped his mouth with his sleeve. "Where can we get some sleep?"

"And get some food?" added Klaus.

The farmer nodded and bent to pull back a small rug. He lifted a trap door and gesticulated with his head that down below was where they should hide. Wary and none too happy, Ernst and Klaus descended into the dark, where they found by feel a mattress and a couple of blankets.

Klaus lay down and folded his arms behind his head. Staring up at the ceiling, he said, "I don't like this. What if that guy is a phony?"

"It's an easy mission. Don't be such a *dummkopf.*"

"What if the war ends and we get killed anyway?"

"Stop worrying about dying," Ernst scolded. "Worry about not living."

"You're getting your rocks off transporting this crap, aren't you?"

"Yeah, I sorta am."

Despite there being nothing to eat, both Ernst and Klaus fell asleep in minutes.

Le Petit Oiseau received her second telegram in the middle of the day when no one was home. Upon reading it, she balled it up and tossed it into the fireplace.

PROP ART EN ROUTE STOP
HAVE LOCATED A HELPFUL FRIEND STOP
ADVISE WHEN READY STOP

Chapter Nineteen

Climbing from their hiding place beneath the kitchen floorboards in Larochette the next morning, Ernst and Klaus were invited to sit at a table set for breakfast. The boys, overjoyed to see such a feast laid out in front of them, began to devour the charcuterie, cheese, and two-day-old baguette without even taking a seat. Eventually, the two recruits sank into chairs, fully satiated now that their bellies were full.

"Your next stop will be the *Clinique Française*, on the western outskirts of Amiens," the farmer said. "That ambulance out there is how you're gonna do it." The farmer pointed over his shoulder with his thumb.

Ernst was the first to scrape his chair back and go to the window. A wall of storm clouds hung low over the farm, and the yard was evermore a soupy mess of mud.

"You better get after it," the farmer said. "I've heard there are some American soldiers slinking around town asking questions."

"Army?" asked Ernst.

"Dunno. They're out of uniform, but that doesn't mean they aren't."

"Oh great, just great." Ernst grabbed two slices of ham and stuffed them in his jacket. What was left of the bread, he shoved into his pants pocket. "We gotta leave now!"

Klaus snatched up the cheese and swigged the last of his beer. *"Scheisse!"*

"Dumb asses," the farmer said. "Did you guys fail to notice that ambulance out there? You gotta transfer what's in my barn into it before you go anywhere."

"We gotta do that?" Klaus whined. "I thought another crew was gonna do that while we got us some shut-eye."

"Well, ya thought wrong."

Ernst kicked the chair across the kitchen, strode to the door, and flung it open so hard it hit and dented the wall. He stepped out into the rain. "C'mon, Klaus, we got zero time to waste."

"Thanks for nuthin'," Klaus snarled.

Once Klaus had the barn doors unlocked and slid open, he tossed the farmer's key into the overgrown weeds and ground it into the mud with the heel of his boot. "That'll fix you, you bloody old coot," he mumbled.

Ernst backed the ambulance up to the rear of the lorry inside. At least this way, the boys could pass the crates of art from one vehicle to the other without having to set them down and lift them back up. It was a straight-across operation from one truck interior to the other and took no more than three quarters of an hour.

Klaus stood back to examine their efforts, rubbing his neck. "I'm not sure we should have loaded the smaller pieces first. Shouldn't the big ones be in the back so they're not leaning on the more fragile ones?"

"Who gives a shit?" Ernst grumbled, slamming the ambulance doors shut. "You wanna do it over?"

Ernst and Klaus climbed into the cab and immediately fell into a stony silence. With eyes forward, straining to see the road through the pelting rain, neither one noticed a pair of binoculars trained on them as they made their way through the town's first intersection. Nor did they spy the second pair of eyes watching as they left town a few minutes later.

Le Petit Oiseau tore open the telegram.

OPP HEADING FOR AMIENS STOP

Très bien, the art would soon be in France. Apparently, it was hopscotching its way toward the Atlantic, but where to ultimately was still unknown. It could turn toward the English Channel, head into Belgium or the Netherlands and be loaded onto a ship bound for the North Sea. Or once through France, the prop art could veer south across the Pyrenées and into General Franco's Spain, whose official status with the Nazis had been for the most part neutral. No sense worrying about it, though, because the Americans were clearly hot on its trail. She did wonder, though, if she should alert them that their "helpful friend" had already arrived safely. No, if they knew where the art was, they probably knew where their SOE agent was, too.

Billy

April - May 1945

Chapter Twenty

Outside, a steel-wool sky swallowed Mount Rainier while the endless rain struck the windowpane. Billy sat in a corner of the hospital patient lounge reading the *Seattle Times*. The newspaper lay open on the table so that he could turn the pages with his good hand. His left arm, what remained of it, rested inert at his side. Across the room, an unfamiliar man was staring at him. If it weren't for the article with its riveting good news, Billy might have spent more time wondering who this fella was and why he seemed so interested in him.

"Can I buy you a drink?"

Billy looked up, startled. "Who's asking?"

"Larry, but it's not my real name." A short balding fellow slid into the banquette with Billy. "Like what you're readin'?"

Billy looked the guy over. He was a short, bespectacled fellow with a round head, round torso, and pigeon-toed feet. Since the accident, he'd been skeptical about anyone getting too close. "I'll take a Scotch. Neat."

"A man with a sense of humor," Larry said. Alcohol was not permitted on army hospital grounds.

"It's pretty much all I got left," quipped Billy.

"I want you to consider what I have to say." Larry smiled a tight grin, more an affectation than anything sincere.

"Okay, hit me."

By way of a preamble, Larry nodded at the newspaper. "Some story, uh."

According to the paper, nine hundred and fifty Flying Fortresses had just rumbled over Berlin in broad daylight, laying waste to the city yet again. It appeared Germany's defeat was imminent, and the demise of Adolf Hitler's Third Reich was all but certain.

...the boulevards leading to and from the city center were distinguishable landmarks even at high altitude. Had it not been for Adolf Hitler who had rebuilt this linden-treed avenue for his vainglorious marches and propaganda parades, the U.S. Army's B-17 bombers might not have been blessed with so clear a target. And by a stroke of serendipity, the Reichstag, Reich Chancellery, Goebel's Propaganda Ministry, and Göring's Air Ministry were all centrally located. Two thousand, two hundred and seventy bombs pummeled each one of these government buildings. Berlin is decimated.

...twenty-one direct hits leveled Germany's Central Bank to a smoking pile of rubble. an unnamed resource on the ground reports that Germany's national wealth—its deposits, reserves, gold, cash and bonds—lies unharmed in vaults below ground. Never doubting there would be another strike and that this time the assets would be completely obliterated, Hitler ordered his assets be moved to an undisclosed location for safekeeping.

Larry waved the waitress over. "Gimme a soda water and . . . what'll ya have, Billy?"

"Water, please. No splash, no rocks." One could only imagine a stiff drink.

The man pointed at Billy's newspaper. "Wanna hear the rest of that story you won't find anywhere else?"

"Sure," Billy replied.

"On their way to Berlin April 4th, General George Patton's 90th Division happened to march into a little old mining town called Merkers and captured it. Shortly thereafter, a pair of young women walking home past their curfew were given a lift by two American GI's. These chatty Patties told our troops that Germany's state reserves were hiding in the nearby mines. You can imagine how fast this news zoomed up the chain of command. The Kaiseroda Mine was immediately placed under heavy guard. But guess what? They failed to do it right away."

Billy let go a whistle. "That's one hell of a discovery."

Larry nodded. "The next day, top brass showed up. Generals Eisenhower, Bradley, and Patton; all of 'em. When they descended a twenty-one-hundred-foot shaft to a series of salt rock caverns below, they found a horde of wealth winking in the torch light. Baled paper currency from around the world. Trunks gaping open with diamonds, pearls, and other precious gems. They were spilling onto the dirt floor like pirates' treasure. Thousands of watches, eye glasses, and gold wedding rings along with gold fillings still embedded in extracted teeth lay in mounds as high as the generals' knees. Sacks of gold bullion worth an estimated $240,000 were heaped in rows along the walls of Room #8."

"Holy shit!"

"There were crates of silver and gold plate, presumably awaiting smelting."

"Did these valuables belong to all those Jews the Nazis sent to the camps?" Billy's forehead creased.

"I'm afraid so." Both men paused for a moment to reflect on so horrible a situation. Larry resumed, "Bradley is rumored to have muttered to Patton, 'If these were the ol' free lootin' days when a

111

soldier got to keep his loot, we'd be the richest men in the world!'"

"I don't need to know this. It's kinda gallows humor, don't you think?"

"Yeah, well," hedged Larry, "ya know how the military gets kinda crass."

"How come I get to hear all this and the rest of the world doesn't?" Billy asked.

"Hold your horses, cowboy, I'm not finished." He gulped his soda and water, wiped his mouth with the back of his hand, and inhaled. "Priceless masterpieces by Pablo Picasso, Marc Chagall, Salvador Dali, Henri Matisse, Renoir, and Vincent van Gogh, which had all been stolen from either Europe's galleries or families' private collections, were found leaning against stone-cold walls of adjoining vaults. Antiques, fine china, and crystal were strewn everywhere. Vintage tapestries and Oriental rugs lay on the floor buried under layers of dust and spiderwebs." He stopped abruptly. "Ya wanna prove yourself, doncha Billy?" This was more a statement than a question. "I have the perfect mission for you."

Billy was suddenly alert. "Why me?" Billy lifted his half-arm as if Larry needed to be reminded of his disability.

"Three reasons. One: no one knows you survived that crash, everyone presumes you're dead." Billy looked away, annoyed that this guy knew so much about him. "*You* wanted it that way," Larry reminded him. "Why you've withheld this information from your family is none of my business. "Besides, your anonymity suits our needs to a tee."

"The second?" Billy cleared his throat, a habit he had when cross. His lips were drawn in a tight line.

"Everything housed in that damn Kaiseroda Mine stinks of the Final Solution. As a man with no history other than the one we will fabricate, you're the mensch who can help us to make sure there's no Fourth Reich. No more genocide."

"And the third reason?"

"Your daddy'll be seriously proud of you when he finds out what you've accomplished for the United States of America." Larry thumped him on his good shoulder. "The whole world will thank you."

How in the world did this fellow know it mattered to Billy what his father thought?

**General Dwight D. Eisenhower surveying
stolen art in Merkers mine**

Gold Bullion and Currency discovered in The Merkers Mine

Painting by Édouard Manet Discovered in The Merkers Mine

German Gold Stashed in The Merkers Mine

115

Chapter Twenty-One

The next morning, Billy found Larry pacing back and forth in front of the entrance to Rhododendron Glen in the Washington Park Arboretum.

"You're late," Larry groused.

"I got lost." In truth, Billy hadn't been at all sure he wanted to pursue further discussion with this strange little man.

"Let's stroll, shall we?" The two men, one tall and the other barely reaching his shoulder, began to walk side by side. Billy was bent at the waist in order to better listen to what Larry had to say.

Larry surveyed the area to see if there were any visitors within earshot, then looked up at Billy and wagged a finger close to his face. "You'll keep your voice down. Is that understood?"

"Got it," Billy said gruffly.

"We want you to go undercover." Billy stopped in his tracks and lifted his abbreviated arm. *What kind of question was that to ask an amputee?* But Billy merely said, "Go on."

"I cannot specifically tell ya in what capacity we'd use your talents, but should you be willing to train for an operation that may or may not happen, show up at this place and on this date." Larry pressed a small business card into Billy's hand.

Billy read the address. "Jesus H. Christ! Northern Scotland?" he fairly shouted. "That's halfway around the world!"

"Shush!" Larry clapped him on the upper arm and quickly scanned their surroundings. The two walked further down the path. "Give it some thought. If you do decide to contribute to the war effort, there'll be no telling nobody nothin' about where you're at neither."

Billy, who never read a book and was usually pretty laid back, winced at the horrendous grammar.

"Understood?"

"What if I decide to not be dead anymore and I want to go home to my wife?"

"Then you're dead to me, pal." And with that, Billy's short little incognito acquaintance veered off the path and disappeared into a grove of red cedars.

Billy sat on a bench where the stream emptied into a shallow pond surrounded by Japanese maples and other small trees. A gurgling stream with its springtime music was irritatingly cheerful. His heart began to gallop as he contemplated what was being asked of him. *Why me*, he wondered, *why now?* The war's end seemed imminent, so what could possibly be happening in the European theatre? Or in the Hebrides, of all godforsaken places? Or would he be sent to the Pacific theatre where the war labored on?

That April, the Allied offensive had already begun in northern Italy. American and British troops were liberating occupants of German death camps in Ohrdruf, Buchenwald, and Bergen-Belsen. The horrors discovered there were reportedly indescribable. Bratislava had fallen into Soviet hands as those troops pressed westward toward Berlin. A race was on among the Allies to reach the German capital first, and it was said the Nazis preferred to be overtaken by the Americans over the Soviets, because the latter's retaliatory tactics were rumored to be far more ruthless. Bombing raids from Tinian in the Mariana Islands were a nightly occurrence, and the Battle of Okinawa was raging. What was to come next in

Japan was anyone's guess.

The disconnect was how hellish the world had become, though not where Billy sat at that very moment. Rhododendron Glen had opened up into a valley bursting with color. Flowering cherries, islands of trees and shrubs, and swaths of green lawn spilled down to another pond bordering on Azalea Way. It seemed bizarre to be surrounded by so much beauty, and yet east and west of him war was ravaging nations, leaving unspeakable death and annihilation in its wake.

"Damn that Hitler," Billy muttered under his breath. "He's gone and polluted the whole damn world. Same with that foolish little Emperor Hirohito and his power-hungry henchmen." Billy looked up at heaven. "Tell me, God, if you even exist, why?"

Billy thought back to his days in hospital. When he had finally broken through the fog of a prolonged coma, he learned he had not only half his arm, but that his spine was in traction, and he had a brain injury which the doctors hoped was only temporary amnesia. Severely afflicted with anxiety over not being able to remember a thing, as well as traumatized by the loss of a limb, Billy was capable only of expressing his fevered wish to die. Consequently, the doctors and nurses had no other recourse than to keep him heavily sedated. For no known reason at the time, the army had aggressively concurred.

While Billy languished, and unbeknownst to him at the time, a funny little bespectacled fellow from Langley, Virginia, had stepped in to supervise his care. He stayed in the background, but as a representative of the United States government he had plans for Billy—should he emerge, that is, from his present condition. He forbade the hospital staff, including Billy's commanding officer, to relay to anyone and specifically Billy's family that he'd been found and was alive. It was best that not only Billy's family, but also the whole world not know what was in store for Billy. Until further notice,

Billy was to remain dead.

At the time Larry was floating around at the hospital, Billy hadn't known that it was he orchestrating his care and keeping the truth from his family. He thought the doctors and nurses were honoring his own stated wishes to not contact his family. He wasn't ready for Claire or his parents to come rushing to Seattle to slather sympathy all over him. Crippled and unseemly, Billy really had been harboring a strong desire to simply disappear. So, he was treated with anti-depressants and forced to visit with a psychotherapist. The shrink's verdict was that Billy was suffering from survivor's guilt, a condition occurring when an individual believes he has done something terribly wrong by surviving a traumatic event when others, who were with him, did not.

Once Billy was living as an outpatient in a nearby hotel he still felt as though he were neither here nor there. He was without purpose, and lonely from his self-imposed isolation. And now, he found himself in quite the pickle. If he did tell Claire about Larry's proposition, how could he leave her yet again? Claire would never understand. She hadn't wanted him to serve in the first place. She'd argue he'd been given a medical discharge due to the loss of his lower left arm, so he was free to come home. She'd rail, *What is stopping you?* And he'd be obliged to fight back, *It's what every patriotic man is supposed to do, especially if he's fighting for a free world! And isn't every patriotic wife supposed to support her husband's wish to serve?*

Billy continued along the path meandering through the heart of the arboretum. It featured every color of azalea in the rainbow. Pink and white dogwoods were in full bloom, their delicate blossoms fluttering in the breeze. Up ahead, a governess in full gray and white nanny regalia, replete with perky cap and short cape, was pushing a baby carriage. Wham! A terrible reminder of loss hit Billy smack between the eyes. He scuffed angrily at the gravel pathway with the toe of his shoe.

Here again, Billy had no compelling reason to go home. Without the promise of children to color his and Claire's future—their not having agreed to anything other than a stalemate—the years ahead seemed bleak. To boot, the socialite lifestyle of the Campbells could never fill a childless void. Of that Billy was certain. Plus, Larry was right. Billy needed to be needed. He clearly gravitated toward the notion that if his country and fellow soldiers needed him, he should honor them. "Do it for the guys who died." Larry had said. "Do it so they aren't forsaken." It was what an army officer did—he honored the fallen and if possible, never left a fellow soldier behind. This work was far more noble than the vacuous life of a socialite back at home. Here was a chance to reinvent himself.

Guilt nagged Billy. *Maybe, I should tell Dad I'm alive, and just swear him to secrecy.* Billy was wavering again.

It had begun to rain, and Billy exited the Seattle park at a jog. He dashed across the rain-splattered street to his hotel. Once inside, he crossed the lobby and signaled the concierge behind the desk that he wanted to use one of the telephones in a long bank of booths at the back of the lobby. He plopped down heavily on the triangle-corner bench, slid the bi-fold door closed, and lifted the receiver.

"Operator."

Billy craned forward to speak into the mouthpiece mounted to the phone on the wall. "AM 4598," he said hoarsely, tears welling up.

"One moment, please." Billy blew out his cheeks and waited. "Connecting AM4598."

His parents' phone began to ring. "Operator? Never mind. Cancel that, please."

Chapter Twenty-Two

As they were buckling into their seats on the Boeing 314 Clipper, Larry scolded, "That was a bad move, Billy."

How the hell did he know? Billy knew he'd been out of line, but all he'd wanted was to reassure his father before he boarded the flying boat to Scotland that he was alive and kicking. "I didn't let the call go through."

"Yeah, but you were real close." He shook his head and sighed. "I'm not sure we can trust you to keep your mouth shut."

"You can trust me." Staring out the window, he added, "Try to understand how I might feel just a tad guilty about letting my family think me dead. For all I know they've given me a big fancy send-off at Saint Pat's, settled my estate, and gone into mourning. Is that really fair?"

"They did," Larry said flatly. "Though I'm not sure they've been able to do anything with the dissolution of your trust fund."

They were on their way to Europe, using one of the North Atlantic air ferry routes originally developed by the US to securely shuttle aircraft manufactured in America to Great Britain and France in '41 and '42. They were flying on what was known as the Crimson Route from Seattle via Montana over Canada to Greenland and across the Atlantic into Scotland. In 1945, the Crimson Route was officially defunct, which was precisely why they were using it.

Billy and Larry were alone on the flying boat and it would be a mistake to say Pan Am's luxurious layout wasn't impressive.

"I could get used to this," Billy said, nodding his head.

"As if Mr. William Wentworth Campbell III isn't accustomed to comfortable travel," Larry scoffed. "Just know, where you're going it ain't the Ritz."

"Take it easy," Billy said, laughing. "I was just paying your outfit a compliment."

Larry decided to reveal a little more information. "You'll be training with Churchill's secret army." Impressed, Billy sat up straighter. "Agents of the Special Operations Executive, otherwise known as the SOE. They gather intelligence and perform sabotage operations such as blowing up munitions factories and bridges, or fun shit like derailing trains. Their purpose is to slow the advancement of the German Army across France and destroy supply lines."

"I get to work with them? Now you're talkin'!"

Ignoring him, Larry droned on. "You'll receive basic training at Dunrobin Castle, which, along with its grounds and five miles of coastline, has been commandeered for use as a facility where candidates are evaluated for physical and psychological soundness to perform as operatives in enemy territory."

Billy's heart pounded with excitement. "Where's Dunrobin Castle?"

"In the county of Sutherland in the Scottish Highlands, overlooking the North Sea. Dunrobin is one of Scotland's oldest continuously lived-in houses, dating back to the 1300s."

"That's pretty remote."

"Which is the point."

"You ever gonna tell me your real name?" Billy asked, determined to remain cheerful.

"Candidates and their handlers are not permitted to divulge their names or any details of their personal lives to each other. Agents are not to know where you come from or where you went to school, not even your favorite book."

"I don't have a favorite book," Billy admitted freely.

"We know."

"Oh, ha ha."

"It's for an agent's protection. You'll understand soon enough."

Billy closed his eyes and leaned back against the headrest. Several minutes elapsed with his being deep in thought. He envisioned the Kaiseroda Mine filled with those precious belongings of the Jewish people. It was outrageous. "I can't help but wonder, as I'm sure everyone has, how in the hell did Hitler ever convince an entire country that *Lebensraum, the need for more room*, was a good thing?"

"Goes to show you can never underestimate the power of propaganda."

"I'd like to think that by their silence, the German people didn't know what was happening or what they were condoning."

"All I can say is they don't need to be repeatin' this history."

"You can say that again!" Billy replied.

The Highlands proved to be as beautiful a landscape as Billy had ever seen. Nothing in his experience compared to the color and texture of the mountains, moors, and beaches of Sutherland. As if the scenery weren't magical enough, Dunrobin Castle with its fairy-tale turrets rose above the North Sea like a picture-book illustration.

In the great hall of Dunrobin's entrance, Billy gaped as he turned three hundred and sixty degrees. A frieze of armorials belonging to past Earls and Dukes of Sutherland, going all the way back to 1401, graced all four walls.

Billy grinned appreciatively when a pretty redhead approached.

As was the norm whenever he encountered a female, she became flustered. So, to fill the void left by her discomfiture, he said with a grin, "Dunrobin is such a charming name. What does it mean?"

"It means Robin's Hill in Gaelic," she said, averting his eyes.

"I'll leave you here," Larry said. "And Billy? Number one rule? Don't get entangled with the gals."

So this was Britain's espionage headquarters, as remote and hidden as any stronghold of agents in training there ever was. Billy soon learned that there was not a single résumé which made for an ideal agent. No special degree, no particular background or upbringing. It was simply a matter of who could do the work or who had nerves of steel. If there were a type, he or she was smart, adaptable, and proficient in powers of persuasion. He or she could tell a lie with a straight face, pick a lock, or summon enough courage to risk capture. It didn't hurt to be motivated by a deep-seated hate for a mass-murdering tyrant, either. As far as Billy was concerned, anyone who sought to rob him of everything he held dear was looking for a punch in the nose or better yet, a kick in the balls. Billy was put through rigorous physical exercises which tested both his nerve and stamina. He learned how to translate in code and operate a radio. He became an expert at breaking into buildings to steal and/or photograph documents. He was drilled in weaponry, field and trade craft, intelligence-gathering, and reporting. The final class was make-or-break in the elimination process. Fail this segment and he'd be going home, wherever that was. Pass, and he'd be assigned a mission.

The last test came in the form of a stress interview in which he was subjected to a mock Gestapo interrogation. Billy suspected the instructors would come at him hard given his history with depression, but Billy made it through with surprising poise. Apparently, his charm had stood him in very good stead. While Billy waited to hear how he had fared, he dedicated the final weekend to perfecting his reflexive memory of his newly assigned name and identity.

Memorizing so many details was one thing. Incorporating them as his own, and reflexively so, was another.

He passed with flying colors.

That Sunday night, just one week before VE Day was to mark the end of World War II in Europe, William Wentworth Campbell III signed his real name for the last time. He officially became Buck Connor, the American ex-pat and committed Francophile, whose landscape art was much admired by the art community in Paris and Provence.

Buck's mission was to prevent the flow of Nazi propaganda art out of Germany to parts unknown. He was billeted to Kersaint, a quaint fishing village in the northwest corner of Brittany, France. When his instructors raised their glasses of Montrachet to toast him, Buck beamed. He was about to do something very important. Dispossessing Germany of its best tools of propaganda meant Buck was safeguarding the future welfare of Europe's people as well as those of the United States of America. Should Germany's intent to resurrect its empire of tyranny be taken seriously—a Fourth Reich—then all the more reason to lock up the propaganda and never let it see the light of day. Hitler's Thousand Year Reich be damned!

In advance of Billy's arrival in France, his contact, Le Petit Oiseau, received a telegram from Dunrobin Castle.

FORTY-EIGHT HOURS STOP

March 1945

Chapter Twenty-Three

Aboud, swarthy and smelling of lemons, held open the door to the jeep for Madeleine. He had told her very little about their outing. The only hint was that she bring nothing but the clothes she was wearing and expect to see the most exquisite scenery in all of north Africa.

Aboud was a vision in blue. His gandoura, a loose-fitting cotton tunic with three-quarter- length sleeves, complemented his light-skinned complexion. Underneath, he wore a pair of *quandrissi* pants and ochre slippers.

"You look like Aladdin," Madeleine giggled. He was not amused. " . . . a very handsome genie who makes magic with my heart," she quickly corrected. Heaven forbid she ruin this, their first outing since that day at the market. Aboud, who had avoided her ever since she'd pushed him away at the height of his ardor, had finally ended his punishment.

Aboud smirked and spanked her bottom as she clambered into the jeep. "Behave," he admonished.

Madeleine intended to play it demure on this date. She knew now not to tease him, so today she was the essence of femininity, dressed in a Delft-blue jumper with little yellow flowers over a short-sleeved white blouse, open at the collar. A mere filament of a gold chain encircled her neck, and in the hollow of her throat nested a single white pearl.

"You'll need this where we're going," Aboud said as he handed her a *melhfa*. Protection if we encounter rough winds." She looked quizzical. "Sandstorms."

A silver single-engine bi-plane glinted in the sun.

"Ooh, you must be really rich if you own this," Madeleine cooed. Aboud barely smiled. "May I ask how you've come by your wealth? I know it's rude, but I'm not one to hold back."

"Oil," he said gruffly. Unaided, she climbed onto the wing and into the open-air cockpit.

"Surely now you can tell me where we are going," she asked sweetly.

"The Sahara desert, my pet. You're about to see the most exquisite scenery in all of Africa."

"And?"

"To a hideaway so secret nobody will know where to find us." He looked over his shoulder.

"Oh."

"You're not yourself today," Aboud observed. "You're very quiet."

"I'm on my best behavior."

He put on his goggles, signaled for her to do the same, and turned back around to face the controls. Once the propeller on the nose started to turn, the engine roared to life. Madeleine covered her ears against the roar and tucked her chin down as the plane started to roll forward. Jostled like a rag doll over the uneven tarmac, she braced herself against the sides of the fuselage with both elbows and knees. It wasn't long before Madeleine and Aboud were crossing over the first dunes of the Sahara, which, according to Aboud, covered over three and a half million square miles. An unfathomable stretch of ivory desert lay before them like an ocean. From time to time Madeleine shut her eyes against the fierce glare of the sun off the hot, white sand. Still, the desert's dazzling light seeped in behind her closed eyelids.

"Can you see my little oasis below?" Aboud shouted above the clamor. He pointed to their two o'clock. Madeleine craned her neck to look. A Berber tent, its red and black stripes stark against the pale sand, was nestled against a crescent of dunes rising as high as five hundred feet. A pair of camels was tied to a railing.

Aboud banked the plane left and pushed the stick forward. He lined the aircraft up with a sand-covered airstrip lying camouflaged on the desert floor. The landing was cushion-soft, but the blizzard of desert sand was brutal.

Aboud lit a campfire. As the sinking sun retreated with the last of the day's heat, he and Madeleine sat on a rise, their bare toes buried in the cool sand. To the west, past ridgeline after ridgeline of dune, the setting sun began to ignite the desert. Soon, the landscape and horizon were in flames of red and orange.

Madeleine turned to Aboud in amazement. *"Comme c'est magnifique!"*

They sat entwined as a full moon rose and a canopy of stars hung low over their heads. The desert's silence was loud and resounding

Aboud finally spoke. "I've waited long enough. Come." He stood and pulled Madeleine to her feet. Taking her hand, he led her down the sandy slope to the tent. Once inside, he spun her around and grasped her head with both hands. Tracing her jawline with his thumbs, he surveyed her face. Then he tilted her head back and kissed and bit her neck. Pressing his lips to hers, offering at first a warm and wet caress, he turned hungry, sucking her bottom lip and driving his tongue deep into her throat. His fingers dug into her arms and he ground hard against her hips.

Abruptly, Aboud backed off and fell backward upon a mattress of quilts and kilim pillows. "Undress," he ordered.

Madeleine slowly shed her clothing, all the while keeping her green cat's eyes on his face. Once she was naked, she reached around to the back of her head and unfastened her barrette. A curtain of gold cascaded to her breasts like a waterfall. Aboud's mouth fell open and, wolf-like, he licked his lips.

Madeleine was curled in the fetal position naked and alone when she woke. It was still dark, and it was freezing cold. She was bruised and torn and frightened. Rising from the mattress, she found her clothes and hastily dressed. With arms wrapped around herself, she stepped from the tent. Aboud sat cross-legged in front of a freshly laid campfire enveloped in all the quilts from inside. He spread his arms wide and, reluctantly, only because the desert morning was so inexplicably cold, did she sit within his lap. He closed the blankets around them both and dropped his chin on her shoulder. They sat in silence, she curling her toes in the sand, waiting for the sun and wondering how last night could have happened.

Despite the beauty of the view of the desert endlessly unfolding in wave upon wave all the way from the eastern horizon, Madeleine was too wounded to be impressed. The silence of so vast a place did serve, however, to accentuate how Madeleine felt: very small, incredibly vulnerable, and full of regret. She didn't think her abused body or soul could take much more, but she refused to cry.

Aboud kicked sand over the fire with his foot. He flopped down on top of her. "Why are you dressed, *ma petite*?" She could feel his arousal. "I'm not finished feasting."

Madeleine gritted her teeth. "Since you refer to me as a meal, I will tell you you've had quite enough."

"I can have my way with you whether you like it or not," he snarled, "but on second thought, you aren't worth my time." Aboud shoved her away and stood up. "Let's go." Those sultry cerulean eyes in which Madeleine had lost herself that first day were now as hard as iron.

Keeping up a front of indifference, Madeleine shrugged and said, "Yes, I think so."

Chapter Twenty-Four

Back at L'Auberge Marrakesh, Madeleine raced up the stairs to her room, slammed the door, and threw herself on the bed. Sobbing into the sheets, she never heard Aboud slither into her room.

He loomed over her prostrate body and bellowed, "*Ferme ta gueule*. Shut your trap!" Alarmed, Madeleine flipped over and backed against the pillows. "Stay away from me!" she screamed, tears coursing down her flushed cheeks.

"Worry not, *ma belle*. I only came to tell you that a car will be ready in the morning to take you to the airport."

"But I'm not leaving."

"Yes, ma petite, you are very much leaving." His white teeth gleaming in the semi-dark made Madeleine recoil deeper into the pillows. "I've chartered a private plane to fly you back to France." He stepped away from the bed. "A small price to pay for your oh-so-sour cherry."

"How dare you speak to me that way!" Madeleine's temper was kicking in. "You and I are over, but I'm still here on holiday." It was an irrational choice, but she was not to be bullied.

"And you will be gone from my premises, effective tomorrow."

Madeleine wanted to be gone too, but she didn't want this odious man to have the last word. "Get out!" Madeleine hurled the bedside lamp at Aboud. It crashed to the floor as the door closed behind his retreating back. *"Espèce de cochon!* You disgust me!" she shrieked.

When Madeleine awoke the next morning, a little hung over, the sun was small and already boiling hot. Slipping into a sleeveless saffron yellow shift—culture be damned—and a pair of espadrilles, she checked herself one more time in the mirror and went downstairs. She had no intention of settling her bill.

A black Renault with brown leather seats sat idling under the porte-cochère. Aboud stood by the rear passenger door, his eyes flashing under their straight black brows. Madeleine glanced at him. His gaze was unblinking.

"Espèce de con," she muttered as she climbed into the backseat of the car.

Aboud chuckled at the insult, content to watch her long comely legs fold up into the backseat of the Renault. As the driver climbed into the front seat, Aboud blew Madeleine a kiss and kicked the door closed.

Madeleine flinched but kept her eyes forward.

At the furthest point of northwestern France, where the English Channel meets the Atlantic Ocean, a tray of gunmetal gray clouds hung low over the port of Brest. As Madeleine looked down at her beloved homeland, her heart swelled. Even though the Nazi destruction could be seen for miles, this was home. As the plane banked and straightened out for its final approach, her heart thrummed faster with anticipation. She thought to herself, *My precious Brittany, you are such a sight for sore eyes.*

So, the wonder of camels, the drama of sandstorms, the fragrant perfumes of mimosa or the theater of fiery desert sands be damned. Aboud Mohammed Abbas, you be damned too. It was exciting at first but disastrous in the end. Never would she admit it to her mother. Her homecoming did present problems, though. While she relished listening to the chirr of crickets at dusk or smelling the pungent aroma of purple lilacs and yellow honeysuckle outside her bedroom window, she didn't look forward to her mother's nagging. Listening to the surf whisper as it kept time with her breath, she vowed to forget Aboud. Madeleine slept fitfully. When she awoke to the soft cooing from a pair of mourning doves cuddling in the clematis, she burst into tears. She went to stand at her gable window and watch the sun rise in a pink sky against the gray backdrop of the English Channel. Seagulls were playfully plunging headfirst into the waves. She felt utterly alone. When Sophie barged into her room with a tray of piping hot coffee, baguette, and homemade blackberry jam, she barked, "Go away!"

Claire

April - May 1945

Chapter Twenty-Five

It was past midnight and as usual, Claire's efforts to fall asleep had failed. Neither the hot bath in her clawfoot tub, nor the steaming cup of chamomile tea, nor even a dull textbook could lull her into the oblivion she sought. To her dismay, the doctor had refused to prescribe any more sleeping pills.

So, Claire rose from her bed, wrapped herself in Billy's gray and crimson Harvard bathrobe, and paced around the apartment. Her feet slippered in a pair of argyle socks, she crossed to the pair of Palladian windows looking down on Madison Avenue. The commotion of a city which never slept was drowned out by the churning of Claire's mind.

Claire sank to the floor and covered her face with her hands. Billy's death had resurrected the agony of other tragedies she had suffered growing up. She was convinced the Lord in whom she had once believed had it in for her. Claire Fitzgerald. What had she ever done to deserve such punishment? Snatching Billy from her when she was a mere twenty-two was horribly cruel. Four years earlier, he had cheated Claire out of ever having children of her own. And when Claire was six, God had seen fit to call her mother to heaven during the second influenza epidemic of 1928. When would it be enough?

All Claire had of her mother was a faded photograph of her

standing on the Gapstow Bridge which curved over the neck of The Pond at 59th Street in Central Park. She had taken it when she was nine years old, with her brand-new Brownie camera. The air had been spiced with the aroma of vendors roasting chestnuts and baking salted pretzels stationed several thousand feet or so apart. An aromatic woodsmoke had hung in the half-naked trees, a blue haze caught among the rattling branches. Periodically looking for Mommy by looking at this black and white photo of her was where Claire had always found solace.

Like now, Claire sought comfort by gazing into Billy's eyes. She wondered if he had meant it when he said he'd forgiven her for not telling him prior to their marriage that she could not bear children. It was wrong to have kept that information from him, she knew, but what was a girl to do if she wanted to catch this man? Claire studied the other photos of the two of them. They were staged elegantly in their silver frames on the credenza. Pictures of the smiles they'd left behind: on the Ferris wheel at Coney Island, in black tie in the Rainbow Room at Rockefeller Plaza and the two of them, so happy, on their wedding day.

Claire's struggle to come to terms with the fact that her life would never be the same again was more than she could stand. It seemed easier to give up. Claire knew in her heart of hearts she'd always passively relied on what life brought to her, not what she could bring to it. She'd never explored all the possibilities lying open to her and she'd never determined any serious goals for herself other than being a model or wanting to marry well. Smart enough to know those were pretty shallow endeavors, she felt stupid for not knowing how to go forward.

Downstairs, Claire heard Boots open the front door. Judging from the high heels clicking against the marble-tiled floor, Caroline Campbell was marching toward her bedroom. Claire ducked under a pillow as Caroline entered without so much as a teeny knock.

"Enough is enough! You've wallowed for far too long." Caroline pulled the draperies open, and a flood of sunlight poured into the room.

Claire peeked above the counterpane and squinting into the glare, mumbled, "What time is it?"

"Way past noon. Time to get up!" Caroline tossed a robe over her daughter-in-law's body. Never one to tolerate laziness, Caroline could get quite gruff. Since Billy's death, kind words of commiseration had only served to fortify Claire's justification for doing absolutely nothing each and every day. "Lord knows Billy's passing has been difficult," she paused to inhale, "but at least you have two beautiful homes, considerable wealth—."

"*At least.*" Two annoying words Claire had heard countless times since Billy died. *At least you have youth on your side* or *At least you don't have children. At least the Campbells are there for you.* Not to be ungrateful, but really, had any of those factors made it easier to withstand her loss?

"It's not healthy to languish like this," Caroline said, pulling back the covers.

Claire flipped over to face her mother-in-law. "When Billy and I were married, I believed in magic. I believed the universe would take care of me." She paused to consider what she was going to say. "Now I think we were always meant to say goodbye."

"Goodness, what a thing to say." Caroline sat down on the side of the bed. "Just the other day, you told me you see Billy everywhere. That you think he might still be alive."

"Well, I don't anymore."

Isabel entered the room holding a mug of hot chocolate in each hand. "Miss Claire, if ye don't mind me sayin' Mr. Billy wouldn't care to know ye been actin' this way. He'd want ye to make right his death."

Claire turned to look at Isabel with surprise. This perspective had never occurred to her, and instantly, she felt ashamed.

Isabel, as stunned by her own spoken candor as was Claire hearing it, continued, "Grief is like fracturin' a bone. Ye have to set it right or it'll hurt ye forever." She handed Claire one of the mugs. "Drink this up now, like a good lass."

Claire took the cup from Isabel and nodded almost imperceptibly. "The rest of my life stretches out in front of me as vast and empty as the Sahara Desert. I want to fill it, but I don't know with what."

For the first time, Claire noticed Caroline's posture. Her head was bent. So too, her frail shoulders. She was pale and thinner than usual. She looked every bit a mother deeply anguished. It wasn't right that a child predecease a parent. "I've been selfish," Claire whispered. "What has all this been like for you?"

"Excuse me?" Caroline seemed confused.

"To lose a son,"

Caroline withdrew her hand and remained silent. Her pain was etched in every fine wrinkle lining her cheeks. It lay just behind her thin pursed lips, huge but under control.

Claire got out of bed. As she padded across the Aubusson carpet to the bathroom, she said over her shoulder, "Give me a few minutes to freshen up and then we'll go out. How does Barbetta's suit? Their truffle risotto is delish!"

Dropping a face cloth into the sink, Claire turned on the hot water and let it run while she smeared a thin layer of Vaseline from her forehead to her ears, and down around the mouth and chin. Then wringing out the hot cloth, she draped it over her face and held it there for a steam cleanse. This was a routine she hadn't performed in weeks. When she was done, Claire cleared the fog from the mirror, gazed into it with a critical eye and sighed deeply. *Darn, if Isabelle isn't right.* Ever so slowly, the icicles surrounding Claire's heart started to melt.

The next morning, Claire moved out of the Campbells' and back into her pied-à-terre.

Chapter Twenty-Six

Sunday dinner, or *Family Night* as it was known, was a Campbell tradition and Claire was late, but at least not a no-show this time. The Campbell house on 68th Street was an impressive brownstone occupying almost a fourth of the city block between Madison and Park Avenues. Inside, plush oriental carpets, carved Queen Anne side tables and chairs, and oversized furniture upholstered in floral chintz made for an eclectic décor. Brass fixtures, crystal lamps, velvet-framed photographs and needlepointed cushions adorned the rooms in layers of comfortable luxury while mullioned windows looked out onto the tree-lined street, and portraits or landscapes graced the walls. Parquet floors of Brazilian walnut gleamed chocolate brown; the marble foyer of black and white diamonds shone. But the thing which impressed Claire the most was the distinct smell of books. Billy, she remembered, had always found that curious, as he didn't think books smelled like anything. As she entered the vestibule, she inhaled deeply and sighed.

Boots appeared. "Good evening, Miss Claire. It's good to see you looking so well." Pale and painfully thin, she didn't look at all well, but Boots was always such a kind soul. "May I take your coat?"

Claire shrugged her mink into his hands without making eye contact. It was difficult to meet Boots' sympathetic gaze as it reminded her too much of Billy, the two of them having been each other's sidekick since Billy was a little boy.

"The commodore and the missus are in the library. I should warn you they have a guest."

"Thank you, Boots." Claire started up the stairs, then hesitated. "Male or female?" she asked, leaning over the bannister.

"A young lady, Miss Claire. From England."

"There you are!" Commodore Campbell said, waving her in. "Come, dear, I want to introduce you to Hermione Brigstock."

Claire crossed the room to kiss Caroline on the cheek and then shook Hermione's hand.

"You're in uniform. Are you with the RAF?"

"Miss Brigstock flew for the Air Transport Auxiliary, the ATA," the commodore butted in. "She belonged to a British organization of mostly women pilots who ferried new, damaged and/or repaired military aircraft all across the British Isles."

"Women were not allowed to fight," Hermione added. "So, to answer your question, Claire, I am not with the RAF." She paused. "Would've rather liked to have been, though."

"Heavens," Claire exclaimed. "You must have already known how to fly?" The notion that women could fly airplanes, not to mention want to engage in wartime air battles, was startling to Claire.

"Yes. All of us aviation nuts—men and women—were terribly eager to serve our country, once the Battle of Britain and the Blitz began."

"Hermione has flown Mosquitos, Hawkers, Spitfires—."

"Randall," Caroline said softly. "Let Miss Brigstock speak."

"It's quite all right, Mrs. Campbell." She smiled benevolently at the commodore, then turned toward Claire. "We flew just about everything there was to fly between factories and airfields, service assembly plants and squadrons."

Claire chuckled inwardly as Randall, who couldn't help himself, started in again. "These gals flew in open cockpits, without instruments and no defense weaponry."

"Goodness gracious!"

"Yes, it was quite frightful, but exhilarating all the same," Hermione agreed.

"They were on twenty-four-hour alert, often flying as many as ten days in a row and then racing back to base in order to do it all over again."

"Randall!" Caroline wagged a finger at him.

Isabelle stood in the doorway. "Dinner in half an hour, ma'am." Moving over to the marble coffee table and setting down a salver of canapés, she asked quietly, "Is there anything you need?"

Caroline declined.

"I'm impressed." Claire said with genuine awe. "Obviously, you are very brave."

"Not really. I simply have a skill I could contribute to the war effort."

"Yes, but still . . ."

"When a Nazi tyrant and his Axis of Evil threaten your freedom, you do whatever you can to stop it. I, like every other Brit, am not going to tolerate speaking German or *heil-Hitler-ing* for the rest of our days. Besides, men and women are dying all over England, France, the Netherlands, and Poland."

"Germany too," Claire uttered. All three looked at Claire in surprise. "What?" she asked, her petulance barely contained. "Just because the Germans are our enemy doesn't mean we can't be sympathetic about them dying. You have to admit it's the same tragic waste of life."

The commodore's forehead creased into a frown, pulling his bushy gray eyebrows into a single seam. The tufts of gray hair behind his ears, usually lending a playful appeal, now looked like thunderclouds hovering over his face.

Claire, usually submissive in instances like this, tonight had no intention of backing down. What had gotten into her, she wondered. This woman, she presumed, but why exactly, she didn't yet know. Claire crossed her slender legs tightly and folded her arms across her chest. "All lives are sacred," she fumed. "Not just the Allies'."

"I completely agree with you," Hermione said. "I just wanted to say that I was compelled to do something. No matter what the cost. Many felt—still feel— the same." Hermione paused. "Like your husband, I imagine."

At the mention of Billy, a heavy blanket of silence dropped over the library. Claire froze and simply stared at Hermione. Now that was going too far, resurrecting her dead husband's memory when it wasn't her place. Clearly nervous, Caroline reached for a cracker of caviar and cream cheese, and popped it whole into her mouth. Absentmindedly, she reached for another. The commodore removed his spectacles, blew on each lens, and then polished them with a handkerchief from his breast pocket before returning them to his nose.

"You have absolutely no idea what motivated my husband, Miss Brigstock." Claire swallowed hard. "And you might be very surprised if I told you what did," she added ominously.

"Right you are." Hermione took a long sip from her gin and tonic. "I'm frightfully sorry. I dare say it was most difficult for any American to endorse a war which hadn't yet reached her continental shores or directly threatened her loved ones."

"Are you implying—?"

Caroline quickly interjected, "Claire, dear, Hermione means well. She simply meant—."

"Did you not do more than ferrying planes?" interceded the commodore.

"Yes. I flew for Coastal Command."

Bully for you. Claire was beginning to feel as though Hermione had been put in front of her for some deliberate reason. Was it to change her mind about the war? Give up her America Firster leanings? She'd never been particularly vocal about her politics in front of her in-laws, out of respect for Billy's wishes not to confront them. Perhaps, Billy had told his parents about her political leanings and had asked that they not press her too hard. How about that? Billy was gone, so now his parents seemed to be acting as though they had carte blanche. Well, the commodore anyway; maybe not her mother-in-law.

Caroline picked up the silver tray and passed the hors d'oeuvres to Hermione, nodding encouragement for her to continue. She then took yet another canapé and laid it on a cocktail napkin in her lap.

"Carry on, shall I?" She sipped her drink. "Most of my missions involved flying very low over the Atlantic to keep the bloody U-boats from surfacing. When they're under the water, you see, they are forced to go more slowly and cannot recharge their batteries."

"It's thanks to you, Miss Brigstock, that our American and Canadian convoys were able to make it safely across the Atlantic." Claire was certain the commodore was making a dig at herself.

Hermione was quick to return the compliment. "And without your Merchant Navy bringing us supplies, Commodore, we Brits would've starved."

Claire uncrossed her legs and sat forward on the edge of the sofa. "What brings you to America anyway?" If it sounded rude, Claire didn't care.

"Wait," Randall said, reaching across the sofa cushions to enfold her small hand in his bigger one. "Miss Brigstock isn't finished. She also flew clandestine missions across the Channel for the SOE, didn't you?

"Please, sir, I insist you call me Hermione."

"Winston Churchill has referred to the SOE spies as the 'unknown warriors.'"

That's pretty cool, thought Claire, but why was her father-in-law literally promoting this woman's accomplishments? Miss Brigstock's curriculum vitae definitely was impressive, but the telling of it felt so staged. There was something contrived about this woman being a guest at the Campbells' Sunday dinner when customarily guests were never included on what was traditionally accepted as *Family Night*. Claire was increasingly certain she was being manipulated. But why? On the one hand, Claire was loath to play along, but on the other hand, Hermione was actually capturing her imagination. She wasn't particularly eager to fly planes like this gal, but she had accomplished things most women to date never had. *How terribly liberating.* Claire decided to tamp down her unpleasant attitude and let good manners prevail.

"What's the SOE?"

The commodore opened his mouth to answer, but Claire put her fingers to her lips to signal that she wanted Hermione to answer, not him.

"SOE stands for Special Operations Executive. It was established at the beginning of the war, and we were known as the 'Baker Street Irregulars' due to the location of our London-based headquarters. I preferred being called one of 'Churchill's Secret Army,' though."

"Fascinating," murmured Claire, enthralled. "How many of you were there?"

"Thirty-two hundred of us women," Hermione replied, glancing at her hosts, who had shifted in their seats. Claire ignored the knowing look she could read being exchanged between Randall and Caroline.

"Go on," Claire said, leaning toward Hermione.

"Our purpose was to work with local resistance movements across Nazi-occupied Europe. We hatched all sorts of plots of subversion behind enemy lines by blowing up bridges and railway depots, planting hidden radio operators in plain sight who transmitted coded information such as Axis co-ordinates and troop movements. We listened in on Nazi soldiers while they drank and dined. Some of the girls even slept with the enemy in the hopes of hearing useful pillow talk released during the afterglow."

"Oh, my," Caroline uttered, blushing crimson.

"Tell her about your training, Miss, Brig—I mean, Hermione," Randall prompted.

"My training was a grueling six weeks long. We ran miles upon miles every morning at dawn. It didn't matter if the skies were spiting hailstones. We learned how to escape and evade, cope under torture…" Claire's brown eyes rounded to the size of dessert plates. "We were taught how to make Molotov cocktails, pick a lock, and handle a Luger." Hermione paused, clearly enjoying, at least to Claire's way of thinking, her rapt audience. "Kill, too, if necessary. With either a gun, or close up with a knife."

"Good grief!" Claire cried out. "I don't know how anyone could manage such a thing!"

"Fortunately, I was never so in danger that I had to kill anyone." Hermione dropped her canapé into her mouth. "I was lucky, as my orders were not on the ground but in the skies. I dropped agents into France, usually at night with only a moon to light my way, or extracted them when they were either wounded, dead, or their identities had been compromised."

Claire shook her head. "I must say, you really are one very plucky lady. *Chapeau!*"

"I don't think of myself as particularly brave, but as I said before, when you've seen what I have, you just do what you must. The total devastation wrought on the city streets of bombed-out London or the port of Liverpool would break your heart. Witnessing the fight by ordinary people combing through the rubble of what were their homes, searching for loved ones or any precious family heirloom is a daily affair. Having a front row seat to the screaming dogfights over the White Cliffs of Dover . . . One simply cannot turn away."

Claire's eyes had suddenly filled with tears.

"But the most frightful?" Hermione continued. Claire squeezed her eyes shut in anticipation. "Were the bodies. All the dead bodies of men, women, and children jammed into cattle cars, heaped on top of each other and spilling out onto the tracks. Naked bodies gathering flies stacked in piles waiting to be shoveled into mass graves. Too, too many bodies, too many to count..."

Claire's mouth gaped in horror. Claire had been quick to discount the rumors about the death camps, but hearing this woman, an eyewitness, speak of it, was a shock.

"Do you want to know what I did see that was bright? Actually, the only thing during this whole bloody awful war?"

Claire shook her head, then nodded.

"Spiked concertina wire coiled like a snake and glittering above a chain-link fence."

Claire leapt from the sofa, tears streaming down her face. Overwhelmed and hardly able to control herself, Claire summoned what restraint she could feel slipping away. Softly she requested her in-laws, "May I please be excused?"

Not waiting for an answer, she strode from the library, her hand covering her mouth which now stretched into a grimace. Crossing the foyer past Isabelle, who had come to announce that dinner was served, Claire stumbled up the staircase to the third floor and rushed into the suite of rooms reserved for her and Billy. She fell across the bed and facedown, so her sobs would be muffled, she bawled.

Claire barely heard the knock or noticed Caroline coming into her room. She sat on the side of the bed and gently stroked Claire's back. "There, there," she crooned. Claire lay still, tense with anguish while her mother-in-law patiently waited for her to calm.

Eventually, Claire sat up. "I'm mortified," she lamented. "How could I have been so shallow, so insular, so terribly selfish?" Claire wrung her hands and waved her arms. Normally reserved, she knew Caroline was seeing a side of her that she herself hardly recognized.

"You mustn't be so hard on yourself, dear."

"No, but really. What's been happening in Europe has fallen on deaf ears! How could I have shut that out so successfully and for so long?" Claire punched a pillow. "Billy knew. Why didn't I?"

"I'm going to hazard a guess that your unfortunate start in life, with so many tragedies already logged at a young age, meant you were unwilling to acknowledge, never mind embrace, any more suffering." She paused. "It was easier to ignore or deny it; pretend it didn't exist." Claire's sad eyes drank in every word. "You shouldn't blame yourself, dear." Caroline pulled her into her arms and rocked her back and forth.

Claire dabbed at her eyes and blew her nose. "That Hermione is one remarkable woman! What courage!"

"Yes, indeed."

"We're British," announced Hermione who had come to stand in the doorway. "We tend to soldier on. It's what we do. Have done for centuries, actually."

"Come in," beckoned Claire. "Sit." She pointed to the foot of the bed. "I've been very rude. Please forgive me?"

"It is I who must ask you for forgiveness," replied Hermione, appearing very contrite.

"How so?" Claire asked, despite knowing what she was likely going to say. Sitting up against the pillows and folding her slender gams beneath her, she raised her eyebrows to signal her to go on.

"I'm going to let you two talk," Caroline said and left the room.

"The commodore invited me here tonight to sell you on the idea of enlisting in the war effort."

"I knew it!" Claire hooted. "This whole evening, no offense to you, has felt terribly contrived." She tossed her head back, letting her wavy hair escape the tortoiseshell combs at her ears.

"I'm sure you felt manipulated," Hermione said.

"More like my naïveté was exploited." Claire rolled her eyes. "Nothing I haven't seen before coming from my father-in-law."

"He thought if you heard about my exploits, you might be tempted to come back to England with me and learn how to fly."

"Are you serious?" She blew her cheeks out. "The commodore ought to know by now I'm the biggest sissy in the world!"

"I'm so awfully sorry." She hesitated. "It's just that who knows how much longer this infernal war will last, and we're so dreadfully desperate for more pilots that I didn't think beyond my own agenda."

"Hermione, listen to me." Claire reached for Hermione's hand. "I most assuredly am not pilot material. I'm a former fashion model and an unapologetic, avid reader, which most people would say makes me an oxymoron, but…"

"Don't sell yourself short," Hermione said. "You've got both brains and style."

Claire sat up straight to signal that what she was about to say was important. Significant to her, that is, given her previous antipathy to war and her own aversion to physical risk. She took a deep breath. "Your over-the-top, graphic descriptions have paid off." Claire was staring at her lap. "I think I'd like to volunteer. Gently, though. No guns and definitely no planes." She sighed heavily. "You see, my husband was killed in a plane crash, so I simply couldn't bear it."

Chapter Twenty-Seven

Claire threw off the sheets and swung her feet out of bed. Pausing for a moment to scratch her head, she surveyed her bedroom. Yesterday's clothes lay across the back of a chintz armchair, a cream-colored linen skirt and a lightweight turquoise sweater. She pulled them on, deciding to forego sorting through her closet for something else. Claire glanced in the mirror and saw she was still as pale as the underbelly of a fish. She splashed some water on her face, dusted her nose with powder, and said to herself, "That'll have to do."

Both Boots and Isabel were in the foyer as Claire click-clacked across the parquet floor in her Ferragamos. Isabel handed her a pain au chocolat wrapped in a paper napkin, along with a thermos of coffee. "Ye must eat to get your strength back, Miss Claire."

Boots opened the apartment door to the outer vestibule. "Your chariot awaits, madam." With a flourish he waved Claire into the elevator. "I've got the car double-parked, so we must hurry, Miss."

The ride downtown to Lower Manhattan was slow thanks to the mid-morning traffic. Staring out the car window, she considered what Caroline had suggested. It had sounded like a good idea the day before, but now Claire wasn't so sure. Did she really want to join the Red Cross Rest and Relaxation branch?

"So, Boots, what do you think about me joining the Red Cross?"

"Splendid, Miss Claire, if it's what ye want to do." They were stopped at a red light on 59th and Lexington Avenue, which was besieged by foot traffic outside Bloomingdale's.

"I can't see why they'd hire me."

"Because you're still in mourning?" He glanced in the mirror, his expression avuncular.

"You understand," Claire said in a low voice. "I'm grateful."

Boots looked at Claire from his rearview mirror and said, "Mr. Billy used to say, 'The only thing stopping you is you.'"

Claire's eyes flicked to his. "He did, didn't he?"

"And ye be a mighty strong lass when you want to be, Miss Claire."

Seeing the grief in Boots' sad eyes, Claire sat forward and patted his shoulder. "You're a good man, Boots."

A short, heavyset woman of around sixty greeted Claire as soon as she entered the busy little office. A network of small fissures pleating the corners of her eyes coalesced as she smiled. "I'm Nurse Taylor, but feel free to call me Laura. We don't stand on ceremony around here." She chuckled. "I'll need you to undress down to your bra and panties. If you feel more comfortable keeping your slip on, I won't object." She indicated a screen in the corner of the room.

The preliminary questions of name, age, and marital status were dispensed with while Claire undressed. When she emerged, she was invited to sit at the end of a doctor's examining table. Her foot nervously bobbed up and down as she waited to be poked and prodded.

"What made you decide to enlist with the Red Cross?"

Claire twisted her gold wedding band round and round. Her knuckles were prominent and her fingers colorless. "I didn't decide. An English pilot—female, I'll have you know—inspired me to do something for the war."

"A woman pilot? That's unusual." Nurse Taylor warmed the stethoscope in her hands. "But I must ask," she paused, "are you volunteering because *you* want to?"

Claire spoke to the floor lying between her bare feet. "It was my housekeeper who said my husband would want me to justify his death by doing something grand in his memory; that it would bring me closer to him." Claire's eyes began to water.

"Wise words."

Claire asked, "What does this Rest and Relaxation entail exactly?"

"You and several other girls would be required to set up a whole host of entertainments for the soldiers requiring rest and recreation during their furloughs from the fighting on the ground in Europe. It's up to you what you organize, but such things as tea dances, tennis matches, scavenger hunts, rounds of golf, bridge tournaments, or quiet getaways are what our boys need. You might help them to translate from French or German into English, compose a difficult letter home, be a good listener, direct them to the appropriate resources for the help they specifically require."

"How many men at a time are at the facility?"

"Around two hundred."

"That's a lot of fellas for just a few girls."

"Indeed it is. Come. Let's get you on a scale, shall we?"

Claire stepped on the scale and waited as Nurse Taylor slid the large counter weight closest to what she estimated was Claire's weight. Then she slid the smaller weight slowly along the scale, watching the balance beam and waiting for it to stop. It took several adjustments until the beam rested horizontally in a straight line.

"Oh my!" Nurse Taylor exclaimed. "You only weigh one hundred and one pounds."

"Is that so bad? I'm five foot five and a model."

"Technically, if you are interested in being at a healthy weight, for every inch over five feet and starting at one hundred pounds, you should weigh five pounds per inch. In your case that would be one hundred plus five times five inches equals one hundred and twenty-five."

"I'd be a blimp at that weight!" Claire decried. Too late, she realized she'd probably insulted the good nurse.

"The Red Cross won't take anyone under one hundred and ten." Nurse Taylor said peering over her owlish spectacles. "What a pity. We have a vacancy needing to be filled. With your looks and social skills, not to mention facility with the French language, you would have been perfect for the job."

"Where would you have sent me?" It sounded as if it were France.

"I'm afraid I'm not at liberty to divulge that information. Besides, I cannot sign you on unless you weigh one hundred and ten."

Claire hopped off the table. "That's so unfair!" she said. "How can you base a job on a gal's weight?"

"Listen, dearie, the ship sails in around three weeks. If you can tip the scale before she departs, the post is yours. I'll have a ticket waiting for you right here on my desk."

Boots was already at the curb when Claire emerged from the Red Cross offices, scowling.

Once she was ensconced in the back seat, Boots asked, "From the looks of it, Miss Claire, the interview did not go as well as planned?"

"If you can believe it, Boots, there's a minimum weight requirement. According to their scale, I am nine pounds shy of the job!"

Boots kept a straight face, his eyes darting over the traffic and pedestrians jaywalking at the intersections.

"Are ye wantin' the job, Miss Claire?"

"I think I do, yes. The ship sails in less than a month, but I'll never get to one hundred and ten by then." Claire slumped in her seat.

At home later that afternoon, Isabelle knocked on Claire's

bedroom door where she was once again sequestered.

"Boots, he be a-tellin' me what happened downtown." Isabelle placed a small tray on the bed next to where Claire was propped up against a stack of pillows. "I've got just the remedy for what ails ye, Miss Claire." On the plate were slices of ripe banana, a Hershey bar broken into segments and a tall glass of whole milk.

"Eat this three times a day plus your dinner and I guarantee ye'll put on those nine pounds ye be missin'."

"In time for the ship's sail?"

"In time for your next adventure, I reckon. Yes, Miss Claire, yes."

Chapter Twenty-Eight

Claire's three o'clock train chuffed its way into Grand Central. Soldiers in uniform bounded onto the platform with wilted daisies in hand as tired and rumpled-looking as their uniforms. Whoops of joy and women and girls flinging themselves into the men's arms were the sweet reunions Claire would never know.

Claire searched the faces of her in-laws, assuming these displays were just as hard on them as they were on her.

"After Hermione left for Virginia, I holed up for few days because I wanted to remember Billy. Picture his face. Feel his warmth if not just his sweet kiss." Mercifully, the train blasted its steam obscuring all their faces, particularly Claire's, whose expression belied her words. She wanted to leave them with a favorable impression of how she felt about their son. Not the terrible fact that no matter how hard she had tried to conjure him, or feel, she couldn't anymore. His ghostly appearances on Madison Avenue or at the theatre or painting by the bay window were no more.

The commodore held Claire by her upper arms. Even though he had a commanding hold of her, he looked sheepish. "Now that you've chosen to join the Red Cross, can you forgive me for manipulating you from your doldrums?"

"In time," Claire replied with a twinkle in her eye. "But you must know you are terribly bossy." She'd surprised herself with her candor, but then Hermione had shown her by example that today's woman was permitted many transgressions from what had been traditionally forbidden to women.

"Yes, but I got you to see the light, didn't I?" He'd brought his face in close as if to taunt her. The unabashed Commodore was back. Claire sighed and subtly extracted herself from his grip.

"Randall, dear, spare the girl your bullying." Caroline reached for Claire's hand. "When you can, dear, please let us know when you've arrived in DC. Do you have any idea how long you'll be there before departing?"

"No, Mumsy, I don't." A whistle blew and a conductor shouted the *all aboard*. "I don't think they'll even tell me from which port we sail or where we disembark on the other side." Claire looked behind her and up the track. "It's all terribly hush-hush." The train cars were shuddering into motion. "I must go."

The commodore tried one more time. "Dearest Claire, you've lost a husband. I just wanted you to know that Mumsy and I both want you to cut your losses and move on." Claire looked at him quizzically. "You will always be a daughter to us, but you are young. So . . ."

"So smart and beautiful, too," Caroline interjected. "You're being clumsy, Randall. Say what you mean."

Randall scolded his wife with a withering look. "You've got your whole life ahead of you. Run with it, dear girl. Run!"

Claire returned his surprising affection with a ghost of a smile. Was this her permission to let Billy go? Maybe fall in love again? "Thank you, Commodore. If there's one thing I know, it's that you do mean well." She stood on her tippy-toes and kissed his wizened cheek.

Hugging Caroline and Randall in a rush, she boarded the train and found her reserved seating quickly. As the train began to roll out, she pulled down the window, leaned out, and shouted, "I promise I won't forget to write!" But her words drifted on the wind, no doubt unheard.

Claire sank down on the banquette. Her heart was pounding in her chest; she was nervous at being so suddenly thrust out into the big, bad world. She dropped her head into both hands. She struggled to hold back the sobs, it being unseemly to cry in public. The Campbells had been so good to her. They'd been like the parents she had lost. How could she tell them that she was coming to the conclusion that she'd probably married Billy for the wrong reasons? That wealth, social standing, and handsome looks were not the be-all and end-all.

Claire shook out her thick wavy mane and sat back, crossing her legs, folding her hands in her lap and gazing out the window. Soon enough her thoughts moved from the guilt she couldn't resolve to a pride that made her smile inwardly. She had actually cast aside her self-pity and all that self-defeating wallowing in exchange for a sense of purpose when she'd joined the Red Cross. Though her work had yet to begin, it already felt remarkable. Being in charge of her life, having direction, and knowing she was going to do good had lifted her spirits to a new level of high. Thanks to Hermione, she'd realized that she didn't want to look back over her life and regret having done nothing to help the suffering. Of course her in-laws had played a role. Boots and Isabelle, too.

Buck

April - May 1945

Chapter Twenty-Nine

Buck was on the last leg of two days of travel, having started his journey on a narrow gage out of Aberdeen across northern Scotland to Ayr, connecting in Glasgow, continuing by trawler on the Inner Seas, where the Germans weren't patrolling, around Land's End in Cornwall to England's south port of Plymouth. From there he'd crossed the English Channel, which had been less dangerous than expected due to the Nazis' all-consuming focus on defending Berlin. It had been a nauseating business thanks to the habitually rough sea, but who was he to complain? The advancing American troops from the west and the Russians from the east had provided Buck with good cover. Now Buck was in the back seat of a Citroën, having hitched a ride with a pair of schoolteachers on their way to Brest.

Buck looked down at his lap where his right hand lay open, his five slender fingers splayed across his knee. The ghost of the other hand lay on the other knee too, the fingers surfing the warm summer breeze wafting through the open window of the car. He swore he could feel the wind's teeth on that hand, but no, it was simply a phantom sensation. The military doctors had said it was normal to experience pain signals—some sharp, others dull—for up to six months post surgery; that Billy's brain was undergoing a "rewiring" of sorts due to its sensing something was wrong. Damn straight, something was wrong! "Deal with it, soldier," the army doc had said. "At least you have a spare!" *Very funny.*

During a spell like this, Buck forced himself to think of other things. His last two billets came to mind. There was nothing to miss about the Aleutians. Thank goodness he was gone from there. The rugged, treeless tundra and almost perpetually foul weather had been as hostile a spot as any active war zone, yet when he was there the Japs had already been flushed out. All that he had encountered was a landscape of many shades of gray. Cowering under slate gray skies, working with gunmetal-gray machinery among boats dotting a washed-out coastline on a base where he'd been stationed had been a gloomy grind. How anyone could carve out a living on those godforsaken islands and not go mad for want of sun and color was anyone's guess. And while Billy recognized that much of his disdain for the place stemmed from his accident, he forced himself to focus on the fact that he had left with most of his body intact. Yay, psych docs who'd encouraged him to engage in positive thoughts. *Uh-huh, right. Not doin' a real good job right now . . .*

The Scottish Highlands, where Buck had received his rushed SOE training, were a different story. There, the terrain was rugged but beautiful. The sea off the coast of Dunrobin Castle caroled mystical songs as the waves crashed against the shore, the terns overhead calling in two- and three-part harmony.

Buck raised his good hand and examined it. *Thank God I can still paint,* he said to himself, patting his paint box lying on the seat beside him. When he caught a glimpse of himself in the Citroën's rearview mirror, he had to suppress a chuckle. Equipped with all the trappings of an artist, Buck wore a pair of loose-fitting jeans and a traditional blue-and-white Breton striped sweater, a row of buttons at the shoulder. The beret he'd been given in order to be better recognized by the Resistance as a *friendly* rested atop his duffel bag. His bare feet were nestled in a pair of brand-new espadrilles, artificially stained with ochre to appear old and beat-up. Buck closed his eyes, satisfied that he looked the part of an American expat artist. Bemused by the fact that he'd not had to fake his newly manufactured persona too much because it was so like his authentic self, he smiled to himself. How easy, really, was it to go from being a footloose man of leisure with nothing better to do than paint while others labored nine to five than pretend to be just that? He tucked his nub in the cradle of his armpit. This had become a habit after the amputation, not so much to get it out of sight as much as something to do with his useless arm. Buck pretended to doze in case the teachers wanted to ask questions.

Buck let memories of the home he grew up in creep into his mind. A broad expanse of cascading lawns, the plush greenness being what typically accompanied wealth, in a village of the right sort of people. Billy's grandparents had been in Amagansett since 1927, back when it was still technically a hamlet and before it became one of the finest residential districts in the Hamptons, if not New York. Buck had never cared about any of that. He may have enjoyed his childhood friends at the beach or on the tennis courts, but in general, Long Island's posh lifestyle wasn't his scene.

The insipid lifestyle bored him to sobs. Everyone was determined to outshine everyone else with their affected lockjaw and up-speak cadences. Flaunting one's newest car or motorboat and droning on about such things as the poor service at the Gritti Palace in Venice over Easter was just folks showing off. And yet, chest-thumping conversations of this kind seemed *de rigueur* if you wanted to belong. A true Ernest Hemingway devotee, he yearned to live life to the fullest, not somnambulate through it. Since childhood, he'd felt fervor for most everything. It was in his art, his recklessness on the ski slopes, mountaineering, flying, even running the bulls in Pamplona like his idol—never mind that he fell early on and was rescued by onlookers—and last but not least, partying. His passion burned like fire. And though he knew his zest for action and risk was a dangerous thing because it usually zoomed out of control, he still relentlessly pursued it. Perhaps that's why he chased girls—blondes in particular, because they were his type. Buck had lost count of how many he'd bedded, but he stopped, just like that, when he met Claire. Brunette temptress that she was, he'd have done anything to make her his. Including waiting until they were married. He wanted to be her first, and of course, her last, too.

Shortly after they were married, however, Buck had begun to wonder if he could ever be truly happy with Claire over the span of his lifetime. As he reflected now, the Citroën rattling over potholes down a poplar tree-lined road, he realized that once upon a time, he'd thought it heavenly waking up beside Claire, one long leg slung over her hip, his hands possessively cupping each of her breasts. The very thought of sex filled him with a warm glow, so he shifted his cramped position in the backseat to one where he could stretch out.

Desires aside, Buck tried to make sense of why he had been so willing to go along with his fake death. For starters, Claire had lied to him. By omission. She had danced her nubile, hard-to-get petite little self right into his life and secured a marriage without so much as a word about there never being any children in his future. Was he being selfish to take this line of thinking? Perhaps. But wasn't he entitled to have this information prior to making a contract for life? Buck didn't take kindly to being duped.

If he were to focus on what part *he* had played to bring about the demise of his marriage, he'd have to admit his ego and hormones were largely to blame. Claire had been one of New York's top models, a fashion sensation. She was a beauty who had beguiled him from the moment she sashayed down the runway. He'd had to have her. When she wouldn't sleep with him, he married her. *Guess I should've looked under the hood, first,* he mused. She hadn't shown any initiative in bed, and that had disappointed him. That she was a voracious reader with a myriad of topics he couldn't share with her was another bad sign, but did he take notice of that as a non-reader, himself, before their wedding vows? No. Finally, Claire was too reserved for his tastes. He liked spontaneity, spunk, and passion. She had shown him nothing but a passive, submissive and go-along to get-along manner. At first, he had liked showing her off, introducing her to his world. Ultimately, though, he'd grown tired of it.

"*Vous* étiez *un soldat?*"

"*Oui, blessé,*" he replied in his badly accented French, lifting his wounded arm. "*Je suis ici en vacances.*" The two women cringed as if they'd just heard fingernails on a chalkboard.

"Where does *monsieur* want to go on his vacation?" asked the younger one, looking over her shoulder. Evidently, she thought it better to proceed in English.

Buck sat forward and said, "Drop me off in Ploudalmézeau. I don't want you to go out of your way." The women exchanged a look. "You've already been too kind."

"*Bien sûr,*" the older one said with a business-like nod. Of course.

Buck couldn't tell if the teachers suspected anything, so he filled the void with more gab, a definite no-no according to his training.

Chapter Thirty

Night had fallen by the time Buck stepped from the car and bid his traveling companions *au revoir*. A scrim of cloud obscuring the light of a new moon forced him to carefully feel his way along the narrow road toward Kersaint and Portsall. Once closer, the Channel's salt smell rising from the little harbor brought him the rest of the way. At the outskirts of Kersaint, Buck could make out a tangle of limestone houses with slate roofs and branches of fragrant lilac dangling across the sand-dusted country lanes. L'Hôtel de Bretagne was a boxy structure at the town's center. It boasted a small flagstone terrace with a few metal tables, wine barrels overflowing with white petunias, fern, and impatiens, and the local wino slumped on the threshold, snuffling in his sleep. Two rows of windows, each sporting cornflower shutters, faced the street and the Notre-Dame de Kersaint Chapel nestled under a stand of oak trees across the way.

Buck stepped over the drunkard and let himself in, knowing that at the top of the stairs he'd find a key taped to the back of a hallway dresser. If the key was missing, he'd be warned to leave immediately. It was there. Buck unlocked a door not much bigger than a hatch at the end of the corridor, where another set of stairs led to an *atelier*. Buck squeezed his six-foot-two frame through the opening and found a garret which lay close to a low, sloping roof. The place was meagerly furnished with an iron bed, table and chair, and a wash-stand with a small round mirror hanging above it on the wall. Buck dug in his pockets for a book of matches he'd been given and told to always have at hand. He lit the solitary candle, and the room was instantly bathed in a soft light. It wasn't the Ritz, but Billy Campbell, aka Buck Connor, felt pleasantly cocooned by this intimate, albeit spartan, little hideaway.

Buck parked his artist's box in the corner and tossed his duffel bag onto the bed. Rummaging through his clothes and toiletries, he found his papers and sat at the table to recheck them: identification and ration cards, travel permits. Then he crawled under the table, no easy feat with only one hand to support his folded body, in search of a removable floorboard. He located a short wooden plank and pried it back. By patting around the innards of the hole, as he couldn't see inside, he found a narrow tin box and lifted it out. Tucking it under his arm, he backed out from under the table. Inside the flat box were two guns packed in cosmoline, a brown gelatinous substance like lard, which would have to be stripped away somehow. Buck recognized the firearms immediately. He had trained with these .32-caliber MAB's at Dunrobin. *Good,* he thought, *I know how to shoot these puppies.*

Buck yawned long and wide. He licked his fingers and pinched the wick to snuff out the candle. Tomorrow would be a busy day of reconnoitering the town and dropping clues that he was an American artist fresh from Paris, living among other ex-pats dodging the war and currently in search of a seaside landscape, or maybe a muse. When he approached the little sink, Buck was touched by the gesture of hospitality lying on a small plate. It was a yellowed and cracked bar of soap which wouldn't afford too many more lathers, it was so worn down, but the generosity of so rare a luxury was not lost on him. *Hmmm,* he wondered, *a woman's touch, perhaps?* Buck inspected his reflection. Dark stubble lined his jaw and the circles under his eyes were pronounced. He turned his head from right to left and frowned. Gray was beginning to streak his jet-black hair at the temples.

Buck crawled between the muslin sheets and folded his arms under his head. After an hour had passed, he was still staring up at the ceiling, sleep eluding him. He attempted to conjure images of making love to Claire, but no stirrings were forthcoming. Not even a whisper. This was a first. Frustrated, Buck jumped out of bed and began to pace.

He didn't want to revisit his wife's duplicity. He needed to keep his focus on the mission. He was an agent now, trained by specialists of Winston Churchill's SOE, and recently made an associate of the Army's Monuments, Fine Arts, and Archives Section. He wasn't like most of the agents from the SOE who'd come into France as part of the unit called "F Section." Mostly there were British men and women who had been tasked with sabotaging Nazi-occupied infrastructure and arming French partisans in advance of the anticipated Allied invasion. But very much like the agents before him, Buck did need to interact with the locals in order to get information. After all, it was folks like the waitress in Saint-Malo overhearing the German officers' chatter at the café, or the farmer noticing changes in the schedule of trains passing by his hayfields, or the observations of locals which often yielded unexpected but highly valuable information. SOE agents were also required to make contact with the *réseau*, the local networks of resistance, in order to strengthen every effort at subverting the Huns. Who was his contact, he wondered.

The Monuments Men, on the other hand, were volunteers who had already rescued countless artworks from the Nazi regime. These men and women were educated architects, archaeologists, curators, and art historians who had willingly put themselves in harm's way to protect Europe's priceless treasures. In 1944, General Eisenhower had ordered his commanders to protect "historical monuments and cultural centers . . . which symbolize[d] . . all that we are fighting to preserve." Whether it was preserving the Ponte Vecchio in Florence, cathedrals across war-torn Europe, or placing da Vinci's Mona Lisa into protective custody, the Monuments Men were eventually tasked with safeguarding smaller treasures too. They were leaving no stone unturned, especially since Hitler had instructed his troops to destroy the stolen art if the Reich should fall. Never did the US government expect to find a cache of propaganda so inflammatory that it needed to be removed from German control.

And this was where Buck's mission came into play. The Germans were absconding with it to parts unknown. And since it was already on its way out of Germany and presumed, though not yet confirmed, to be in France, President Truman's fear as transmitted from General Eisenhower was that it was heading toward a hiding place, never to be seen again. Not until the Germans tried to launch another thousand-year Reich, anyway. As an aide to the Monuments Men, Buck felt his assignment was a good fit, his passion for art making him truly invested in the success of his efforts. Not that he placed any high esteem for the propaganda art itself. No, not at all. According to samples he'd been shown before departing Dunrobin Castle, it was cheap and simplistic, an insult to any talented or trained eye. Paintings of the farmer in his hay field with scythe in hand, pronounced chest muscles visible behind an open shirt; the farmer's buxom wife with babe at the breast; or men and women made to look like Greek Gods or Roman warriors? What made this phony-baloney art unique, however, was its effectiveness in evoking a blind devotion to its evil narrative. *Deutschland* Über *Alles*, Germany above all, was what the art professed. A line originally referring to a desire for the unification of all German peoples sung in their national anthem, its more sinister meaning of Germany above all *else* could not be mistaken.

Madeleine

May 1945

Chapter Thirty-One

Germany surrendered on May 8, 1945 and *grâce à Dieu* Hitler, along with his wife of fewer than forty hours, Eva Braun, were dead. At least in Europe, the war was over. Church bells tolled throughout France. Charles de Gaulle said in his address, "Honor to our nation, which never faltered, even under terrible trials, or gave in to them..." This was debatable, given that the whole of the south of France had become Vichy—a puppet government for the Nazis—but Madeleine, ever patriotic, didn't quibble about this fact on so joyous an occasion. De Gaulle also remarked, "Honor to the League of Nations, which mingled their blood, their sorrows, and their hopes with ours . . ."

Madeleine had so hoped to be in Paris for VE Day (Victory in Europe) celebrations, but Annabelle had forbidden her any more travel. After all, it was going to be a madhouse. Instead, mother and daughter sat by the radio and vicariously joined in the exuberance. The city was a jubilant riot. Apparently, servicemen and giddy girls created a conga line down the Champs-Élysées and as night blanketed the city, the Eiffel Tower was lit after having been dark since the beginning of the war. There wasn't a soul who wasn't drunk with joy or cheap Beaujolais.

In Kersaint's town center, revelers jostled every which way. High-spirited cries of *hoora*, profuse tears of joy, and villagers hugging villagers filled the streets. Dogs scampered alongside their owners wearing tricolored bows, while little boys and girls held balloons and blew on their kazoos. They began to cheer in one voice and it echoed across the bay to Portsall. So, Madeleine along with her mother and grumpy old Sophie, walking arm-in-arm, three abreast, let the tide of glad madness carry them out the door and down to the beach.

Madeleine and her mother huddled together to watch a fireworks display over the harbor between Kersaint and Portsall. A velvety blanket of stars hung low over the water and all the fishing boats moored there at high tide were pointing to the North Star. It was as though they, too, were standing at attention, in awe of the auspicious occasion.

Amiens,
France

May 1945

Chapter Thirty-Two

Klaus, as skittish as ever, begged Ernst to take the southern route out of Larochette through the smaller villages, so they crossed the border into France at Dudelange. It was a much longer distance to Amiens than the one heading across Belgium, but he felt that he and Ernst would be safer staying off the main thoroughfares. Besides, those roads were packed with hundreds of displaced peoples trying to get home now that the war was over.

When Ernst drove the truck through the Somme Valley on their final stretch into Amiens, both men were uncharacteristically silent. This once bucolic countryside was where many of the vicious battles of World War I had been fought. Each of the boys had lost a member of his family here. All around them the terrain was marred by shell holes and the vestiges of trenches, not to mention the haunting echoes of silent screams. Coming into the city, the destruction wrought by first the invading Nazis and then the Allies in their recapture of the city during this current world convulsion was fresh and no less shocking. It gave them pause.

Ernst reached into his shirt pocket for his pack of cigarettes. He shook one out and put it between his lips and then patted his chest in search of his lighter. Klaus leaned across the seat and lit it for him with a gold Cartier lighter.

"Whoa, where did that little treasure come from?" Ernst asked

"Where do ya think?"

"You stole it?"

"Tell me who's gonna miss it and I'll put it back."

"Smart ass."

The cigarette took hold and Ernst sucked in a deep breath. Through a blue stream of smoke, he said, "Weird, there's no one here." He inhaled again and looked down the streets to his left and right as he rolled through one intersection after another.

"This place gives me the creeps."

"Everything gives you the creeps."

"Yeah, well, I guess I'm not blessed with your courage." Ernst inhaled once more and tossed the butt out the window.

"If it makes you feel any better, my father told me courage is just a lie. All you gotta do, he said, is ignore the fear."

"For once would you just shut the fuck up?"

Ernst slammed on the brake and both men were thrown forward. An avalanche of crunches and the sound of broken glass in back ensued. "Now look what you made me do!"

"Look! There's the *Clinique*." Klaus pointed in the direction of two o'clock. "Should we go around to the back?"

"Great idea, Einstein."

"Listen, your stupid bromides are driving me nuts!"

"For what it's worth, *Klaus-ie*, hanging out with you is no picnic either."

As soon as he was chastised, Klaus changed his tune. "I shouldn't have yelled at you, Ernst. I'm sorry."

"Show more respect, would ya?"

When they drove to the back of the clinic, there was a Renault bus waiting under a *porte- cochère*. Standing next to the open cargo bay at the back was a tall, buxom Valkyrie of a woman. Her lips were drawn in a sneer as she glanced at her watch and then glared at the boys through the windshield.

"That's some piece of ass!" Klaus said, chuckling.

"That may be, but I highly doubt she's gonna put out. Not for you, anyway."

"You are over two hours late," the Valkyrie stated as Ernst and Klaus hopped down from the cab. "Which means you've got only one hour now to move the cargo from in there to in here." The boys looked inside the bus, whose rows of bench seats had been removed.

"*Mach schnell!*" she barked. "Hurry up. I haven't got all day."

"Jawohl, Brünnhilde," Ernst muttered under his breath.

"What did you call me?" She stormed toward Ernst and towered over him.

"Nothing," he murmured, "but do you mind telling me why we aren't being offered a bed to sleep in for the next few days?" Both boys looked up at the second and third story windows of the hospital. It was only natural to presume there were beds inside.

"We are being watched," Brünnhilde said. "At this very moment, for all I know." She scanned the overgrown and weed-infested gardens, searched the edge of the woods on the other side of a little pond smothered by algae. Looking down her nose at them, she said sternly, "You can't stay here. Your instructions are to proceed to Brittany. No more dilly-dallying." She extracted a postcard from her nurse's smock.

Without so much as an *auf wiedersehen*, the Valkyrie with the big bosom and stout legs was gone. Ernst read the name of the destination and then turned the card over. A photo of Rue des Trois Cailloux from prewar Amiens shone brightly in Kodachrome. It was obvious that when this picture had been snapped, those had definitely been happier days.

Le Petit Oiseau ripped open the telegram.

UNMARKED TRUCK IS LATEST TRANSPORT
STOP DESTINATION AND ETA STILL
UNKNOWN STOP

She tore the yellow sheet of paper and its matching envelope into a million pieces and walked them out to the back of her garden where she buried them in her compost pile. Swatting away the flies, she brushed her graying hair from her brow. *Hopefully, that movie star of an agent they sent me is worth his salt,* she said to herself.

Chapter Thirty-Three

"Ernst?"

"Now what?"

"I'm worried about what's going to happen to us afterward?"

"After what?"

"After we deliver this shit?"

"I keep telling you, stop calling it *shit*. These works of art are vital to the next Reich." Ernst glanced away from the dark road for a moment. He could barely make out Klaus' face, but his oily, white-blond hair in the eerie illumination of the dashboard lights made him look crazed.

"You're as white as a ghost," Ernst said, his eyes trained on the beach road leading to the walled city of Saint-Malo. "And with that hideous grimace of yours, anyone would think you're heading back to the Russian front."

"Forget it . . ."

"The war's over, buddy." Ernst laughed. "Besides, we're almost there."

"Then what?" As the bus rolled down the poorly patched road, hugging the coastline of the English Channel, they were both silent as they observed in shock the shelled remnants of a city.

After a while, Ernst offered another one of his platitudes. "Ya know, seeing where we're going isn't any better than knowing where we've already been."

"Jesus Christ!" Klaus exploded. "You're doin' it again." He punched Ernst in the arm. "Can't a guy express himself without you having to follow up with some philosophical bullshit?"

"I'm pulling over here." With a yank on the steering wheel, Ernst drove off the road and brought the bus to a stop on the beach. "You're getting far too paranoid, and I'm too tired to put up with you. We both need a few hours of sleep."

"You're gonna park us here in plain sight?"

"Yup. C'mon."

The boys found enough pieces of driftwood to build a campfire and soon, they were settled in front of it. The fire snapped cheerfully, and periodically it sent up a drift of sparks. Staring at it seemed to have a hypnotic effect on Klaus.

"Feeling better?" Ernst asked. For once, he was willing to show Klaus a little empathy.

"Not really."

"Oh, for God's sake, Klaus. This mission has been a piece of cake."

"Easy for you to say."

"All we gotta do now is find that Father Gilles fellow in Kersaint and dump our load on his doorstep. How could it get any simpler?"

"I can think of a million things that might go wrong, which you don't seem to think about at all. That makes me nervous. Real nervous."

"Sod off!"

"I count on you to handle the rough spots, but if you're not prepared for any of them, then we're sunk!" Klaus flopped back onto the sand and stared up at the stars. "Does that make sense?"

"No. It's dumb." Ernst pulled the collar of his jacket up around his ears. There was a chill in the air.

"You should know I've had a premonition," Klaus announced.

"Yeah? Like what?" Ernst scoffed.

"Like we're gonna die once this is done. And you know what else?"

"No idea."

"No one's gonna give a shit."

"I'm confused. You worried about dying or no one giving a shit?"

"Both."

"Well, here's what I got to say on that."

"Oh, no. Please don't," Klaus begged.

"Too bad." Ernst cleared his throat and paused. "You die once when your last breath leaves your body. Nothin' you can do about it. But you only die for real when the very last person on earth speaks your name."

"You're not making any sense."

"After what we've accomplished? Saving this art for the Fatherland? The world will never stop *speaking* our names. We're gonna be heroes, Klaus-ie baby. You and I are gonna be forever immortalized!"

Klaus looked dumbfounded.

"We're never ever gonna die. Got that?" Klaus nodded slowly. "Now get some sleep."

The next morning, the beach was saturated with sunlight. Up above, a cloudless sky made the Channel a dazzling blue.

Ernst stretched with arms wide and instantly burst out laughing. "The end is nigh, Klaus!"

"That may be, but I'm hungry!" Klaus hugged his grumbling stomach.

"Yeah, a cup of coffee would sure hit the spot. Let's hope we find a bakery."

"If there's one open," Klaus rejoined, always the pessimist.

Four hours later and running on fumes, the boys limped into Portsall, the sister village to Kersaint. They parked behind a row of shops on the quay.

"That's as far as we're gonna get," Ernst declared. "We are outta gas."

"But how are we gonna get this crap to where it's s'posed to go if we can't roll?" Klaus whined.

"You're gonna stay here and guard the art while I go over there . . ." he pointed to the little harbor, "and then I'm gonna steal a boat and go siphon me some gas. Might decide to take a tour of the place while I'm at it. Can you handle that, Klaus-ie?"

Madeleine

May 1945

Chapter Thirty-Four

S ummer unleashed a punishing heat on Kersaint. Slumbering late every morning unless rousted by Annabelle, and retiring early, she felt drugged by the high temperatures, if not by an overabundance of sleep. Loneliness weighed her down too. Not that she'd had any social life before the war—she'd been too young—but she had so looked forward to one now that the war was over. With none of the younger men home yet, Madeleine was beginning to think she'd never fall in love.

Ever making the effort to be away from Sophie's shuffling grouchiness and Annabelle's nagging, Madeleine liked to take long walks in the morning. She especially gravitated to a path along the edge of the cliffs facing the English Channel. Less than a week after VE Day, Madeleine took a picnic up there. On her way, a single tern surfed slowly by on a light breeze. It stayed parallel with her, and every now and then Madeleine had to wonder if this were an omen. In the sparkling sunlight, the cliffs were particularly distinctive, their rosy hues banded with pink granite, which had made Brittany's coastline famous. Though Madeleine felt restless, the rhythms of the sea radiated permanence, which was comforting. When she reached the famous St. Samson Chapelle, its stone cross and holy well, she sat down amid the flowering heather, its rosy blooms in full splendor.

According to the history books, St. Samson was a wandering

Celtic missionary, an ascetic who was born in Wales around 490 and who died in France in 565. He wound up in Brittany, where he became Bishop of Dol. It was said he had spent much time in the Finistère department of Brittany and had performed many a miracle of healing. Madeleine thought the general malaise she was experiencing needed attention. Perhaps, a trace of his supernatural powers might still be hanging in the air. After all, legend had it that Samson, one of the most highly venerated Celtic clerics of his time, had crossed the English Channel in a boat made of stone.

Once she said her prayers, Madeleine wandered down a steep path to the tidal pools below. The tide was far out, and as she walked barefoot, the suction in the sand tugged noisily at her feet. Standing quietly in two inches of salt water, she watched tiny minnows dart between the sunny spots and shadows, even between her toes. She giggled.

"You are amused, Fräulein?"

Madeleine spun around, her long ponytail whipping across her face. A chill ran down the open neck of her blouse. In the shadows, a lanky fellow, not much older than she, with a sweep of blonde hair across his forehead, was pressed against the cliff face. He was dressed in slate-gray Nazi fatigues and was barefoot. He pushed off from the rock wall and squatted on a piece of petrified driftwood.

"Who are you?" Throughout the occupation, Madeleine had studiously tried to ignore the German boys patrolling through town. Today, however, she wasn't afraid to look this German boy in the eye. He was scrawny, with too big a nose for the shape of his small face. She didn't hide her revulsion. Who cared? Her side had won the war.

"My name is Ernst." His eyes lingered a little bit longer on her. "Anyone ever tell you you're really pretty?"

Ignoring his question, she stated, "The war's over. Why are you still here?"

"I like French girls." He licked his lips. He stared unabashedly at her tanned legs.

Madeleine stepped backward toward the path heading to the top. "You Jerries are not welcome here."

Ernst pouted dramatically for affect. "Ah, Fräulein, you may think you French are liberated, but the Reich will never fall. Hitler has lost this battle, but Germany has not lost the war. We Germans are too strong, and certainly, we'll return."

Madeleine stopped in her tracks. "Is that so?" she asked. "Well, you don't scare me." She looked him up and down again. "Judging by the looks of you, you're a nobody. I suspect you're probably AWOL, scared you'll be shot if you go home. After all, you deprived your team of its win, didn't you?"

"And you, you foolish girl, talk with the swagger of a Maquis. Or were you one of those radio operators who floated down from the clouds to frustrate us?"

"Radio operator, you ask?" Madeleine sniggered as if the suggestion were offensive. "The Resistance did more than that," she argued. "I'd run along now, if I were you." She waved the back of her hand at him as if to shoo him away.

"So you were a spy!" Ernst laughed. "And such a pretty little thing. How did you ever escape attention?" He rose from his perch and made to follow her.

Madeleine immediately realized her mistake. All that bravura, having him believe she was a member of the Resistance, was not at all what she wanted him to think. She wanted him to think of her as a nobody and to go as far away from Kersaint as his dirty feet would take him.

Madeleine used every bit of willpower to maintain a leisurely pace as she climbed back up the path to the top of the cliff. Heaven forbid she exude any hint of fear. When at the top, though, she took off at a run, her hair unraveling from its ponytail and flying out behind her. Past the patch of artichokes, she pushed through a fence and cut across a pasture of cattle. They scattered into a cluster of bovine protest, lowing loud enough to alert the Nazi of her whereabouts. Looking back to see if the Nazi was following, and seeing no one, she slowed to catch her breath. Her chest burned and her breathing was ragged. Though eager to be home, Madeleine opted for the longer route and turned left where limbs of horse chestnut trees stretched across the narrow lane and provided her with a semblance of cover. She stopped short when a group of boys, kicking a soccer ball and colliding into each other in intentional scrums, barreled down the track and knocked her over.

A man standing at an easel in front of the Château de Trémazan ruins saw Madeleine fall and rushed to her side. Madeleine recoiled, her heart galloping. Not recognizing this man, she presumed him another Nazi holdover. But when he reached for her elbow to help her up and her eyes met his, she could not bring herself to pull away. The cobalt sky reflected in his eyes was so bewitching, she allowed his unfamiliar hand to lift her up.

"Are you okay?" She nodded. "Let me introduce myself," the man offered in English. "My name is Buck Connor."

Madeleine could hardly doubt his sincerity his voice was so warm. "*Enchantée*," she replied, dusting herself off.

"And you are?" Buck smiled his encouragement, which lit up his entire face.

Suddenly shy and self-conscious, Madeleine flicked her hair behind her shoulders and gathered it into a knot at the nape of her neck.

Buck watched, mesmerized. "You seemed to be in quite the hurry just now. Are you in distress, *mademoiselle*?" Buck took the liberty of caressing an errant strand. "Your hair is as bright as falling water."

The heat rose in Madeleine. She remained very still as she looked up at Buck. Scanning his strong jawline, straight nose, and high forehead, she marveled at his black eyebrows, arched and perfectly framing electric blue eyes. Butterflies fluttered somewhere deep inside Madeleine's belly.

"Let's sit down over here," Buck said. He guided her toward a moss-covered chunk of castle ruin lying amidst a clump of wild rose bushes and sea grass. "What happened?"

Madeleine's breathing finally steadied, but she was at a loss for words. Both stared into the distance at the fishing boats anchored in the little harbor bobbing up and down like toys.

"There was a German soldier below the cliffs," Madeleine finally said. "He got a little too friendly."

"Did he touch you?"

"No."

"Are you too scared to tell *me* your name?" Buck cajoled.

"Madeleine." She arched her back. "That pig was wearing army fatigues with a pair of swastikas on his shirt collar."

Putting this information on the back burner, Buck teased. "No last name?"

"That's good enough for now, I think," Madeleine said crossly.

Worried that this German soldier was up to no good, Buck said, "May I escort you home?"

"You don't mind?" Madeleine asked with relief. It was when Buck was dismantling his easel and tucking away the little canvas that she noticed his left arm's missing hand. "What happened to your hand?"

"I'll tell you all about it if you'll accept an invitation to dinner tonight."

They had crossed the lane when Madeleine stopped, cocked her head, and looked down at her sand-encrusted bare feet. She could feel Buck's eyes caressing her skin.

"This is where I live." Madeleine announced. She blushed and extended her hand to shake his. *"Merci, Monsieur Connor."* She started up the gravel path to her door.

At the last second, she turned around and called, "I'll be ready at six-thirty."

May 1945

Chapter Thirty-Five

Claire tipped the scales at one hundred and eleven pounds. All she needed now were her military clearances.

To keep busy while she waited on pins and needles to be called up, Claire purchased two more pairs of GI slacks, another field jacket, stadium boots, and a rain hat. She took great care to sew on the Red Cross patches she was given by Nurse Taylor. And though Isabelle had ironed her blouses and hand-washed her lingerie, Claire re-did everything so she could enjoy the effort first-hand. Fussing with packing and repacking, she had added several slinky dinner dresses, more trousers and sweaters. Since she didn't know what she would need first, it was a struggle to figure out if the civvies ought to be at the top of her suitcase or underneath her army apparel.

A day didn't go by without butterflies taking up residence in Claire's stomach. The vastness of the steps ahead was so daunting it took her breath away. Even though Hitler had pulled his troops from Paris in August of ‹44, the previous year, the war was by no means over yet and Claire was now, after all her original objections, voluntarily rushing toward it. Not only that, but Claire had never been outside the country—not even outside New York.

Her imminent departure was shrouded in secrecy. There would be no telling Claire's in-laws or friends when she was leaving or from what port. Nor would Claire know where she was headed until she reached that port on the other side of the Atlantic. All she did know was that she'd be given a twelve-hour head's up for her leave-taking.

On May 5th, 1945, at seven in the morning. Claire got the call to be ready by seven p.m. that night. When the time came for Claire to lug her gear down to the front hall of the little hotel she'd been staying in on Dupont Circle, she glanced around her rooms. Then she looked down at her trembling hands. The three-carat diamond winked in the overhead lights. As if hearing a voice, she obediently twisted the ring from her finger, kissed it, and zipped it into her traveling jewelry pouch.

"Wish me luck," she whispered to Bill's memory.

Claire traveled through the night with other soldiers and Red Cross gals in a motor coach, with blacked-out windows—even the driver and the windshield were curtained off—to a port whose name was never disclosed. With the war still on, troop movements were on a need-to-know basis. While the understandably apprehensive GI's were talkative, the Red Cross girls twittered just as nervously. Clearly, there was no sleep to be had. So, at daybreak when the bus finally pulled up to the side of a massive ship, the young men and women emerged into the sunlight bleary-eyed and yawning. The vessel rose from the pier like a skyscraper, sea birds shrieking over its open cargo bays. The ship struck an imperial and looming pose, its three fat smokestacks painted a dreary navy gray, the hull the same gloomy color. It bore no markings other than a seemingly meaningless number. To Claire, this ocean liner looked like a gray ghost, and she fervently hoped that if the German U-boats did catch sight of her on the open sea, she could at least outrun them.

The only thing Claire was told about their ship was that she had recently undergone a significant refit which boosted her passenger load from five thousand to eight thousand and that she had upgraded her defensive capabilities as well. Before 1942, she had only been protected by a single 4-inch gun and a few scattered Vickers and Lewis machine guns. Now, she boasted armaments roughly equivalent to a light cruiser, including 40mm cannon in five double mounts sited fore and aft, and twenty-four single-barrel cannon emplaced in steel tub mounts along the ship's upper structure. Six 3-inch guns were also aboard, as well as two antiaircraft rocket launchers near the aft funnel. There were, as it turned out, a few things Claire and her fellow passengers were allowed to know. Their ship was renowned for its speed, the primary reason for its being put into service. The other big advantage was that their ship's agility meant that it did not require a surrounding convoy. Claire, ever the pessimist, figured that should they be torpedoed, at least half of them would meet the same fate as those on board the *Titanic*: death by drowning or hypothermia.

Despite their looking like trolls, bent over by all their attire and gear, Claire and the other Red Cross volunteers were apparently a fetching enough group of women, because as they lumbered unaided up the gangway, harmless catcalls and whistles erupted. Claire couldn't resist a smile. It felt good to experience the favor of the male species again. Besides, their flattery lightened everybody's mood. Without too much difficulty, she found her state room and was immediately surprised to find it far roomier than she expected. It looked as though she'd have only three roommates and not the advertised six or eight. There was even a wash basin in the room with both hot and cold running water. Such luxury!

"So terribly swanky," Claire remarked to the army nurses who had entered and were standing in the doorway with mouths agape and eyes big as dinner plates. Could Commodore Campbell have had anything to do with these plush accommodations?

"Hi, my name is Betty," said a tall, big-boned gal coming forward with hand outstretched. "And this is Frances and Carol."

"Claire Campbell. Nice to meet you. Did you three just meet or did you come together?"

"We were together in Richmond waiting our orders."

"Where are we, anyway?"

"No idea."

"I think we're in Baltimore," said Betty. "I went to Goucher College in Townsend. This port looks a tad familiar."

"Ladies," interrupted Frances, "I was informed by one of the officers in charge of our well-being that we are allowed one shower a day and that at the aft of this deck there are deck chairs with blankets reserved for just us Red Cross girls."

Carol gushed, "We were also told that under no circumstances are we to fraternize with the ship's crew or the enlisted troops." She giggled. "Which is such a pity, because some of them are so darn cute!"

"Yes," interjected Frances, "but we're invited into the army officers' lounge. And that is infinitely better, wouldn't you say?" Looking up from the suitcase she was unpacking, she asked Claire, "You did bring a cocktail dress, I hope?"

Claire hesitated, suddenly reminded of her modeling days—the dizziness a group of gals could generate when thrown into close quarters.

"I guess that means we are the high-class group," Carol said with an impish grin. "I'm certainly not going to say no to playing in the officers' lounge."

"Perish the thought!" Frances exclaimed.

"What say you, Claire?" asked Carol. "Will you cut loose on the way over?"

Claire shrugged. "I'm recently widowed, so I won't be jumping into the dating scene, if that's what you're suggesting." She had brought several novels with her, which she now placed on the shelf above her berth. Feeling three pairs of eyes on her, she said, "I'm an incorrigible bookworm."

"Who said anything about dating?" Betty said, hanging her dress on the last hanger in the closet.

"What happened?" Carol's concern sounded genuine.

"If you don't mind, I'd rather not talk about it right now." Claire liked Carol. Her giddy outlook was contagious. Just the ticket if the blahs hit. "Show me your dress," Claire said.

The girls spent the rest of the afternoon getting acquainted and prepping for their first cocktail hour on board the *USS Anonymous*.

Chapter Thirty-Six

Claire stood at the railing watching the sun's last rays dip into the watery horizon. Keeping her eyes fixed on the coast of America as it grew smaller and smaller off the stern, she wondered if she were doing the right thing.

"It's too late to change your mind, you know."

Claire jumped. Standing there with a grin so broad it barely fit between his cheeks was a fellow with a lock of blond hair falling forward across his brow and into kind hazel eyes.

"What makes you think I'm changing my mind?" Her tone was more coy than defensive.

"Oh, I dunno. You looked kinda wistful." He leaned on the railing and folded his hands. In a gentle voice, he probed, "*Are* you feeling melancholy?"

Claire studied her new acquaintance's profile. He bore a slight resemblance to a young Robert Mitchum, only more studious. While his high forehead, spectacles and strong aquiline nose lent an intellectual aspect, it was the dimple in his chin and that runaway lock of hair which gave him a boyishness she had to admit she found appealing. As if on cue, he smoothed his hair aside.

"Name's Scott," he said, turning and offering Claire his right hand. "Dr. Scott Jeffries. Art historian catching a ride with you brave girls and boys."

"Claire Campbell, widow and all-around neophyte heading off to parts unknown." She did not withdraw her hand as quickly as she knew she should. "And no, I don't have a death wish. I just thought I ought to do my part."

"That's very noble . . ."

"Or terribly foolish."

"No, not at all," Scott insisted, touching her upper arm. "Last time I checked, there weren't too many women on troop detachments zig-zagging across the Atlantic Ocean dodging U-boats. I'm kinda in awe."

"Well, don't be." Truth be told, though, Claire was pretty impressed with her newfound courage. A ship's crossing in 1945 was no small potatoes. After all, the Battle of the Atlantic had been called the "longest, largest, and most complex" naval battle in history. The campaign had started immediately after the European War began, during the so-called Phony War and had persevered for more than five years. It had involved thousands of ships in more than a hundred convoy battles and perhaps a thousand single-ship encounters in a theatre covering millions of square miles of ocean. Claire looked in both directions down the length of their ship. Lookouts were posted every one hundred feet, keeping their eyes peeled for enemy periscopes and telltale streaks of a torpedo's wake. She shuddered.

"Important endeavors such as what you and the Red Cross gals are doing involve quite a bit of risk, so . . ."

Claire laughed softly. "You needn't remind me."

With nothing more to say, they looked awkwardly away from each other and stared at the rolling waves. The evening air felt silky, and as they stood in silence, their fingers almost touching, a Johnny Mercer song drifted from the officers' lounge. With a melody like that, romance was definitely in the air, and Claire was not so closed off that she couldn't feel a current passing between this man and herself. But she had vowed to herself that she wouldn't get entangled with a man—not so soon after Billy's death. Besides, what if by some crazy fluke he were still alive? Not that she was "seeing" him anymore, but what if he weren't missing anymore?

Scott touched the back of Claire's hand and when she looked over at him, he gestured with his head toward the deck chairs. She nodded and followed him to where a couple of seats and ship's blankets were tucked out of the wind.

Once they were ensconced in their semi-hidden corner and separately swaddled under plush burgundy and navy blue wool blankets, Scott commented, "I'm thinking these are a dead giveaway that we are traveling on a refurbished ocean liner."

"Very observant of you. I think you're right. The state room I'm sharing with three other girls is far too luxurious to be military digs, unless it belonged to an admiral."

"I think this might be Cunard's *Queen Mary* turned troop ship."

Claire was inclined to agree. "What does an art historian want with Europe at this particular moment in time?"

Scott returned her question with one of his own. "What do you know about the Monuments Men?"

"That they're responsible for preserving the art and architecture from the ravages of war. Are you one of them?"

"You might say so, but I'm on a slightly different mission."

"And what is that, may I ask?" Claire had always held an interest in art, particularly the Impressionist movement. She had been deeply saddened when she'd read about Hitler and Göring ransacking all of Europe's museums for their own private collections.

"You may ask, but unfortunately I'm not at liberty to tell."

"Oh," Claire said, disappointed. She liked this soft-spoken, thoughtful man. He had seemed so open. His shutting her down all of a sudden was a surprise, so Claire scooted to the edge of her seat and made to rise. "I should turn in."

"Please don't go." Scott reached for her hand. "Let me give you a first installment of what I'm up to, and I'll share what I can as events warrant." He smiled his wide, captivating grin. "Deal?"

With no warning, Claire found herself comparing him to Billy. This gentle man was less dashing but seemed more reliable. And Scott was clearly perceptive and empathic, which were not Billy's strong suits, he being too impulsive. Hadn't Scott already picked up on her thoughts twice—without even knowing her for more than a few minutes? Plus, this man was an academic. She doubted he'd ever tease her for reading like Billy had.

"Will you mind terribly if I go into professor mode?"

"Not at all." She smiled. He hadn't let go of her hand and now it rested in his lap with his other hand covering hers.

"Good. Are you familiar with Expressionism?"

"Yes, and it's not my favorite." Thinking better of it, she added, "Probably because it's harsh and escapes my comprehension."

Scott inclined his head. Smile lines appeared around his deep-set hazel eyes. "It's meant to portray society's reaction to the world, but I'd make the distinction that it reflects one's inability to keep up with this crazy world. Man is off balance, maybe even lost."

Identifying with this statement, Claire rolled her eyes. "Who isn't lost and confused with this war going on? I know I certainly am."

Scott nodded his agreement. "Van Gogh and Edvard Munch are credited for starting the Expressionist movement. It was in reaction to Impressionism. They wanted their art to express feelings, not just show superficial interpretations."

"But I love the Impressionists! What's wrong with Monet's lilies? Or Manet's landscapes and cityscapes? I consider Pissarro's pointillism absolutely breathtaking."

Scott ducked his chin and paused to gather his thoughts. He pulled a pipe from his breast pocket and chewed on the end of it without bothering to light it. "Expressionism has signaled an important new standard for the creation of art, which is that art should come from within." Scott thumped his chest with his fist. "Rather than being a mere depiction of an external, it reflects authentic feelings, not necessarily rosy or conventional ones. With Expressionism, the judgment of art is also key. This means that the standard for assessing the quality of work has less to do with the caliber of the painting and everything to do with the artist's emotions."

"That explains *The Scream*," interrupted Claire. "I don't think much of Munch's skill with the paintbrush, but I get where he's coming from."

"And where's that?" Scott asked, his tone softening when he saw Claire's lower lip quivering.

"My husband was killed last year."

"Gosh. I'm so sorry."

Brushing off his sympathy for fear it would only make her cry, Claire asked rhetorically, "Is society really ready for art to make so intimate a public display of emotion? I've come to the conclusion that introspection is an unhealthy waste of time. Even worse, it's terribly bad-mannered to thrust your feelings onto everyone else."

"Adolf Hitler would agree with you."

"Excuse me?"

"Expressionists do use bold colors, harsh brush strokes, and hard lines to convey horror, fear, alienation, and the grotesque. Yes, their subjects are indeed twisted. Broken, even. There's no question Expressionism exposes dark states of mind. But don't you think it challenges society to think, to question, maybe actually get others to respond?"

"But I respond to a Manet or a Degas any day of the week!"

"But they're not provocative."

"What if I want my art to be uplifting, not mentally abnormal?"

"Okay, but art can be a vehicle for social change, too." Claire folded her arms across her chest. "Yes, I agree this is a controversial style," Scott coaxed, "but it's the honesty I admire—whether we want to face the ugliness or not. You don't seem to be ready for such candor." He threw Claire a wink.

"No, I'm not. And if it means I agree with Hitler, so be it." Claire stood. "I really must get to bed."

"Will you talk with me tomorrow?"

Shrugging one shoulder and tilting her head, she replied, "Will you be comparing me to Göring next?"

Chapter Thirty-Seven

On May 8th, three days into their Atlantic crossing, a call to General Quarters blared over the loudspeakers. At first, Claire froze in place, believing that her worst fears were coming true. Her imagination jumped into high gear: they were under attack, a U-boat was lurking off their starboard bow or a torpedo had been spotted, its impending strike streaking toward them silvery-white beneath the dark ocean waters. The ship captain's voice boomed over the PA system. "All hands on deck. Ladies, you too."

As thousands of soldiers and the small contingent of Red Cross women flooded the passageways on their way up the stairs to the main deck, the air was subdued. No one spoke as they crowded into the bow and looked up at the bridge where the captain of the ship stood.

"The war is over! Hitler is dead. Today is Victory in Europe Day!" There was a moment of stunned silence and then the crowd erupted. Sailors threw their caps in the air as men whistled and cheered. Claire's roommates and entourage burst into tearful laughter and hugged each other. The ship's horn blasted its deep, resonant baritone to quiet the crowd as the captain bellowed, "Gentlemen— ahem, excuse me, and ladies—allow me to share President Truman's announcement." The admiral cleared his throat:

" 'Our rejoicing is sobered and subdued by a supreme consciousness of the terrible price we have paid to rid the world of Hitler and his evil band. Let us not forget, my fellow Americans, the sorrow and the heartache which today abide in the homes of so many of our neighbors—neighbors whose most priceless possession has been rendered as a sacrifice to redeem our liberty … If I could give you a single watchword for the coming months, that word is work, work, and more work. We must work to finish the war. Our victory is only half over.' "

He was referring to Japan. A hush fell over the men as they wrestled with their emotions. While today was undeniably a day of joy for all of Europe now that she was free of Hitler, the war in the Pacific raged on. Now they'd be shipped off to the Pacific theater where hundreds of starving American POWs were being brutalized by their captors in war camps. Sure, Truman didn't want the soldiers to lose sight of the endgame, but naturally, the thought of what was happening over there made these fellas cringe. They were hard pressed to think about victory. Claire could see it written all over their faces.

And Claire, couldn't help thinking that victory had come too late for the loved ones who had perished, namely Billy. She bit her lip and tried to smile through her tears, hoping they'd be interpreted as tears of joy. But Scott suspected differently, and appearing out of nowhere, encircled her in his arms. He held and rocked her gently until all the men and women had dispersed and gone inside or below deck. When she looked up from his tear-soaked lapels, her eyes were red-rimmed and her cheeks stained with smudges of mascara.

"Care for a drink?"

"If it's a double, yes please."

While Scott was at the bar collecting their cocktails, Claire fished her compact from her pocket and dusted her nose and cheeks with powder. She examined her face from side to side, applied a fresh coat of red lipstick, and blotted her mouth with a tissue. She patted her hair and then shook her head to throw off the doldrums. When Scott returned to their corner table, her spirits lifted. That lock of hair was in his eyes and he looked adorable.

Scott sat close to Claire instead of taking the seat opposite from hers. As he raised his glass, inviting her to clink hers to his, he shouted, "To victory at long last!"

"And may my friend, Herr Hitler, rot in hell!" Claire teased.

"I guess I owe you an explanation." He mugged a sheepish look. "Last night, I told you I was working with the Monuments Men. Those guys, who are literally soldiers or trained volunteers, are currently trying to find and save the cultural treasures of countries Hitler invaded. My job, which I think it's pretty safe to reveal now that victory is ours, is to round up all the Nazi propaganda art before the Germans whisk it away and try to use it again."

"You mean to tell me the Nazis might strive for a Fourth Reich?"

"Wouldn't put it past 'em," Scott said, taking a long sip. "Generals Eisenhower, Patton, and Bradley think so."

"How do you know all this?" Claire asked. Scott wiggled his eyebrows à la Charlie Chaplin and pretended to twirl an invisible cane. "Oh, stop!"

"Did you happen to read in the papers about the cache found in the Kaiseroda Mine?" Scott asked.

"No."

"Over four hundred paintings stolen from Europe's capitals were found there. Masters such as Picasso, Rembrandt, and Michelangelo are still missing, but the hunt is on."

"*Schweinhunds!*"

"Ditto," Scott said, visibly relaxing. Claire liked to think it was because she was easy to talk to, that he liked her candor. "Imagine precious art being spirited away to hiding places such as salt mines in Austria or the damp cellars of Bavarian castles. Stolen masterpieces are even hiding in plain sight above the living room mantels of unsuspecting farmers who know nothing of their worth or provenance."

"Goodness! You mean to say Johann *und* his dear *vife*, Heidi, have no idea *vat* hangs on *zehr vall*?"

Scott burst out laughing. "I like your sarcasm. That's a pretty good German accent, by the way."

Claire was pleased with herself for having made her professor friend laugh. Engaging in a real dialogue with a man was new for Claire. With Billy, there had always been just a light banter with a whole lot of kissing—rarely any intellectual exchange of thought or ideas. Claire was enjoying being acknowledged for her brain and not simply as a plaything, fondled or flaunted because of her looks. To be fair, though, that's how she let Billy treat her. With the goal of ensnaring him, she'd never used her intellect to attract him.

"Did you know the Monuments Men train at The Coop in New York?" Claire shook her head. "They're working covertly with the SOE now."

"I've heard of them."

"Really? How so?"

Claire uncrossed her legs and leaned closer to whisper, "I was introduced to a young woman who flew with the ATA and eventually the SOE, dropping British agents behind enemy lines." Scott nodded, impressed. "She's the one who convinced me to get off my derrière and volunteer in the war effort." Claire paused to take a sip of her gin and tonic. "Are you with the SOE?"

Scott withdrew his pipe from his pocket and gestured to her

for permission. She nodded. It took a couple of minutes to light, his lips making popping noises as he brought it to life. Finally, he answered, "No, I'm afraid I'm not that daring." He puffed on his pipe. "Churchill's gang of spies—lemme tell you, those are some incredibly brave folks. They hide in plain sight, transmit information on hidden radios, never sleep in the same place for more than a few nights, blow up bridges and train tracks, and generally cause a whole lot of mayhem. If caught, they are subjected to some of the worst torture imaginable."

Claire shuddered. She watched the smoke from Scott's pipe curl around his head. "Let's just say I'm working for the United States government."

Claire's eyebrows shot up. "Well, that's a surprise."

Scott lowered his voice further. "My job is to oversee the rounding up of all the Nazi propaganda art the Reich produced."

"What's so terrible about it that it needs to be 'rounded up?'"

With artificial pomposity, Scott intoned, " 'Art belongs to the whole complex of the racial values and gifts of the people.' So declared Herr Adolf Hitler in 1935."

"Ooh, knowing what we know now about the Final Solution, this doesn't sound good." It had been so hard to comprehend Hitler's barbarism. How could it possibly be true? The faces of the suffering from so far away, when all the while people in America continued to go to the cinema or complain about the shortage of nylons, didn't feel real. Not until the newsreels began to tell a grotesque story could one even begin to mentally grasp the existence of such horror.

Claire settled back against the banquette and folded her hands in her lap. "Tell me more."

"Adolf Hitler proclaimed himself Germany's patron of the arts, and as a formidable spokesman for not only the permissible style and content of German art, he also made himself responsible for delivering its metaphysical message. The first order of business was to ban all of art's 'isms.' Impressionism, Cubism, Dadaism, and especially Expressionism, which he particularly despised." Scott gave her an apologetic smile. "You see, to Hitler these genres of art could never achieve *Zeitgeist*—German eternal truths. Hitler was determined to rid the world of works of art which highlighted human deformity, mental illness, and depravity. Those were 'truths' Hitler preferred to deny. Realities which to him were a lie."

"So styles of art deviating from the conventional or portraying all aspects of the human condition was vulgar?" Claire watched an officer lift her roommate, Carol, up onto the bar where she began to sway to the strains of Les Brown's "My Dreams Are Getting Better All the Time."

Scott nodded. "Hitler also said, 'True art is and remains eternal. It does not follow the law of fashion; its effect is that of a revelation arising from the depths of the essential character of a people.' Something like that, anyway."

"That's utter bunk!" Claire scoffed. "*The essential character of a people* implies an all-encompassing collective. Is there such a thing as generic art?"

"I'm glad you asked—."

"If there were, surely it would be substandard, cheap, and unworthy of even being called art," Claire said crossly. She downed the last of her gin. "I'm confused. I mean, I might interpret a painting or a poem or a person's facial expression one way and you another. There's never any universally understood interpretation."

"Life would be very monochromatic if there were," Scott mused. "But here's the point I'm trying to make." He reached for Claire's hand. "The National Socialist Party of Germany wished for their art to go beyond their history or current reality. Hitler's goal was to extol the sublime."

"Whatever for?"

"To impart a metaphysical message."

"Which was what?"

"The glory of a new German reality, *Weltanschauung*—worldview."

"Why?"

"Hitler used his propaganda art to unite the German people. It was a means to lift them from the doldrums wrought by the Versailles Treaty in the aftermath of World War I. Hitler's art not only justified to the German people his plans of conquering Europe and finishing what the first war never did, but also gave reasons for the Final Solution."

"Reasons or excuses?" Claire was growing angrier by the minute. "How outrageous!"

Scott signaled the private second class on duty behind the bar to bring another round of drinks. He then slid his arm around Claire's shoulders. "I'm changing the subject."

"Good idea," Claire conceded, watching out the corner of her eye as Frances and Betty joined Carol on top of the bar. All three of them were dancing to the music.

"Would you mind telling me how your husband died?"

Claire fell silent. Eventually, she said, "His plane crashed into a shoulder of Mount McKinley. There were nineteen on board. Sixteen dead, three missing."

"And was—?"

"Billy's body was never located."

Scott shook his head and sighed. "I'm so sorry."

Claire's eyes glistened. "Billy deserved to witness this day."

"Of course he did." Scott retrieved his pipe from his breast pocket, and gripping it between his teeth, relit it.

"But I'm here now. In this banquette. With you. The past is in the past."

In between puffs, Scott dared to ask in staccato, "Does this mean you're ready to maybe possibly sorta-kinda think about dating again?"

Yet again, he'd read her mind.

Glenn Miller's "In the Mood" suddenly sprang from the phonograph. Claire's roommates began waving and calling to her. She demurred.

"C'mon, Claire, we need you for the harmony!"

Scott turned to Claire while someone shone a spotlight on her. "Let your hair down, kiddo. Go on!" cajoled Scott. "Celebrate the day!" And before Claire could protest, he pulled her from the banquette, scooped her into his arms, carried her across the crowded salon and hoisted her up onto the bar top.

The men went wild, whistling and clapping their approval as Claire, Betty, Frances, and Carol all sang "In the Mood," each one of them belting out the lyrics while pantomiming holding mics. When the song ended, shouts of *encore* rang out, so the girls consulted with the DJ and they sang "Boogie-Woogie Bugle Boy from Company B." Everyone was dancing the jitterbug. Scott leaned against a column, with his hands shoved in his pockets and a grin that wouldn't quit.

The girls hopped down when "Moonlight Serenade" began to play. Scott was right there to enfold Claire in his arms. With his hand closed around Claire's and curled against his chest, Scott slid his other hand around to the small of her back. Not since her wedding had she slow danced with a man. Her breath came a little faster, sensing the citrusy aftershave on his skin. Scott led Claire around the dance floor with all the grace and expertise of a Gene Kelly. Cheek to cheek, both became oblivious to what was happening around them.

"Before this ship sails into port I have a mind to make you my girl, Claire Campbell."

"I'm flattered. Truly, but it's too soon." She meant every word. "I'm just not ready." Claire bolted from his hold.

Claire stared out at sea, her hair and clothing blowing in the cold wind and ocean spray catching in her thick lashes. Gunmetal-gray waves stretched out like a desert, mile after mile, with no landfall yet in sight. Scott stepped close behind her, opened his coat, and enveloped her in his warmth. She clasped his arms to her chest and allowed him to rest his chin on her shoulder, their cheeks touching. Claire liked this man, more than she thought she should for the few short days they'd spent together. There was a calmness about him that seemed to center her.

She and Scott stood at the stern under a soft blanket of stars, the ship's wake a churning cacophony of foam and roaring engines. The contrast was emblematic of Claire's emotions. On the one hand she felt herself falling for the professor, and on the other she couldn't help wondering if Billy were still alive. If he were would he come back to her? Would their marriage survive the lie she'd told? Would she even want Billy back if he were alive? That was the biggest question, and she had no answer for it.

Scott turned Claire around to face him. Tucking a strand of her hair behind her ear, his eyes caressed her face. Then sweeping his thumb across her jaw, he wove his fingers through her thick auburn hair and whispered hoarsely, "May I kiss you?" Almost imperceptibly, she consented.

It was as if she knew how the kiss would feel, as if they were made for each other. It was the most gentle and sincere kiss Claire had ever experienced.

When Scott withdrew his lips from hers, a shiver ran down Claire's back. She felt a profound sense of guilt. "I think I should turn in."

She stepped back, but Scott grabbed her hand to stop her. Claire looked down at his long, tapered fingers encircling her wrist. How

218

she loved elegant hands. It was the first physical attribute she noticed in a man. The second was how good a dancer he was. On the dance floor, Scott was elegance personified. Claire hesitated.

"Tomorrow, then," Scott said, letting go. He watched her reluctant retreat, but before she disappeared below deck, he called softly, "Claire?" She paused at the hatch. "Take all the time you need."

Once again, he seemed to know.

Claire tiptoed into her stateroom and undressed by the light of a setting moon. Slipping between the cold sheets, she lay on her back and stared out the porthole next to her berth. With eyes wide open until a faint daylight began to seep under a dawn that was slow to rise, she struggled to understand the tangled thoughts running through her mind. Maybe, she ought to live while she could, and accept love while it was offered.

May 1945

Chapter Thirty-Eight

A pair of turtledoves pecked on the ledge where Madeleine had strewn breadcrumbs outside her bedroom window. She chattered to them as she ransacked her armoire looking for the perfect outfit to wear on her date with Buck. Determined to shut out the memories of the fiasco in Morocco, she was willing, nonetheless, to admit she'd been a fool. Tonight was not going to be the same. She just knew it.

"The yellow dress to go with my hair?" She held it up to her and swished this way and that. The doves made no response. Tossing it on the bed, she held up a turquoise blouse dotted with tiny pink roses and scalloped capped sleeves. "Too many buttons," she concluded, not realizing her own subconscious thread of thinking. "What about these cropped white slacks and a striped t-shirt? No, white at a picnic isn't a good idea." She threw the articles over a chair and stomped her foot. "*Merde, merde, et re-merde!*" she cried.

The turtle doves startled and took flight.

"À *bientôt,*" she trilled. She picked up the yellow frock again and dropped it over her head. Suddenly, a wave of nausea took hold and bile rose to the back of her throat. Thinking she was about to vomit, she ran to the chamber pot stored under the corner wash basin and bent over it. She threw up and greenish-brown fluid and sputum, but remained kneeling over the bowl for a few moments longer until the queasiness passed. Then she stood up on wobbly legs, rinsed her mouth and splashed her face with water.

Strange, she thought, *how can I feel right as rain one moment and then sick the next?* These sudden bouts of queasiness had been going on now for almost a fortnight. They didn't feel like food poisoning or gastric problems, and her appetite had been good. From out of nowhere, she suddenly remembered something her mother had told her: *I was as sick as a dog with you, but I always felt fine as soon as I threw up.*

And then with a sharp intake of breath, it hit her. It was in early March when last she'd worn pads. Frantically, she counted the weeks on her fingers. Seven or eight weeks, give or take, had passed since her last period. Madeleine rushed over to the mirror and turned sideways. She lifted her dress up to her waist and examined her profile. She smoothed her hand over her belly. Her skin felt the same—soft and smooth—but then she saw a thickening that wasn't there before.

Quel horreur! she cried inwardly. *I can't be pregnant! Not now.* She let the dress drop back down and stomped her foot. *"Merde à la puissance treize,"* she hissed. Shit to the thirteenth power was just the half of it. She'd have to figure out how to make it go away. That thought startled her. How could she be so dismissive? But dammit, how would she ever be able to blot out the memories of Aboud if there were a baby to remind her of him? This baby wasn't made in love. It was conceived in cruelty.

She'd figure something out, but not tonight. Tonight, she was going to fall in love with a delicious American artist.

Buck spread a blanket in the shade of an oak tree adjacent to the crumbling tower of the Château Trémazan. All around them, Mother Nature seemed to be dancing to a happy tune, a bright sunny day having transitioned into a lively evening. Red and yellow poppies fluttered in the breeze, while low clumps of sea thrift poked their pink flowers on long slender stems between the fallen ruins of the castle.

The history of Trémazan was closely linked to that of the Châtel family, who had built and made it their principal residence in the thirteenth century. It was erected over the ruins of a sixth- century *castellum*. The origins of this dynasty were still shrouded in mist, but it was said that Tanneguy du Châtel, founder of the Abbey at Saint-Mathieu, was born at the castle. The Châtel family became so prominent that the Châtels rose to take their place in high Breton aristocracy.

Madeleine watched Buck as he pulled from his rucksack a baguette, a quarter wheel of creamy brie, a garlicky saucisson, and a jar of cornichons. His bright blue eyes, almost electric against his swarthy complexion, elicited in her an attraction she had not felt since Morocco. What was it about that dark-haired, blue-eyed aesthetic? The two men were different, though. With Aboud, there had been a sense of danger, which while it had initially been arousing, had turned out to be disastrous. With Buck, his allure felt safe. She'd missed the signals then. She hoped she wasn't misreading them now.

"What was it like here after the invasion?" Buck asked. He tucked the baguette under his arm and tore off a tranche of bread and handed it to Madeleine. "I'm afraid I haven't mastered the art of one-handed slicing," he said, shrugging apologetically, handing her the knife.

Madeleine cut a few slices off the saucisson. "I was fifteen when rationing began. Fortunately, everyone here was either a fisherman or a farmer, so we didn't want for too much. Plus, there was a flour mill just outside of town, so we had bread. Food was scarce, but we were resourceful. At least, that is, until the Nazis arrived and ate everything in sight."

Madeleine smeared a *soupçon* of gooey cheese on her bread and layered the sausage with a cornichon on top. Balancing it carefully, she then dropped the whole thing into her mouth. She knew her pursed, pouty lips with the tiny opening in the center had Buck's full attention.

"And what was that like?" Buck asked. He opened the Bordeaux by gripping the bottle with his feet, screwing the metal point of the corkscrew on his knife until it was firmly embedded in the cork, then extracted it with a pop.

Madeleine watched in fascination. *"Bien joué!"* she exclaimed, impressed that a one-handed fellow could open a bottle so expertly. Well done. She wanted to ask how he'd lost his hand but was afraid the topic of his injury might ruin the mood. "Wherever there was a dearth, someone had something to trade for what they needed. If Madame Colbert needed eggs and Monsieur Jadot needed a light-bulb, they could barter."

"Very resourceful, but who would organize such a thing?" Buck sniffed the cork, then poured a little into two glasses he'd purloined from a café. He handed her one and tapped his against it. *"Santé,"* he said.

"Maman, of course," Madeleine replied proudly. "She ran the communication network and I fulfilled the errands. It wasn't always easy, as I had to move around right under the Huns' noses."

"I bet, because there's no way anyone could not notice you, *ma belle.*"

She smiled at the compliment. "I made myself as drab as possible, even down to rubbing coal dust on my cheeks. We lived under a relative calm compared to other towns. Call it a sinister one, but none of us was particularly suffering. Angry, certainly. Worried too, but not adversely affected."

"I suppose all things are relative."

"Yes." Madeleine took a big sip of her wine.

"You've been very gutsy," Buck said, his eyes, once again, fixated on Madeleine's sensuous mouth.

A pair of thrushes began to call to each other. Madeleine looked up and said, "Maman says you can make believe there's no war on when you hear the birds singing."

"What a charming notion," responded Buck.

"Anyway, our invaders were really quite polite and well disciplined. No doubt grateful, I suppose, to be stationed in this beautiful part of France."

"Yeah, but I bet the officers took over the vacated holiday homes and helped themselves to all the contents."

"How'd you know?" She sipped her wine and looked into Buck's face over the rim of her glass. Batting her long lashes over dilated pupils, she unconsciously unfolded her legs.

"Common tactics of an occupier. They gotta live somewhere." Buck sipped more wine. "*C'est la vie, c'est la guerre, non?*" That's life, that's war.

"Soon enough they were indeed looking for billets for all their troops. Fortunately for Maman and me, our house was too small."

Buck scooted closer to Madeleine, and bringing his face up to hers, his breath warm on her cheeks, he paused teasingly before dusting a bread crumb from her mouth.

"You're not eating anything," she said accusingly. "*Pourquoi?*"

"You ask 'why.' I guess it's cause I'm too busy looking at you."

"It's embarrassing." Madeleine said, not in the least bit discomfited.

"You know you're gorgeous."

"You're not too shabby yourself."

Buck pushed the picnic to the side, and backing up against the oak's massive tree trunk, he pulled Madeleine between his long legs so her back was up against his chest. "Finish your story," he said.

Madeleine felt the heat of Buck's body behind her. Haltingly, she continued. "So we didn't have a Nazi in the house, but we had one on top of our roof. A sentry was installed on the flat part of our roof. There were two, actually, who alternated patrols night and day, peering out to sea in search of any English who might come ashore. There was a tent up there," Madeleine pointed at her cottage across the road, "a siren, and a machine gun. With all the constant stomping of boots over our heads it was impossible to sleep. As you can imagine, there were a lot of false alarms."

Buck had begun to stroke Madeleine's hair. She, in turn, became more distracted.

"Maman went to the *Kommandantur* to complain and next thing we knew, a few soldiers arrived to pour sand over the roof to deaden the noise."

"Did it work?"

"A few days later, on his way back from the beach, the Commander saw my mother, and inquired if she were sleeping better. He also asked about my father's whereabouts. And do you know what she said?" Buck shook his head. " 'Your people killed him at Verdun.' "

"Whoa! That was asking for it," Buck exclaimed.

"Sure, but then you don't mess around with my mother, either."

Buck surveilled their surroundings. "Will she be cross if I do this?" Buck cupped Madeleine's breast on the outside of her dress.

"Probably..." Madeleine murmured.

"And this?" Buck slid his hand inside her shift. He groaned when his fingers touched bare skin. Madeleine, like most French women, was not wearing a bra. And as he began to lightly trace a circle around her nipple, she arched her back and pressed her head against his shoulder.

"You're irresistible," Buck moaned in her ear. "And all I want to do is show you." He stroked her face. "May I make love to you?"

Madeleine hesitated as if considering something.

"Say 'yes,' " Buck urged.

Chapter Thirty-Nine

The following morning, when Madeleine finally emerged from the best sleep she'd had in weeks, the sun was high in a crystal-blue sky. Finally, she had slept without a single nightmare. Neither her maman nor Sophie was home, so Madeleine dressed quickly, grabbed a tartine from the kitchen, and left the house before she could be stopped and told to do her chores.

A very happy Madeleine skipped down the sandy lane, past the château and neighbors' houses. Making every effort to close her mind against her condition, she focused instead on still being in Buck's arms. She hadn't known until Buck made love to her that sex could be so sublime. His attentions had made her feel as though she'd fallen over a precipice and down an endless chute of sparkling water. Her body was still tingling, and she couldn't wait to lie with him again.

At the end of the lane where the beach began, pheasants clattered from their hiding places within a copse of yew trees and thorny bushes. Startled, Madeleine jumped, thinking it was that creepy Nazi fellow sneaking up on her again. It was nothing, though. The Channel glistened, its incoming tide a series of rolling waves painted golden. On the opposite shore in Portsall, the slate and tile rooftops shone. As she made her way across the sand already radiating its heat, and climbed the rocks to what she liked to think of as her very own private ledge, the chapel bells rang eleven o'clock.

Based on the snippets of conversation she and Buck had shared during the afterglow, she gathered they were cut from the same cloth. For one, they both came from money and could not care less about it. Agreeing they preferred an uncomplicated lifestyle without all the silly trappings and annoying obligations associated with wealth was what they had laughed about until the wee hours of the morning. Sharing similar outlooks, having an innate joie de vivre, they discovered they both had a knack for quickly moving on from a troubling situation; maybe even avoiding it altogether. "Sans souci" or no worry was a motto they had lived by. Well, up until the Germans started conquering Europe, anyway. Finally, they seemed to share a love for the outdoors, golf and tennis, and horseback riding . . . And then, there was that undeniable and unabashed affinity for the carnal.

Her thoughts naturally turned to her condition. To Madeleine's way of thinking, this pregnancy was an obstacle to her happiness. How was she to move forward with Buck if pregnant? Put the baby up for adoption? Or get rid of it? Or could she try to pass it off as his.

Madeleine reflected on what it would feel like to give up a child. She had heard somewhere that adoption was noble. That there was no other act more generous or selfless, and she had agreed. She admired the girls who found themselves in this particular kind of trouble for making that painful choice. Nevertheless, how hard was it to go through an entire pregnancy only to give the baby away? It defied human nature to separate from one's infant. She didn't think the virtue of giving the baby away so it could have a better life could ever compensate for the loss she'd feel.

Madeleine remembered meeting a young woman who'd been adopted. She had confided that she'd grown up feeling invisible, doomed to never belonging anywhere or to anyone. She had said she felt so robbed of an identity that with every birthday it became imperative that she find her birth mother so she could know herself. Yet wanting to search for her birth mother had made her feel enormous guilt and shame. She was mortified that she wasn't more grateful for her adoptive parents. She felt caught. Included in her mixed bag of emotions was that she was angry at her natural mother for giving her up. Yet as she complained she also had to admit, «What right do I have to blame my birth mother for giving me a chance at a better life than any she could have provided?" Madeleine had been deeply saddened by this girl's confusion. She didn't think she could bequeath such a mess of emotions to her own child.

Madeleine thought about an abortion and shuddered. The ordeal of plucking out her baby from her womb seemed barbaric. Never mind, it was against the law. Besides, where would she go for such an operation? How would she manage it without her mother knowing? She certainly couldn't trust anyone in town. Gossip was a staple at every dinner table this side of Brest. Madeleine knew she could neither tolerate the shame nor the pity. In the end, she couldn't fathom an abortion any more than she could envision giving up her own flesh and blood.

An early-afternoon fog began to roll in across the shore. It matched Madeleine's state of mind so well that she felt as if she were stumbling around in her own head. In this mist of raw emotion and confusion her muddled thoughts yielded little clarity. Guilt was creeping in. She just couldn't go through with either an adoption or an abortion. Looking down at her belly, instead of dismissing it as readily as she had the night before, Madeleine began to think of the life growing as a baby, her baby, and not an *it*. She caressed her midriff. And in spite of it all, she began to feel an unexpected compassion for this little life. She even began to speculate on what kind of mother she'd be. A plan began to germinate. Buck's and her desire for each other was beyond question. They could very easily have a future together. If they continued to have sex like they did the night before, she could probably pass this baby off as his. Could she live with this option for her predicament?

It didn't take long for Madeleine to figure out her best alternative.

Chapter Forty

The silence of the night was as boundless as the ocean in front of them. Madeleine, wanting to share her favorite place with Buck, brought him to the shores of Little Beach. They stood at the water's edge, holding hands and letting the gentle ebb and flow of the wavelets wash over their bare feet. The rhythmic rolling in and rolling out reminded Madeleine of their lovemaking just the night before.

She felt a tug from deep within her and turned to face Buck. He bent his head to kiss her. His lips on her skin felt like a branding iron, and she moaned. As his hands began to greedily reach for her breasts, she stepped back. With eyes never leaving his, she pulled her dress up and tossed it onto the sand. Then stepping out of her panties, she spun around and ran at full tilt into the dark-blue waters of the cove.

"What the hell?" Buck exclaimed.

Madeleine swam far out until she was out of breath. She flipped on her back to face the beach and called, *"Viens, mon amour!"* Come, my love.

Buck needed no invitation. He tore his shirt and jeans off as fast as any male in lust can strip and plunged into the water.

Buck

May 1945

Chapter Forty-One

Buck couldn't stop marveling at Madeleine's lustiness and penchant for spontaneity. Her wild antics like the one last night amazed him. How could he be so lucky to have found a woman so uninhibited? What a difference, he mused, from Claire's distaste for the outdoors or anything athletic. Madeleine personified total abandon, which was so exciting; his wife, now that he was thinking about it, was more about restraint, even cowardice.

"I dare you to join me for a picnic," challenged Madeleine out of the blue. On colt-like legs, she was trotting backwards a few paces in front of Buck, taunting him yet again. Her rucksack, slung over one shoulder, looked heavy hanging on this slim girl who was all arms and legs, but it seemed not to weigh her down.

"That's hardly a dare," Buck laughed. He closed the distance between them in three long strides. "I'd follow you anywhere."

"Yes, but when you hear where, you might think differently."

"Okay. So where are you taking me?" Buck's eyes danced with amusement.

"Here!" She stopped and pointed at a spot inside a massive oak tree whose many beefy arms began four feet off the ground. Before Buck could answer, she jumped up, swung her leg over the lowest bough, and pulled herself up.

Buck looked up at her and began to laugh. "I'm loving your

impromptu choice, but how do you expect me to get up there with only one hand?" He waved his abbreviated arm at her.

"Oooh, I don't know." With a puff, she poofed her blonde bangs out of her eyes. "Desire, perhaps? Maybe a *soupçon* of determination?"

"Is this some sort of a test?"

"Probably." She extracted a pre-opened bottle of wine from her backpack and pulled the cork out with her teeth. "Have you ever had sex in a tree?"

"Game on!"

Buck walked to a point fifteen feet away, turned to face her and scraping the ground with his foot like a bull staring down a tore-ador's red cape, he charged. When he was almost there, he hurled himself at the branch in one flying leap. Managing to drape himself over it at the waist, he paused as if the wind had been knocked out of him. "I can't believe I just did that," he said, gasping for air and still facing the ground.

"Are you going to remain in that position? It's hardly suitable if you plan on joining me for a swig of wine and a diddle."

Buck wrapped his one good arm around the tree branch, hooked his left leg over, and with sheer force of will, twisted around and sat back up.

"There!"

"I'm over here, silly." Buck was facing the wrong way. Madeleine bent over, howling.

"Dammit!" In one more herculean effort, Buck swung himself around to face her. He expelled a big whoosh of air. "Crazy woman!"

Madeleine passed him the bottle and he took several gulps.

"This is just the best," Madeleine sighed. "I'd take all my meals here if I could."

"Not fond of forks and knives, are we?"

"It's not that, so much as the formality of everything. *Chez moi,* it's always *comme il faut* morning, noon, and night."

"I know what you mean. Propriety gets in the way of being natural or honest about things."

"Or even about oneself. You can never say what's on your mind, either. You have to couch it so gently you might as well not say it at all."

"And what good is that?"

"You have to dress to impress or 'appropriately' for whatever occasion. Who cares?"

"Seems you and I are cut from the same cloth, Madeleine."

"I think so, my handsome American." She smiled impishly. "How did that happen?"

They sat in silence, staring at each other, while above their heads in the thick branches, the wind sighed a lullaby.

"I can just barely hear the roar of the surf," Madeleine said. "Can you hear it?"

"Just," Buck said. "The gulls must be following the fishing boats in, because I can hear them, too."

"If we stay here long enough, we'll hear the night music of crickets and frogs. They'll provide us with a different kind of concert."

"Do you come here often?" Buck asked, studying her face.

"I've never climbed this tree," she replied.

Never? "You mean to tell me, you just decided at the last minute to picnic in a tree?"

"Is that so terrible?" Her blue eyes sparkled.

"You're somethin' else!" He leaned across the divide between them on the branch. "Now show me how we're gonna make love up here."

Kersaint

May 1945

Chapter Forty-Two

As Ernst and Klaus tiptoed up the narrow wooden steps toward the small balcony cantilevered over the altar at the Notre Dame de Kersaint Chapel, Klaus gestured to the rood screen behind the podium. Ernst's gaze followed in the direction Klaus was pointing.

It looked as though someone were standing in the shadows behind it. Was it Père Gilles, their contact? Surely, if he could observe them climbing the stairs, he'd come out to greet them. What was he waiting for? If he weren't going to make himself known, then who was hiding there? The boys didn't feel comfortable calling out his name. Nor did they think it wise to draw attention to themselves, because just below them in the second pew, an elderly woman was kneeling in prayer.

The boys shrugged and sat down on a small bench to wait for Père Gilles to make his appearance. Klaus, taking advantage of being in God's house, closed his eyes, bent, and laced his fingers together. Praying like he'd never prayed before as he endured the most heart-pounding, nerve-wracking four-minute ordeal of a waiting period, he didn't notice the priest when he finally did show up.

"Where did you leave your truck?" growled a slight man in a black cassock and priest's white collar.

Ernst stood up and puffed out his chest. "Who wants to know?"

"Père Gilles. Isn't it obvious?"

Ernst curled his lip. "In a parking lot behind the *crêperie*. In Portsall. We walked across the harbor."

"Ah," the priest said, nodding. "Tide must be all the way out."

"Well, we're sure as hell not Jesus."

"And we drove a bus, not a truck," corrected Klaus. "So, no one's gonna suspect anything."

"No need for blasphemy," said Père Gilles. With movement coming from below, he held his finger up to his lips. Casting a cautious look over the balcony, he noticed one of his parishioners, Annabelle de Beaulieu, riffling through the pages of her Bible.

"That old gal is harmless," the priest said in a low voice, "but let's not linger."

"Good plan," Ernst said.

Père Gilles pulled a large iron key from his pocket. "If there are any firearms in your shipment, you're going to have to stash them at Saint Samson, a little granite chapel up on the bluff. I won't allow for any guns or cannon in this church."

"Now wait just a minute!"

"No, you wait a minute!" barked the priest. I draw the line at keeping armaments on this sacred ground."

"But—."

"No buts!" Père Gilles snapped. "It's where I made the last group store their guns and that applies to you two also." It was news to Ernst and Klaus that there'd been other missions transporting German property.

"You just said Saint Samson is a chapel," countered Ernst. "Isn't that a holy place too?"

"Yes." His glare dared Ernst to pursue the argument. "As for your precious artifacts, come back in a few days and I'll be free to help you unload your cargo into the crypt."

"That's hilarious. Try again, Père."

"Nope."

"Three days? This art is Germany's most prized possession. We can't keep it hidden in the bus for that long!"

"And how are we supposed to get crates of munitions up a bluff?" Klaus chimed in.

"Figure it out." Père Gilles handed the key to Ernst. "You've got plenty of time to work out the details. Bunk in the crypt if you need a place to stay. *Au revoir*." He glided away before Ernst and Klaus could protest any further.

"Bonjour, Madame de Beaulieu," Père Gilles whispered, inclining his head as he passed by her pew. She looked up, seemingly startled, from her prayer book. "May God be with you, my child." He made the sign of the cross in the air above her and then slipped behind the chancel.

Chapter Forty-Three

In the early mornings, as was typical for northern Brittany, mist engulfed the coast in grayness. Ernst and Klaus carried one crate after another out to the little motorboat they had stolen before dawn. The tide was out, so the distance across the damp sand to the water was longer than it would have been had the tide been in. The beach was littered with broken shells and crab claws Seagulls flew low overhead, arguing with each other over their windfall.

"Damn birds! I can barely hear myself think!" Klaus bayed.

"Don't think. Leave that to me."

"Oh, ha ha."

"You know where to go, right?" Not waiting for Klaus to answer, Ernst blathered, "You're gonna head out into the Channel, turn left around that rock island sticking out of the water, and head west. Keep your eyes open for that granite Saint Samson chapel sitting up top of the cliff. There's a tiny beach you can pull onto."

"Which way is west? Left or right?"

"Dammit, Klaus! Please tell me you're kidding."

"You should be doing this, not me."

"I have to watch for any trouble on the bluff. I'm better at handling that than you."

"Thanks a lot."

"Remember to moor the boat first. Come up the cliff steps before you unload. You wanna make sure the coast is clear."

"Aye-aye, Captain," Klaus saluted, climbed into the boat, and sat in the stern, grabbing the tiller as if it were a handle. As Klaus waited for Ernst to shove him out into the white-capped surf, he looked up at the sky, at the breeze-pushed clouds, and said a quick Hail Mary.

Much to Klaus' surprise, the motor caught the first time he pulled the cord. It sputtered and belched smoke, but it came to life, making Klaus very happy that he wouldn't be drifting out to sea rudderless. So, in his exuberance, he pushed the throttle too far. Instantly, the boat banked sharply. Ernst, aghast, watched from Little Beach as the engine screamed and his sidekick was almost tossed out. That Klaus let go of the throttle when he tumbled off the bench was indeed for-tuitous, as the boat immediately slowed to an idle and many crates of arms and ammo were spared a watery ruin. Tentatively, Klaus ac-celerated out of the cove, eventually riding up and down the waves and into the Channel.

Once Klaus was out of sight, Ernst turned toward town and broke into a run.

Buck

May - June 1945

Chapter Forty-Four

It wasn't simply a matter of lust with Madeleine anymore. This was love. He was genuinely falling for her. There was something very real about this girl. She lived life in the moment, unashamed and spontaneous. Perhaps, her upper-crust British heritage gave her the confidence to be brazen, but he didn't care. In other words, despite her lineage, which was much like his, she didn't make any effort to be anything other than what bubbled to the surface. He, too, was prone to acting on impulse. In his marriage to Claire, he had been well aware that she was interested in his family's wealth and social standing in New York society, but he had ignored it because he was intent on possessing her. Buck never doubted Claire's love for him personally, though. Now that he was falling in love with Madeleine, he feared that his subterfuge both as a dead man and a married man was going to bite him in the butt.

As for Madeleine, she was one sexy numéro. And yes, Madeleine was very young. At twenty-three, she was four years younger than he was, but it was that very gamine demeanor which made her seem so uncomplicated and very dear. He concluded there was no artifice about her. He admired that aspect a lot. And in so thinking, it occurred to him he'd better come clean about his marriage. But what did that mean? Would he ask Claire for a divorce? And how could he do that if he were dead? After only a few dates with Madeleine, he was already prepared to never look back. Yes, it was soon, but Madeleine was his perfect soul mate.

Buck set up his easel by the stone wall of the Notre-Dame de Kersaint Chapel. His hope was to give the impression he was simply painting a typical French market in the village square, and not actually on the lookout. Competing thoughts, though, of Madeleine in his arms the night before and Claire mourning his death had him so distracted, he was unaware that he was slapping globs instead of dollops of oil paint onto his palette. And as his confusion gathered steam, he found he was haphazardly slashing his painted market-goers with a putty knife into sharp ridges, instead of a brush. The scene he was inadvertently creating looked more like a riot than the cheerful market day playing out in front of him.

Buck bit down hard on the brush he held between his teeth. He was tormenting himself by mentally replaying the past, wishing he'd been less impulsive about joining the army, about faking his death, choosing to serve his country, save the world by presumably impeding the escape of Nazi propaganda, possibly opting out of a marriage or potentially hurting a truly decent girl if he didn't. In Claire, he'd first seen a beautiful woman who had saved herself for him. But there had been much to her that was hidden from view. She was still that wounded girl who'd lost her parents and all the damaged self-esteem that went with so horrible a loss. The most unfortunate thought of all was that once he'd married Claire and put an end to her hard-to-get antics, he found he wasn't all that interested anymore. And finally, it still burned to know that if he stayed with Claire, he'd never enjoy being a father. He didn't think he could ever come to terms with parenting another man's child.

The nurses had told Buck he was too independent for his own good, which was true. He could just imagine that when he went home Claire would read every book she could find on amputation and then fuss and flutter. Buck flexed the fingers on his good hand, then rubbed the nub of his other arm where the ghost of feeling still lingered. He recalled how he had felt and still did from time to time if he allowed himself the privilege of self-pity. *Do I really deserve this bullshit? Especially after having served my country? Not fair!* It was then that he determined *home* wasn't an option. And who'da thunk he'd be given an out by Mr. Larry from some branch of the US government and the SOE? Snatching the brush from his mouth, Buck flung it at his easel. A passerby, startled by his outburst, scooted past him looking over her shoulder and shaking her head in displeasure.

Madeleine had been so sweet after the second time they'd made love and he'd reluctantly explained how he lost his hand. Her first words had been, *What an absolutely terrifying ordeal for you. Your missing hand is not the first thing I notice about you, though.* And as she kissed Buck's eyelids she said in between each kiss, *It's the courage residing right in these divine blue eyes. I thank God your life was spared to be here with me now.*

Suddenly, Ernst burst from the crowd like a fox from the shadows. He seemed to be on a mission, running down the main road lined with chestnut trees and up the hill toward the cliffs. Buck was lucky to have noticed him at all, he was so preoccupied in his introspection. Tossing his brushes and palette into its paint box, Buck shoved his still wet and goopy canvas under his arm and hurried after him. Keeping his distance, Buck turned left on the lane where Madeleine lived opposite the château and kept his eyes fixed on Ernst, whose pace was picking up speed. *You're in a big hurry, buddy. Where ya headed?* Up on the cliffs, Buck could see the white caps on the Channel, hear the spank of the surf on the rocks far below. Salt wind clung to the stubble on his unshaven cheeks, and he was alert with what he was certain would be his first encounter regarding his mission. He not only felt exposed on this treeless bluff but also a little nervous about confronting this fellow who was the hostile he was instructed to waylay.

When Ernst stopped at the little stone Saint Samson chapel, Buck, having nothing behind which to duck, quickly opened his artist's case, unfolded the spindly legs of his easel, and propped his canvas on its shelf. Pretending to study the vista where gauzy clouds had begun to drift across the churning sea, Buck was able to openly observe Ernst. Daubing at crusty lumps of paint already dry on his palette and applying nearly no color to his painting, Buck looked over his shoulder to make sure no one coming up behind him could see his subterfuge. Ernst leaned on the wall, repeatedly glancing at his watch or reading entries in a small notebook. Suddenly, another fellow popped up from below the cliffs. Ernst said something inaudible and quickly withdrew a key from his pocket. Quite a bit of effort was required to get the lock to submit, but eventually both men were inside. They left the door ajar.

Buck was compelled to get closer, even if it meant risking his identity—but risk it he must. Shoving his palette under his arm, Buck picked up his easel, and while balancing the canvas on top, carried the whole thing as one piece to within eight feet of the chapel doorway. Setting it down, Buck barely had enough time to sketch a rough outline of the chapel in the midst of his chaotic and hopefully unrecognizable market scene before Ernst and his buddy came back outside. Going on the offense, it being the best defense, Buck strode toward them. "Bonjour!" And hoping the sun in their eyes might disorient them after being inside so dark a chamber, he walked right up to the chapel and poked his head inside.

"*Mein Gott im Himmel!*" grumbled Ernst, swiftly swinging around and pulling the heavy door closed. "*Dumme Esel!* What is it with you? You're always showing up where you're not wanted."

"What can I say? I'm just a dumb-ass painter, who loves these pink cliffs." Buck pointed to the west where an early afternoon sun shone brightly on the blush-hued sand and rocks. "Look there," he said. "Can you blame me for wanting to paint Brittany's famous Pink Granite Coast?" Not wanting to linger, Buck went back to his easel and began to pack up his things. "Who's your buddy, Ernst?" Buck was pretty sure Ernst wasn't really Ernst, so didn't expect the answer to be true. "And what's in there that has your interest?"

"Klaus."

"Morning, Klaus.

"He's like me," offered Ernst, "and doesn't want to return to Germany. We thought we might find shelter in this old heap of stone. Turns out it's inhabited by rats."

"Unwelcome in town, huh?" Buck scratched his head. "Can't fault the Bretons for not wanting you here. Best go where you'll be welcome." Buck, choosing to come across as nothing more than a gloating American who'd won the war and not an agent tasked with investigating people like Ernst, faked a thoughtful mien. "Hmmm. I can't think where that might be, though . . ."

Ernst exploded. *"Schweinhund! Komm, Klaus, verschwinden wir."* Let's get out of here.

"Yeah, that's a good idea," Buck said. "Say, where'd you get that key?"

"The priest in town thought we might want to shelter here, but no thank you. It's an empty shithole inside."

As for what Buck had seen inside the chapel, it was stuffed to the gills. From floor to ceiling and wall to wall, there were crates and more crates of what appeared to be a weapons cache, a swastika stamped on the side of each one.

Chapter Forty-Five

The grassy meadow behind the church bobbed with white daisies. Madeleine sat across from Buck, perched like a sparrow with her legs folded and her slender arms wrapped around them. Her chin rested on her knees. Night was falling fast.

The smoke from Buck's cigarette plumed over his head and it gave off such an acrid odor that Madeleine pinched her nose. Buck turned his head away and exhaled one last stream of smoke. "I keep telling you if you have one," he said proffering his pack, "it won't be so smelly."

"No thank you!" Madeleine choked as another wave of nausea rolled over her. She changed the subject. "You're growing a beard." She cocked her head from side to side to study his face. "It suits you."

"Thanks," Buck muttered self-consciously. Madeleine continued to stare, dreamy-eyed. "C'mere," he said, pulling her to his side of the blanket. He lay on top of her and began to push down against her body. "I can't get enough of you," he groaned into her ear.

"*Moi non plus,*" she whispered, arching her back. *Me neither* was all the permission he needed to lift her sundress out of the way.

Headlights stabbed the semi-darkness as a truck lumbered round the back of Notre-Dame de Kersaint Chapel. Brakes squealed and Madeleine and Buck jerked away from each other to see the sound.

"Stay down!" Buck hissed, quickly zipping up his pants. "And stay there." On hands and knees, he crawled to the stone wall and peered over the top. Never one to do as she was told, Madeleine scrambled to his side.

"I've seen that kind of truck before," whispered Madeleine. I think it must belong to that sleazy Nazi."

Buck tugged on Madeleine's arm to pull her out of sight. He yanked Madeleine below the wall. "Do you want to get shot?"

Two doors, one after the other, clunked closed and footsteps crunched on the gravel. German words were exchanged in low voices. As far as Buck could tell, the men were Ernst and Klaus, but they were both cloaked in black from head to toe. One of them moved to the rear of the truck and the other started poking at the ivy-covered wall of the church.

Buck's heart pounded as he waited to see what these two were up to. Finally, an iron door was revealed behind the curtain of overgrown clematis. Very slowly, the two men hauled it open. At this point, Père Gilles hopped out the back of the truck. He pulled out a large six-by-eight-foot slim package wrapped in brown paper. It was cumbersome enough that he needed Ernst or Klaus to help him carry it. Sidestepping with their cumbersome load, they disappeared through the door gaping on its rusty hinges.

"Oh my God," Buck gushed, sinking back on his haunches. "It's really happening."

"What's happening?" Madeleine demanded, a few decibels too loudly.

"Shh!" Buck hissed again. A flashlight suddenly cast its beam in their direction.

An eerie silence enveloped them as Buck and Madeleine held their breaths and waited to be found. Luckily, they only had to wait in their cramped crouching positions, not daring to move even a finger, for the next forty-five excruciating minutes. When the truck finally drove away, Buck and Madeleine collapsed onto their backs, exhaling one giant sigh of relief.

"What was that we just witnessed?" Madeleine clamored. Buck remained still, speechless. Madeleine persisted. "You said something that made you sound like you expected what just happened." Buck ignored her, so she slapped Buck's arm. "Tell me, Buck." And when he still didn't utter a word, she began to whimper. "What are the Germans doing in my church? Madeleine had never been particularly religious, but nevertheless she couldn't help feeling territorial about her village chapel. It's where she had gone every Sunday as a child, taken catechism lessons, and been confirmed. Her chapel bore a long Celtic history. It felt violated, and she was pretty cross about it.

"Stop whining!"

The rebuke startled Madeleine, which in turn made her angrier. "Then I'll leave you be," she said, standing. Buck made to rise. "No, don't get up," she said, gesturing with her hand that he stay right where he was.

"But it's pitch dark. And Ernst could still be nearby." Buck reached out to her. "I'm sorry. I shouldn't have snapped at you."

"Well, you did, and I've had enough upset for one night." Madeleine bunched the blanket in her arms.

"Where are you going?"

"Wherever you aren't!" Madeleine spat. She scurried across the meadow to her back yard and slipped through a hole in the hedgerow.

Chapter Forty-Six

B uck stood outside the de Beaulieu cottage with a bundle of white peonies wrapped in newspaper. Staring up at what he presumed was Madeleine's open bedroom window, he whistled softly, hoping it was enough to wake her. When Annabelle, Madeleine's mother, appeared in the doorway with elbows akimbo and a cross expression on her face, Buck nodded sheepishly and turned to walk away.

"Come inside, you silly man. I've something I'd like to discuss with you." Annabelle stepped back to let Buck pass through the door. "We're in the salon."

Madeleine's mouth, full of croissant, fell open when Buck entered. She blushed a deep crimson.

"Darling, have you lost your tongue?" Annabelle scolded. "Do me the kindness of introducing me to your young man."

Madeleine dabbed at the corners of her mouth with a napkin and got up from the table. "Mummy, this is the man who rescued me from that dreadful Nazi the other day, Buck Connor. Buck, my mother, Madame de Beaulieu."

Annabelle extended the back of her hand, clearly indicating Buck should kiss it. He hesitated, unfamiliar with this Victorian formality, then obliged her with the old-fashioned form of greeting. "Enchanté, Madame."

"My daughter tells me that our church received some unusual guests last night." Buck's eyes rounded in surprise. It had not occurred to him that Madeleine would talk about what she'd seen last night, so he had to punt.

"It was just some delivery truck, that's all." Even in his ears, Buck could tell how lame his fib sounded. "Probably a shipment of new Bibles. Maybe some wine . . ."

"Come now, Mr. Connor. Late at night? And to the back hidden behind a thick panel of purple blooms and an iron door so heavy it takes two to open it?" Clearly, Annabelle was not to be fooled. "Try again," she coaxed, smiling oddly.

"What makes you think I know anything more than what Madeleine told you?"

"Because I know who you really are, Mr. Connor."

"Madame?"

"It's plain you don't know who I am." She folded her arms across her chest and scowled. "I would have thought by now, you knew."

Oh Jeez! What kind of game was this? Buck shrank from the glowering Madame de Beaulieu. *Now I know where Madeleine gets her feistiness.* With eyes fixed on the worn wooden floorboards, Buck pondered his next move.

"You're SOE." Annabelle declared. She took a long sip of coffee, surveying Buck over the rim of her cup. "Though you're not a very good one, are you?"

One could have heard a pin drop. Even Sophie, hesitated in midpour of the coffee, waiting to decipher Buck's response. Madeleine sat on the edge of her seat, looking less angry at him as she was now feeling sorry for him. Annabelle was formidable. There was no trifling with her.

Buck inhaled sharply. His eyes slid over to Madeleine, whose green eyes were glittering with tears about to fall.

Throwing his head back and releasing a hearty *ha!* Buck then beamed his movie-star grin. "Guilty as charged, Madame, but I assure you as an American, I am one of the good guys."

"What?" Madeleine shrieked.

"How did you ever guess, Madame?" Buck asked.

"Guess, Mr. Connor?" She spread her arms and pantomimed the flapping of wings. "I'm your *petit oiseau*."

"My who?"

"Did you not know you would have a little bird waiting for you here in Brittany?"

"No, Madame." Buck scraped his fingers through his hair.

"You're Resistance?" Madeleine jumped up, spilling her cup of coffee.

"Not now, darling."

"You forbade me . . ."

"For good reason, *chérie*."

"But why?"

"You are too impetuous and emotional."

Sophie smirked and left the salon to fetch more bread and cheese. She understood the word "emotional."

Without going into any detail about the crash over Mount McKinley, Buck relayed that his recruiter's name was a certain "Larry," that he'd had the most basic of training in Scotland, and was detailed to France to await word from a Professor Jeffries about the propaganda art.

Annabelle de Beaulieu scoffed. "Not mentioning me. Hmm. A bit of a communication failure, wouldn't you say? Ah, well."

"Madame, you have been wronged."

"So, you're a spy, too?" Madeleine looked from one to the other.

"Guilty as charged," Buck replied.

"So, what's this propaganda art?" Madeleine asked crossly.

"Hideous propaganda used against the people of Germany," Annabelle said brusquely.

"How so, Maman?"

"Without it, the German *volk* were incapable of absorbing the information necessary for comprehending why a second war was necessary."

"To be fair, Maman, maybe the Germans didn't want to go to war again, especially so soon after the first one."

"Madeleine has a point," Buck said, smiling indulgently at her. "But so, too, does Madame. According to Joseph Goebbels, the Minister of Propaganda, people will believe anything if you repeat it loud enough and long enough."

"Just draw them a picture!" cackled Sophie, who had clearly understood what was being said. "*Quels idiots!*"

Buck took a sip of his coffee. He felt a modicum of relief wash over him. To have the truth of his mission out in the open felt good; it felt right. Now, he no longer needed to pretend he was someone different than who he really was. Of course, he still had to reveal his real name and tell Madeleine about his life in the US before the war. Hardest of all, he'd have to inform her that he was married. He was neither sure how he should tell her nor looking forward to her reaction. Knowing Madeleine as he already did, it was likely to be explosive.

"I might need your help, Madame." His gaze slid over to the housekeeper. "Yours, too, Sophie. And yours, *ma belle.* I'm not sure in what way yet, but would you three be willing to jump in if I require something? Nothing too dangerous, of course."

"Very few things in life happen without a cost, Monsieur Connor, but you can definitely count on me," Annabelle said. "After all, I am the one who asked for your help."

"Thank you, Madame."

"I've always believed in peace. More than ever, in fact, since this dreadful war. But I've also learned that pacifism isn't the answer either. Prime Minister Neville Chamberlain got us into this war by appeasing Germany. Monsters like Hitler saw that disgraceful weakness and took total advantage of it. I've been so ashamed of England's foolishness, but thank God for Winston Churchill." Annabelle threw her hands into the air and then brought them down to her lap. "So, if I can help as a deterrent to a Fourth Reich, so be it!"

"Hear, hear!" Buck caroled. He stole a glance at Madeleine, who was still frowning at her mother. "With your permission, I'd like to borrow your daughter? I owe her an apology and want to make it up to her."

"Allez, mes enfants, mais soyez sage." Go on, kids, but be good.

As soon as Buck and Madeleine were out on the road, he took her hand in his. "I am so sorry for speaking to you the way that I did last night." He tucked her hand into the crook of his arm. "Will you accept my apology?"

"Of course. You were under a lot of stress, and I was being a silly twit."

They passed a paddock at the top of the bluff where the vista opened up to the windswept moor overlooking the English Channel. There, two old horses with sunken backs stood head to rump in the corner, snoozing in the sun. Madeleine envied them, praying that her future might look like that someday: trusting, comfortable, and abiding. She needed that for the little one growing inside her. With Buck's sweet and sincere apology, she felt an ever stronger connection with this crazy American. Perhaps, this *coup de foudre* was becoming a deeper and more lasting relationship. Even though they'd met a short time ago, she could feel they were crossing that invisible line from casual lovers out for fun to soul mates with longer term implications.

"I have to make a quick trip to Paris in the morning," Buck said, "but I should be back in a week. When I return, I want to share everything with you. My real name, where I'm from, and what my life has been all about before I met you."

A gasp escaped from Madeleine's throat. If he went to Paris, she feared he'd slip from her grasp. She stopped to wrap her arms around his neck. A sob escaped, so she buried her face in his shirt.

"Hey, hey," Buck soothed, stroking the back of her blonde head. "It's just good ol' *gay Paree.* I'll be back before you know it." Buck stepped back, and putting his finger beneath Madeleine's chin, lifted her face so that he could read her expression. His eyes roamed over her features, eventually settling on her pouty lips. He kissed them softly.

"You should know I'm falling, sweet girl. Hard, real hard."

"*Moi aussi,*" Madeleine whispered. "Me, too."

Claire

May - June 1945

Chapter Forty-Seven

The ship docked in the decimated port of Brest, a coastal city in northwestern France where just outside the harbor, the Atlantic was known to collide with the English Channel. Under cover of darkness, the Red Cross volunteers were the first to disembark. Claire and her roommates wore their skirts over slacks, layered sweaters under their field jackets, liners and overcoats. They shoved their feet into galoshes and stacked multiple hats atop their heads. Slung over their shoulders they each carried a purse, musette bag, gas mask, and a ditty bag. Attached to their suitcases were a helmet, canteen, and mess kit. The women were a sight to behold as they traipsed through the officers' lounge, past the GI's standing at attention at the rails, down the stairs to the main deck. Weighted down like pack mules, they were helped by a number of the soldiers a part of the way. Claire scanned the crowd for Scott, but in the dark he was nowhere to be found.

"See you at the front," one GI shouted. "Save us a croissant and make sure the coffee is hot when we get there!" yelled another. The men had teased the Red Cross about how tough their lives were about to become, but everyone knew what lay ahead for the soldiers: namely, a reassignment to the Pacific. Others cheered the women as they made their way down the gangway. A great camaraderie had developed over the past eight days, so tight throats were felt by all.

Claire stood amid her roommates on the pier, sickened by the sight of so much wreckage. The port had taken extraordinarily heavy bombardment. Parts of broken ships poked blackly out of the water. They looked like behemoth carcasses in the moonlight. Mixed in with knowing the horror wrought by the enemy was the feeling of being so very far from home. Claire was lost in a brand-new country with a foreign language, unfamiliar customs, and topsy-turvy, if not dangerous, conditions.

"Are you feeling like I am? A fish out of water?" asked Claire.

"No pun intended? Yes!" Carol replied.

Suddenly, a jeep sped up to the ship and screeched to a stop beside them and a fellow in a camelhair overcoat and brown felt trilby hopped out. "Any of you ladies happen to be from New York?"

"Scott!" cried Claire. "I thought you'd left without saying good-bye." She threw her arms around his neck.

"Nope, just raced ahead to secure you gals a compartment on the train. I got you some K-rations, too."

"You're a doll," cooed Carol, patting him on the cheek. "This one's a keeper, Claire."

"Let's get these things of yours in the jeep. You girls might have to sit on top of the luggage."

By the light of the moon, the bombed-out electrical grid in Brittany not yet restored, they drove in silence. The train station was in utter chaos. Luggage was strewn along two platforms and folks ran hither and thither trying to locate their belongings.

"Now I know why you recommended we not part with our stuff. This is a madhouse!" Betty said to Claire.

"Advice from the professor, here," Claire replied, smiling affectionately at Scott. "He's taking good care of us."

Carol tilted her head toward Claire's ear. "You, not us," she whispered. "Anyone can see by the way he looks at you that he's in love with you."

"Don't be ridiculous!" Claire protested, batting her away with her free hand. "We hardly know each other." Claire was not as shocked as she let on, suspecting that yes, Scott might very well be falling in love with her, but was she ready to admit it? Was she feeling similarly?

Scott escorted the ladies to their reserved compartment at the front of the train. He made sure all their gear was securely stashed on the netted racks overhead or beneath their wooden seats.

"Claire, would you step out for a moment?" All three nurses giggled.

Out on the platform, Claire and Scott stood in a billow of steam and a blast of whistles. They exchanged a shy glance and Claire's fingers fluttered at her throat where Billy's ring hung on a gold chain hidden under her blouse. The staccato slamming of doors added to the cacophony of porters' trolleys and the surging murmur of voices. Scott pulled Claire into his arms and smiled bashfully. His kiss and embrace shot through her like an arrow from Cupid's bow. She swayed a little and started to say something but thought better of it.

Was he feeling it, too? she wondered. Her big brown eyes searched Scott's tender hazel ones for an answer. He lifted her hand and pressed it to his lips. Then a slow smile crawled across his face, accentuating the dimple in his cheek. "Don't tell the girls, but I'll be catching up with you in Paris."

Paris? Did Scott just say they were headed for Paris? The City of Lights? The capitol of *haute couture* where every ambitious model hoped to work before the war had broken out and dashed her dreams?

Claire climbed back aboard the train, giddy. Never in a million years had she expected to go to the number one destination on her European wish list so early on. She had assumed she'd be working in Nice for at least a year before she'd get a furlough. Paris, according to her in-laws, was the most romantic city in Europe. To think she might be falling in love with Scott in that city set the butterflies to a crazy fluttering.

Doing her best to compose herself before re-entering the compartment, Claire tried to smooth the broad smile off her face. But it was no use. A grin as big as the Cheshire Cat's lit up her face when she slid open the door.

"Oh, my God! Look at you." Carol was pointing a finger at her. "If you're not in love, my name is Grand Duchess Anastasia Nikolaevna Romanov."

"Silly goose! It was just a kiss." Claire plunked down in her seat next to the window. Afraid she might blab their destination, she said, "Let's try and get some sleep, shall we?"

The girls, however, were too excited, so by the light of the moon as the French countryside rolled by, they ate their rations, sang songs, and huddled together to keep their anxiety over the newness of everything at bay. Eventually, one by one, they fell asleep, slumped against each other like a litter of kittens. At daybreak, two Frenchmen in blue uniforms with red trim and shiny brass buttons opened their door to declare in French, *"Mesdemoiselles, nous sommes arrivés à Paris!"*

Chapter FOrty-Eight

S cott and Claire sat facing each other at a sidewalk table outside a café on the Champs-Élysées. Sipping wine and nibbling on Swiss cheese, neither one paid the passersby any mind. They were deep in conversation. Claire was relishing her return to a more cerebral way of life. While modeling had been a means to an end, an income, she didn't miss that world. None of her peers had been readers like her, so conversation, unless trivial, had been infrequent. The same could be said about her marriage to Billy. There had never been any significant discourse—a steady back and forth of ideas or discussions about what one was reading or caught in a newspaper.

"If you'd asked Herman Göring why the Germans followed the Nazis, he would have said that it had nothing to do with Nazism but everything to do with human nature. Scare folks enough and they will follow."

"Yes, I suppose that's true," Claire mused. "People can be like sheep."

Scott nodded, seeming pleased that Claire understood. "What's insidious about propaganda is that in a few short lines or in a picture an awful lot can be said to drive home a point . . ."

"To a public too ignorant," Claire interrupted, "lazy, or unwilling to be informed, to know the background or history well enough to have an intelligent opinion . . ."

"Gee whiz, Claire! Anyone would think you'd taken my course at Cooper Union."

"Cooper Union in New York?"

"It's where the Monuments Men trained. I thought I told you."

"I'm familiar with fashion ad campaigns. It's in the same vein, really. Convince women they're beautiful if they wear this or smell like so or apply such and such eye shadow. Now that I think about it, it's really quite the con job. To think I used to be party to it." Claire started to laugh. "I'm sorry. I shouldn't make this about me. What happened in German-occupied Europe is absolutely appalling."

Scott looked from side to side, then lowered his voice. "Remember what I told you about the Merkers Mine?" Claire nodded. "Those precious masterpieces were found stacked against each other and leaning against the walls of the mine like discarded furniture." Scott shook his head in disgust. "The propaganda art, on the other hand, was wrapped very carefully and nested in straw inside cartons."

"Sounds like somebody wanted to preserve them for posterity," Claire said.

"Precisely! And since this trove of propaganda is likely to have played a big role in Hitler's rise to power, one has to presume the Nazis wanted to save it for future use."

"What's the subject matter?"

"The art exalts German ideals and fosters patriotism to the extreme. And as you might have guessed, it goes so far as to advance racial purity."

Claire winced at the notion of eugenics and ethnic cleansing. These were foul words, especially given what Hermione Brigstock had recounted in lurid detail. Plus, more and more headlines about places like Dachau and Auschwitz. were emerging.

"Put simply, and I hate to say it because it's insulting, the German folk were brainwashed." Scott's hands had balled into fists in his lap. "First there was Hitler's decree promising national pride, national unity, and national purity. Then came this plethora of art commissioned by his stable of nobodies, containing Hitler's latent messages of German glory. This phony art was intended to transcend Germany's 1930s reality."

"That reality being a downtrodden people overwhelmed by the Depression and the unfairness of the Versailles Treaty, right?"

"Bingo!" Scott slapped the table and beamed. "But Hitler was also priming his people for his ulterior motive." He sighed heavily. "The extermination of Jews."

Claire shook her head in dismay.

"Judging by the sheer number of those pieces discovered in Merkers, Herr Hitler obviously had to build an enormous museum. He named it the German House of Art and every year he hosted Great German Art Exhibitions for the entire country. The government even provided passes for those who couldn't afford the train fare to come to Berlin and visit Hitler's cultural sites."

"Goodness!" Claire exclaimed.

"By doing this, art was no longer solely the province of wealthy and educated city dwellers but was available to the farmers as well. Everyone got to see how magnificent Germany was."

"What does this art depict?" Claire asked.

"Heroics à la Greek or Roman Gods, depictions of the Fatherland's lofty and fertile landscapes . . . but here's the rub. Instead of using propaganda to exacerbate attitudes directed outwardly toward an enemy, Hitler's art was turned inward toward his own people."

"That's vile."

"Recognizing that Germans were a beleaguered people, needing a boost to their morale, he saw an opportunity and seized upon it. Hitler fed the people an exaggerated myth of German greatness. He gave them what everyone hungered for and was eager to swallow. He commissioned art for the purpose of inspiring German national pride."

"In and of itself, that's not such a bad thing," Claire said. "All governments should instill pride in their citizens."

"Yes, but while on the surface this credo was manna from heaven to a downtrodden people, Hitler's message of hope and change, plus German invincibility, served a more dreadful and hidden purpose." Scott was so agitated he paused to take a few breaths. "Hitler stoked the German *Volk* to such rapture, to believing they as a nation could do absolutely no wrong, they came to regard their Führer as above reproach." Scott hesitated, then lowered his voice to a mere whisper. "Little did folks know, but it opened the door to wipe out an entire race."

"At the time all we knew was that Hitler wanted to unite Germany and seize control of all Europe. That he intended to eradicate the Jewish population came later."

Scott's eyes glistened with tears ready to spill. "Shit, I'm too worked up to continue. Forgive me."

"Of course," Claire soothed. She massaged Scott's shoulders in sympathy. *Poor man,* she thought. *When you know as much as he obviously does, it's hard to avoid the pain of so much horror. No wonder people like me bury their heads in the sand.* She watched him struggle to rein in his emotions.

"How 'bout we go visit Montmartre, and you have your portrait done by one of those street artists the area is so famous for?"

Grateful for the distraction, he said with gusto, "Let's go!"

Chapter Forty-Nine

Perhaps it was that second glass of Bordeaux which had loosened her tongue. Or maybe it was because Scott made her feel safe, and that's why Claire opened up on their way to Montmartre.

"I'm compelled to confess that when Germany invaded Poland and then France in 1940, I couldn't have been less sympathetic. My attitude was war was a madman's folly. I was against all of it, so I became a non-interventionist."

"Ah, an America Firster," Scott said. "A lot of folks felt that way."

"I was selfish, Scott. That woman I told you about? Hermione Brigstock? She's the one who informed me with her eyewitness experience, but you've enlightened me even more. Why it's taken me so long to truly absorb all that human suffering, I'm ashamed to say."

"Don't beat yourself up. After all, the news was just a trickle. It was only after the Allies landed at Normandy that we got the full measure of the Nazi atrocities. And that was barely a year ago."

Claire appreciated his forbearance. "My point is while so much death, starvation, and terror ruled in Europe, we Americans were going to fashion shows and the theatre, kvetching about the dearth of French perfume and nylon stockings."

"Totally normal. Maybe you were in denial because you were

protecting yourself against the possibilities of it coming to your doorstep."

"Yes, but even after my worst fears did happen and I went through the grieving, I focused on *my* loneliness, *my* isolation. I blamed FDR. I hated him for what he got us into; hated what he did to me. I demanded God explain why he was punishing me."

Not unkindly, Scott chuckled at Claire's outburst. "Where are you heading with all this guilt? You aren't Catholic, are you?" He snapped his mouth shut, clearly surprised. "Forgive me, that was rude."

"No, it's okay. I'm actually a renounced Catholic. And formally so, I might add. Since excommunicating myself from the church, I've decided one only feels guilt if one subscribes to it." She paused. "Which is a hard habit to break, but I'm working on it."

"May I ask a personal question? You don't have to answer if you don't want." Scott was suddenly very earnest. He reached for her hand when she consented. "What was your husband like?"

Claire took a moment to gather her thoughts. Should she be truthful and run the risk of Scott possibly feeling diminished, or should she fudge on the details? She opted for the facts. "Billy was handsome, charming, and rich. He was a gifted artist, decent tennis player, and all-around charmer. . ."

Scott remained quiet, though Claire did notice that his eyebrows had shot up.

"I married him for the wrong reasons."

"And what were those?" he asked.

"Oh dear. You had to ask, didn't you?" Claire gulped, then continued haltingly. "I was desperate to climb out of the hole I grew up in. Billy was my ticket out. I don't think I knew that at the time, but since his death I've had lots of time to reflect on the past and my poor choices. Time to be honest with myself." Claire squirmed. She was about to be brutally honest. "Billy was a superficial bon vivant and I compromised myself. Not that there was anything wrong with being happy-go-lucky, but he wasn't an intellect with any meaningful conversation to offer. When the fun and games were over, there was no counterbalance. He was more of a physical, action-oriented type. I'm a reader and like to talk." She smiled nervously at Scott. "Can't you tell?" Claire couldn't bring herself to confide the bit about not telling Billy she was infertile. It was still too soon to share that bit of news with Scott.

"Well, he did stand up for his country, did he not?" Claire could only imagine what Scott was thinking; that he'd feel challenged by a dead man with whose memory he might have to compete.

"He did, and now, after the fact, unfortunately, I'm proud of him for enlisting." Claire exhaled. "What I want to add is that I'm done drowning in grief. In spite of it all, I'm ready to breathe again. Not be a numb zombie unable to get up in the morning." She surveyed Scott's face. Deciding it was best to get off the topic of Billy, she abruptly said, "Gosh, I do love those laugh lines around your eyes."

"Sure you do." Scott patted her knee. "Anyway, it seems you've coped with your bereavement very well." He stroked her cheek and gazed at her appreciatively. "It couldn't have been easy." He hesitated. "And if you'll permit me to admit, I'm glad you dropped the America Firster mantle. If you hadn't, we might not have found common ground."

"And that would have been a great pity."

"You're beautiful."

Brushing away the compliment, she said, "My shame for being so clueless will never be assuaged unless I contribute to the war effort." Claire's prettily arched brows scrunched into a web of deep grooves. "I don't think I'll ever have closure until I do my part to help our exiting boys get home, visit the death camps, and see for myself the ravaged towns and cities of western Europe."

"That's the ticket."

"I've got a question. About the Nazi propaganda art. If there's stuff in the Merkers Mine, then who's to say there isn't more stashed somewhere else?"

"Uh-huh." Scott pulled Claire away from a group of troops milling about on the steps of the Sacré-Coeur. Scott seemed to be holding his cards close.

"I want to help you find all of it. It needs to be destroyed!"

"I'm going to take you into my confidence, and don't you dare breathe a word of this." He looked around to make sure no one was eavesdropping. "Generals Eisenhower, Patton, and Bradley have unanimously agreed the propaganda found at Merkers needs to be confiscated immediately. Sent Stateside."

He chose not to expand on the potential for a Fourth Reich, but he said, "We think there's more out there, too. In Austria, possibly Poland." Scott looked over his shoulder again. "With the discovery of the preserved propaganda art, we're pretty certain the Germans are trying to protect it for use in the future."

Claire began to pace in place. "So, I was right, after all." She grinned. "Do you suppose they'd go so far as to stash it somewhere *outside* Germany?"

"You're really something else, Claire. You should consider becoming a CIA analyst."

"You flatter me too much." Reflexively, Claire shook out her hair. "But seriously, the Germans could hide it in Spain or maybe even in South America. Isn't Argentina friendly with them?"

"Very intuitive." He threw his arm around her shoulders. "Walk with me." Scott led Claire up a set of steps that wound around the back of the cathedral. "The Monuments Men have advised the generals that the likelihood of the art being transported by ship or submarine to somewhere in South America is indeed extremely high. Their thinking is that the art will be ferried and hidden along the way until it reaches a harbor. We just don't know yet which harbor."

"Wow." Claire stared into the middle distance, unaware that the pigeons were swarming her feet. "Brest is as good a port of embarkation as any," she supposed aloud.

"We've had our eye on those cargo ships and their manifests for weeks now." Scott steered her away from another batch of troops loitering too near. "On the other hand, they may simply stash it somewhere for a few years and ship it commercially once the world has returned to some semblance of normal."

"Good point," Claire agreed.

"Either way, we need to find it."

Scott lit the candles positioned around their suite at the Paris Hôtel Ritz. Shadows ran up the walls while an ambient light illuminated the soffits overhead. Claire poured wine from a carafe on the sideboard.

When "Night and Day" began to play on the radio, Claire didn't need an invitation to walk into Scott's arms. Her breath quickened as he pulled her in tight. Butterflies fluttered in her stomach and she felt giddy as they slow-danced around the living room of their two-bedroom suite.

"I've Got You Under My Skin" was playing when Scott cupped Claire's cheeks between his palms. Gazing into her eyes, he bent his head to hers and kissed her deeply. "I'm falling for you, Claire Campbell."

Scott twirled her around and capturing her in his embrace again, he whispered in her ear, "I hope you don't mind that I am."

After he poured every ounce of his heart into their next kiss, Claire loosed a sigh as soft as silk and whispered, "I'm falling too, but I think it best I retire to my own room before we regret something."

Had there been one more dance or one more kiss, Claire knew she'd be allowing him to lead her to his bed. She hated seeing the disappointment in his eyes, which moments before had held such desire, but go to her own room she must. It was the right thing to do.

Chapter Fifty

The next morning, Scott was hard-pressed to disturb Claire, she looked so adorable wrapped up under her bed covers. However, he was already late for his rendezvous with a contact, so he was forced to nudge her awake. "I have an appointment," he whispered in her ear, "but sleep. I'll bring up a cup of café au lait when I get back."

Claire didn't lift her head from the pillow, but mumbled, "I'll miss you."

Scott kissed the top of her sleep-tousled head. "And I'll miss you," he echoed, tucking the sheet around her bare shoulder.

Scott strode briskly from the Ritz Hôtel, letting the foot traffic swallow him up in its undertow. Keeping abreast of the Ministère de la Justice on his right and the Place Vendôme on his left, Scott forced himself to contemplate his mission. Meeting Buck Connor in person meant he'd be exposing his own identity, which was always nerve-wracking. Trust in this business was never a given, even if one's co-ordinator up the chain of command had orchestrated the rendezvous. Turning his thoughts back to Claire, he decided that the one thing he did trust was the realization that all he wanted when this business was over was to spend the rest of his life with Claire.

It was a shining morning and everywhere he looked it was like a Monet painting depicting the old *gai Paris*. It occurred to him then that in an ironic if not bizarre sense, he could actually be grateful for the Nazis choosing to preserve its beauty, rather than run it over with their Panzers. They had taken over all the finest establishments as their billets and lived high on the hog. It's where the Allies now resided as they helped Charles De Gaulle restore normalcy. Waiting to cross the Rue Saint Honoré, he gazed across the park where the Louvre loomed large and splendid. The aroma of a pungent blend of dark roasted coffee beans and freshly baked bread filled the air and Scott made note of the boulangerie for when he returned. Two blocks later, he was crossing the Rue de Rivoli and entering the Jardin de Tuileries between the matching statues of Mercury on his winged horse.

Scott found his contact sitting on a bench in front of a Punch and Judy marionette stage.

He was surrounded by children sitting cross-legged on the ground while nannies hovered among the pigeons keeping an eye on their protégés. Scott spotted him immediately for the fact he looked so out of place. In his pseudo-Breton garb of blue and white striped sweater, beret, and blue jeans with the cuffs turned up at the ankle, Buck looked like a fisherman from Hollywood's central casting department.

"You must be Buck Connor." Scott sat down next to Buck.

"Is it really that obvious?" Buck asked, waving his amputated wrist and completely missing Scott's meaning.

Scott gave him a watery smile. "How'd ya lose the hand?"

"A really dumb accident, the details of which I don't care to go into if that's okay by you."

"No need to know." Scott said, staring straight ahead at the puppets, ignoring Buck's sour attitude. "I presume you're right-handed?"

"In other words, 'am I able to fire a gun?'" Scott had no idea why he was behaving so temperamentally. Maybe he was nervous?

"It might come in handy. Yes."

"Perfect scores with a handgun at Dunrobin. Gotta a pass on the rifle."

"Good for you." Scott pulled his pipe from his breast pocket and parked it between his teeth. He searched his pockets for matches, but found none. "Got a light?"

Buck pulled a lighter from his pocket and handed it to Scott. "Mind if I ask, since when was propaganda art such a terrible thing? I mean we had Uncle Sam pointing at us from a zillion posters all over New York."

"That wasn't propaganda," Scott replied. "My understanding is that with every stroke of the brush, Hitler's artists were able to bewitch an entire citizenry into believing Germany was superior and their leader infallible if not invincible."

"I've always been under the impression," Buck parried, "that Germany never considered the first world war over. Wouldn't that have been enough to compel them to regroup? There was no treaty, just a suspension of hostilities, a truce of sorts."

"I see you know your history. There was only an armistice with heavy penalties." Scott couldn't help wonder why this fellow seemed so combative. Weren't they supposed to be teammates in their endeavor to wrest the art from the Germans?

"And along with a grotesque inflation and the worldwide economic depression, Germans were destitute. Like I said, they didn't need a great deal of persuasion."

"Yes, but they were wallowing in such despair," Scott rejoined, "that they needed these cleverly crafted works of art to inspire them into believing that Hitler could indeed provide the German unification and glory they so craved, even deserved."

"I guess I can buy that," Buck said.

"The stash our guys found at Merkers is definitely proof of a pervasive and constant stimulus." Scott tamped out the spent ashes and returned his pipe to his jacket pocket.

"Obviously it was successful. To a point, anyway."

"That's why we need to intercept the art," Scott said. "We can't leave a door open for this stuff to foment another uprising."

"You can't mean another Reich?"

"Anything's possible."

"Seriously? Who's got any blood and treasure left to fight these fuckers all over again?"

"The next generation or the ones after would be my guess." Scott pushed his hair off his brow. "You've seen the news reels, haven't you? The euphoria at those media events was insane. Contagious. Germans experienced a spiritual cohesion so exhilarating they became transfixed!" Spittle formed at the corner of Professor Jeffries' mouth. His eyes flashed anger.

"Whenever I think about Hitler getting away with mesmerizing an entire nation of people, I'm dumbfounded."

"Yeah, me too."

"It's pretty heartbreaking to think an entire population of decent people were duped into becoming unwitting accomplices."

"Yup, and right under their noses, which is what makes these pieces of art so insidious! That the joyful *Weltanschauung* of German greatness would eventually include the annihilation of six million Jews demonstrates how everybody was too bloody beguiled to look beyond the barbed wire—."

Buck ogled a pair of twenty-somethings from head to toe as they approached. He smiled appreciatively at the blonde, who brazenly held his gaze. Once they were past and he had checked their departing backsides, he said, "Man, these French girls are somethin' else." He looked to Scott. "Don't you think so?"

"Naw, I'm kinda partial to just one gal, and she's American."

"To each his own," Buck remarked, shrugging. He pondered what Scott had said about the German population seeming to be unaware of their leader's atrocities. "Given what's happened, I don't imagine anyone's in a big hurry to forgive the Germans."

Scott had grown weary of this back and forth. He considered Buck a bit of a lightweight striving to be grander than he really was. "So, have you seen anything out of the ordinary in Kersaint?"

"Yeah, I've seen stuff." So Buck was going to drag this out. "I followed a guy to a small stone chapel overlooking the cliffs above the English Channel."

Scott sat up a little straighter, instantly alert. "How big was this place?"

"You could probably drive a Deux-Chevaux into it. In other words, tiny."

"So why was he there?"

"Why is anybody anywhere?" Buck was having fun messing with this fellow who seemed so serious—a bona fide square.

"Gimme a break!" Scott had taken an instant disliking to Buck, but who was he to care one way or the other. After all, he was grateful to have an agent positioned in Brittany.

"He met up with another guy, who popped up from the same spit of sand below the chapel and Ernst—that's what he says is his name—had a big ol' key."

"Did you get to see what was inside?" Scott was off the bench now, pushing back his unruly lock of hair. He was shifting his weight from side to side.

"I saw a chapel full of wall-to-wall boxes. Nothing that looked like paintings. They were more like crates—mostly slatted, some metal."

"Oh, my God. Sounds like munitions, maybe gold."

"Gold? Really?"

"Well, if you're on the run from the Allies you need money, no?" Scott didn't expect Buck to answer.

"The next night, Madeleine and I saw Ernst entering the Notre-Dame Chapelle de Kersaint."

"And?" Buck could tell that Scott didn't like having to drag everything out of him. *I like playing at cat and mouse*, he thought mischievously.

"You gonna tell me, Buck?" Scott looked at his watch. By now, Claire was probably awake and wanting that coffee he'd promised her.

"Ernst and his buddy entered through an iron door hidden behind a nest of vines in back of the church which we think leads down to a crypt. They unloaded what sure as hell looked like a shit pile of paintings."

"This is indeed good news." Scott sat back down. "I need you to keep a close eye on both those chapels, as it looks as though Kersaint is the final stop on their itinerary." Scott looked like a colt ready to jump a fence. "That chapel on the cliff so close to the sea has me really intrigued."

"They've got two hiding places," Buck said. "I wonder if that means two jumping-off points."

"Be on the lookout for any additional vehicles. And if you can, get inside and take inventory. I need to know if the art is propaganda or stolen masterpieces." Scott handed him a card. Use Western Union at that address."

"*Nürnberg*? Where the trials are being conducted?" Buck asked.

"Göring will be on the stand, and I want to hear his testimony."

Buck whistled. "What I'd give to be a fly on that wall."

"Your job, Buck, is to determine the Nazis' next move after Kersaint."

"You think it's headed for Spain?" Spain had leaned pro-Axis.

Scott's expression remained impassive. "I'll tell you this much. Your country is counting on you. Intercept that art before it leaves France. Got it?"

"I swore an oath to serve my country. Consider it done."

"Say," Scott extended his hand to shake Buck's. "Tell me you and this Madeleine girl aren't romantic."

"No can do, Professor."

"Oh, boy."

"Yeah, I know."

"Then you'd better watch out. Feelings have a tendency to confuse decisions."

Buck was about to head off when Scott said, "One more thing." He scratched his head behind his ear. "This isn't easy."

"What's that?"

"You're dead, remember?"

"How could I forget?"

"No one has a need to know who you are or what you're up to."

"Yeah, well that can't last forever, ya know."

"For the time being it can. So no grand reveals. Especially to that girlfriend."

"You're the boss," Buck snapped.

"You do understand, I hope, that this art needs to be snatched away without anyone knowing it's our government who's commandeering it, right? Europe is in the throes of getting herself back on her feet. Countries damaged by Germany are very vulnerable at this juncture. If they were to know about this propaganda's existence, they may try to claim some of it for themselves, which in turn would expose them to blackmail or worse."

"Yeah, yeah, yeah. I get it," Buck interrupted. "They don't need to know we have it."

"In a weakened state," Scott continued, "a France or a Belgium might give it back to Germany if they were put under a bunch of pressure."

"Makes sense."

"You are a lone wolf in this, Buck. You were picked because your 'death' made you anonymous, nonexistent." Scott patted Buck on the shoulder. "Stay dead, buddy. Okay?"

The two men parted, Scott heading back the way he'd come and Buck toward the Louvre at the far end of the park. Scott crossed the boulevard to join the queue outside the bakery. Once inside, he was jostled by the bustle of women with their net tote bags and shrill gossiping voices. Baguettes poking out of wicker baskets like arrows from a quiver were too great a temptation to resist, so he took one and tucked it under his arm. When it was finally his turn to order, he chose an assortment of pastries and croissants.

"*Merci, Madame, c'est tout,*" he said. "*Combien cela coûte?*" He was so eager to be on his way, he didn't even blink after the salesgirl told him what it cost. Everyday post-war goods were exorbitantly high what with inflation. He had American dollars to burn for his sweetheart, so he didn't mind. Besides, the art had apparently arrived in Kersaint. And the port of Brest was a mere hour's drive away from there. He now had every reason to believe that that's where the propaganda was going to be loaded into a ship's cargo bay and ferried far away.

As Scott walked back to the hotel, he thanked Larry for finding a mensch like Buck Connor to help capture the Nazi propaganda art. Buck was a last-minute godsend, no question. Given that the European government agencies were still trying to reconstitute themselves after liberation and were in no position to help was actually fortuitous. President Truman had no desire for any European government or the international media to get in their way. Should anyone get their knickers in a knot over America's absconding with the art, albeit dangerous Nazi propaganda, it would only put them on the defensive. For now, the Europeans thought of America as the hero who had rescued them from history's trash heap. Again. Truman wanted to keep it that way. Buck Connor would have to make it happen.

Buck had two errands before heading back to the train station. First, he made his way to the Louvre and purchased a ticket. His goal was to see da Vinci's famous Mona Lisa now that she was no longer in hiding. It was a miracle she hadn't fallen into Göring's greedy hands. As a painter, Buck was eager to see the masterpiece up close, appreciate its genius. On his way up the grand staircase, he hesitated in front of the Venus de Milo. Though imperfect—both her arms were broken off—she was breathtakingly beautiful. A thought occurred to him and so looking down at both his arms, a wry smile blossomed. *I guess I'm pretty lucky. At least I still have one arm in tact.*

Next stop was at a pawn shop on the Left Bank. Church bells tolled the lunch hour as Buck arrived at La Banque Buard. Already, a line of people was forming in the cobblestone courtyard. Ever since VE Day, Parisians had been coming here. They brought what valuables they still possessed to trade for quick cash just to buy food. People of all walks of life, best Buck could tell, stood in line while their children made friends with each other—skipping rope, playing games of marbles, or kicking a soccer ball over the cobblestones. When it was his turn inside, Buck was very specific as to what he wanted and very clear on how much he was willing to pay. Pawnbrokers, after all, were just as hungry as everyone else.

He made his transaction and looked anxiously at his watch. His train was due to depart at four forty-five, and he didn't want to miss it.

Chapter Fifty-One

It was only after Scott had tiptoed from her room and gently closed the door that Claire allowed herself a good cry. She wept for a long, long time. When her tears were spent, she dragged herself to a sitting position. Feeling shaky, but oddly better now that her soul was purged of all the heartache it had carried for so long, she took a few shuddering deep breaths. Dared she believe she might be happy again?

Claire glanced down at her hands clutching the bedcover. Splaying her left hand in front of her face, where her wedding band and engagement ring had once resided, the ghost of a pale outline still remained on her fourth finger. With that silhouette fading, so too was her attachment to Billy's memory.

And here she was now, falling in love with Scott. And so soon, too. The guilt ate away at her. She had once loved Billy, or so she thought. But after so many months, she wasn't sure anymore if she had loved him for the right reasons. Good looks, wealth, and a fancy address weren't everything, after all. Conversation, friendship, and emotional intimacy tended to last a lifetime. With Scott, she was experiencing just those things. Sex hadn't even entered the equation yet. With Billy, it had been a big part of the marriage. That hadn't been such a bad thing except for the fact no emotional or intellectual intimacy had accompanied it. *I'm so confused*, she wailed inwardly.

At the time when Claire's marriage to Billy had begun, Claire had believed they'd be together forever because that's what husbands and wives were supposed to do; in spite of any lying by omission or in spite of not being able to conceive; even in spite of a tour of duty with the army. But Billy had never really come to terms with there being no children; not of his own anyway. Claire wasn't even certain he'd ever truly forgiven her, in which case their future was on shaky ground. His death, however, precluded there being any chance to work through their difficulty. And with all this elapsed time since then, Scott had found his way into Claire's heart.

Hadn't Billy's parents as much as encouraged her to move on, live her life? Surely, that included falling in love again. So, should she feel this guilty? No. After all, guilt was for only those who subscribed to it. Could she finally let go? She thought of Scott, the way his hair seemed to always fall in his eyes, the dimple in his chin, and she said to herself, *I think I can, yes.*

It wasn't really until the Atlantic crossing that Claire had fully embraced her new life. Embarking upon a task which forced her to look outward instead of wallowing in introspection meant, she realized, that she was ready to stand on her own two feet. Her fervent hope for a better life than the one she'd had growing up motherless and with an aunt who made her pay rent was up to her now—not the largesse of a wealthy heir whose raison d'être was to move in rarefied circles. Nevertheless, she would never discount the fact that her life had been made far better because of Billy. In fact, one could say it was because of him she was here now, in Paris, and falling in love with a truly good man. Scott seemed to like her as much as he might love her. And that was the best foundation for a long and lasting love.

Up until last night, Claire's feelings for Scott had been an exercise in denial, but now lying here with the sensation of his kiss still on her lips, she felt the full impact of her desire. There could be no denying it any longer. She was in love with him.

When Claire heard the key turn in the lock, her heart skipped a beat. Scott appeared in the doorway, beaming. She leapt out of bed and ran to him. What was it that came over her whenever he was near? She couldn't give it a name, having never experienced anything like this before. He was a safe haven. And indeed, he was a force of nature like no other. Not because he was dreamy-looking or a legacy heir, but because he was smart, down to earth, and dependable. He was genuine. She held her breath as she tilted her head back to let his lips kiss hers.

It was dark when Claire climbed into the taxi, streetlights casting yellow pools on the Champs Élysées. Scott was escorting her to the Gare de Lyon so they could have a few more precious moments together before she left for Nice. Claire's Red Cross cohorts—Betty, Frances, and Carol—had gone ahead to secure a compartment and buy provisions for the long and slow journey south.

As the lovebirds travelled across Paris, victory flags fluttered in the wind from street lamps and almost every window. This was a city still berserk with joy after being liberated from Nazi tyranny.

"Can't you just imagine the sheer elation?" Claire mused. "Cheering crowds, folks singing the Marseillaise, cars honking their horns . . . I swear I can hear it still echoing down these avenues. It must have been utterly insane."

"Indeed," Scott said softly, squeezing her hand. He was preoccupied.

"Church bells tolling, a racket of whoops and song, and applause..." Claire's eyes shone. "I wish we could have been here with the French, caught up in their euphoria... I know I would have besieged the marching ranks of soldiers with flowers and kisses."

"It must have been the happiest bedlam ever," Scott agreed. "A far cry from the flatline reaction our American boys experienced onboard our ship coming over. When they realized the celebration wasn't yet theirs to cheer, they must have been devastated."

Claire nodded. "What will become of them?"

"They'll be reassigned to the islands in the Pacific, but a lot will beg to stay here to help with the reconstitution of the formerly occupied countries. It'll take a while for our guys to demobilize and return stateside."

"I guess that's what the Red Cross has planned for us girls," Claire said. "My billet is for two years."

"You're gonna be awesome at making the fellas forget they're not back home yet," Scott mused. There was just a hint of a lament in his voice.

"You'll visit me, won't you?" Claire said, turning to face him. "Surely the Nürnberg Trials will give everyone a day or two off?"

"I imagine I'll find a way. Maybe, you and I can furlough together. How does a sweep through Switzerland sound?"

"Terribly grand!" Claire cheered. "But I'll go anywhere if it's with you." Claire dropped her head on Scott's shoulder. Tears had begun to pool in her eyes, and she didn't want him to see her being a poor pitiful Pearl, so she bit the inside of her cheek to keep them at bay.

"Would you look at that!" Scott exclaimed. The taxi was pulling up to the Gare de Lyon, a massive train station, with a clock tower atop one of its corners similar in design to Big Ben on London's Houses of Parliament. Claire bent low and angled her head to catch sight of it in the foreground of a setting sun.

"Isn't this where Le Train Bleu restaurant is? I'd love to see that Albert Maignan painting. It's famous, you know. Let's have an apéritif?"

"Darling, we barely have time to get you onto your train." He looked at his watch. "We must hurry."

Claire hid her pout and allowed herself to be propelled into the great hall of the Paris-to-Lyon Railway Station. She was grateful for her Red Cross companions' offer to lug her gear here so that she could not be burdened now as she ran-walked down the platform. Up ahead, Carol was hanging from the window of the fourth rail car, waving frantically. The conductor was shouting, *"Aux voitures!"*— to your cars— and blowing his shrill little whistle.

Scott stopped at the door to her car and pulled Claire into his arms. The two kissed long and deeply while a rain of catcalls tumbled all around them. When Claire finally opened her eyes, she blushed and started to turn away, but Scott gently moved her face back to face his. Her eyes were brimming with tears and he, too, fought to keep his own from falling.

"I've never felt this way before." He swallowed hard. "Promise, Claire, you'll write."

She drew back and stared at him in wonder. "You, Scott Jeffries, are a beautiful man. You live right here." She placed the palm of his hand across her heart, held his eyes with her own for a long moment, and then turned quickly and disappeared into the train.

Not a minute later, the train began to snake its way out of the station and Claire, too overwhelmed with emotion to twitter with the other girls, pressed her forehead against the windowpane.

Humanity—a blur of shapes, sizes, and colors—streaked by. One among the throng with a Panama hat pulled low over his eyes and cheeks covered in whiskers the color of shale, looked oddly familiar. For a second, she thought he even resembled Billy. He wore blue jeans and a striped sweater with the sleeves scrunched up to the elbows and he was carrying a bespeckled artist's box and duffel bag in one hand. Tucked under his other arm was a rolled-up newspaper. *No, that can't be Billy. He's dead.* As the man disappeared from view, Claire sighed, feeling sorry for him. She'd grown up around sorrow, but there was no getting used to how this war had made so many children orphans, so many women widows. And so many men amputees.

Madeleine

May - June 1945

Chapter Fifty-Two

It was mid-morning when the fog began to roll across the Little Beach and the château's solitary tower poked its head above the brume, a veritable fairy-tale image of a castle floating in the sky. As Madeleine sat watching the white ruffled edges of the waves fold on themselves in a hypnotizing sequence of watery whispers, Buck was busy sealing and priming his canvas. Unscrewing the tubes of oil paint with his teeth, Buck squeezed thumbnail-sized smudges of primary colors onto his wooden palette: red, yellow, and blue. Then extending his arm toward Madeleine till it was straight, he held his paintbrush vertically and closed one eye to measure her face for the correct scale as it would appear on the canvas. His eyes darted from subject to easel and back again as he strove to get the proportions right. Madeleine would be his Mona Lisa.

Madeleine squirmed on the warm blanket, then re-settling into a more comfortable pose, she slid her toes into the sand. Not ten seconds later, she plucked a conch from the sand and held it to her ear. When she began to blow it like a trumpet, Buck ordered her to sit still. Chastened, she batted her eyelashes and looked down.

"Yes!" Buck exclaimed, "hold it right there. That's perfect." There was a flurry of strokes where neither spoke, he focused on his canvas and she wondering if her pregnancy showed yet.

Eventually, Buck remarked. "My dad insisted I get over my

passion for art, quit trying to be Monet and come work for him at his bank."

"And did you?" Madeleine asked looking into Buck's eyes, ever the brilliant blue.

"Yup. Until I enlisted, anyway." Buck extended the brush in her direction again. "I hated it. Making gobs of money is not my thing."

"What if your paintings sold for a lot?" Madeleine said.

"That'd be different. I'd feel as though I'd earned it." Buck put his palette and brushes down and walked over to where Madeleine sat. Bending over her, he lifted her braid and curled it around the nape of her neck. Unable to resist a kiss, he leaned down further and grazed her lips with his.

"You taste like Benson & Hedges and café au lait," she murmured.

"And you taste like love," Buck crooned, his teeth nibbling her earlobe. When he started to lick her neck, Madeleine pulled the ribbon from her braid and shook loose her flaxen hair. That was too much for Buck. In one swift move, he flipped her onto her back and began to blaze a trail with his tongue down the length of her.

Afterward, Madeleine lay on her side with Buck spooned behind her, a small beach blanket scarcely covering their half-naked bodies. His hand was fanned across her belly. Turning within the circle of his arms so that they were face-to-face, Madeleine said, "I think I'm pregnant."

Buck didn't move. He didn't speak. He simply stared at Madeleine as her news reverberated in his head like an electric charge. As she nodded an encouraging confirmation, Buck's eyes began to fill with tears. With his only hand, he cupped her belly and gazed at her with such tenderness and joy, she knew she'd been right to tell him. As it turned out, this had been the perfect moment to unburden herself. It was more than she could have hoped for. Obviously, Buck was besotted with her and without her having to go into any details, he had instantly believed the baby was his.

Amazingly, not a single lie had crossed her lips.

Chapter Fifty-Three

Another telegram arrived for *le petit oiseau*. It read:

ERNST SCHNEIDER & KLAUS MEILI OPP
TRANSPORTERS STOP
PÈRE GILLES THEIR CONTACT STOP

Annabelle paced. *That little weasel,* she fumed, *so you're the Nazi I've been expecting.*

There was little doubt anymore that Buck Connor had been sent to the right place at the right time and not to any other towns near Brest. And her suspicions about *Père Gilles* were right after all.

Annabelle struck a match and as it hissed to life, she held it to the wick of a candle jammed in a cognac bottle encrusted with wax. Holding the telegram over the flame and watching it as its corners curled inward, Annabelle pondered how best to deal with this traitor. Her priest, of all people. The one person she and her fellow congregants had trusted throughout the war was *Milice*. That anyone from the political paramilitary organization formed by the Vichy to fight against the French Resistance was here in Kersaint was a devastating blow. She'd had no idea how close the danger had been.

Chapter Fifty-Four

"Tell me about this chapel," Buck said, his eyes roaming over the carved trusses under the ceiling.

"Kersaint was once a center for pilgrims," she began. "The legend of Sainte Haude and Saint Tanguy was the basis for their devotions."

"Were they lovers? Like us?" Billy asked, scooting closer.

"Heavens, no. Now just listen. Around 545, Gurguy beheaded his sister with his sword after he heard rumors that she was leading a decadent lifestyle. But following her death, a miracle happened. Haude was seen holding her head in her hands, and when she restored her head on her neck and accused her mother-in-law of being the one who caused her death by spreading the terrible gossip, the old nag died on the spot. As for Gurguy, who'd been forgiven by his sister, he remained so remorseful that he spent forty days making penance, took the name of ‹Tanguy› and atoned for his crime by founding the abbey of Saint-Mathieu."

"Wow! That's all he got?"

"Buck, *arrête*!" She swatted his shoulder. "Anyway, his repentance was so sincere it earned him sainthood. Several lords of the Château de Trémazan proceeded over the years to take the Christian name of Tanguy."

"Is that the story depicted in the stained-glass windows up

there?" Buck pointed above their heads.

"Yes."

"Seems odd that a depiction of fratricide be in a place of worship."

"It's the Gospels' advocating for forgiveness that's important." Madeleine pointed to two statues on the walls of the nave. One was of Sainte Haude holding her head and the other of Tanguy with his Bible and his staff.

Buck and Madeleine sat in silence, she unusually calm.

Buck clasped Madeleine's slender fingers to his chest. "You are the light of my life, the beat of my heart, and I'm crazy about you."

"I'm in love with you too." Madeleine hesitated.

"What's wrong?"

"But will I be in love with the other you? The one whose real identity I haven't met yet?"

Buck scooted closer to Madeleine on the wooden bench. Lifting her chin up so he could look into her eyes, he said earnestly, "You have every right to know the real me. Let's go sit outside in the sun and I'll tell you." They left the church and settled in the grass outside.

"My name is William Campbell, but everybody calls me Billy."

Madeleine let his name roll across her tongue, a hint of a French accent changing the short *i* to a long one. *"Beeely,"* she said with a giggle.

"I'm married." At that, she sat up straight, her eyes ablaze.

Buck grabbed Madeleine's hand before she could rise and take flight. "And I happen to be dead, too."

A shower of French blasphemies ensued. *"Mort? Ce n'est pas possible! Tu es là, quoi."* Dead? That's impossible. You're here. Madeleine tore away from Buck's grasp and loomed over him like a banshee. *"How could you?"* she hurled at him, turning to stomp away.

"Hey, hey, hey!" Buck implored. "Sit down. Hear me out." He looked so pitiful, Madeleine acquiesced.

Dropping onto the grass with a thump and sitting cross-legged, she began to pull large tufts of grass from the ground and throw them in his direction. "Go ahead," she said petulantly.

"I'm a seventh-generation Campbell whose ancestors came over to America on the Mayflower. That probably means absolutely nothing to you, but for Americans it's the closest claim they've got to royalty. For the record, I couldn't care less about it."

Madeleine rolled her eyes. "You told me this already."

"I was married last October after years of being a devout bachelor."

"She must really be *quelque chose*," Madeleine said grudgingly.

"She was, so I'm not going to criticize her to you. She doesn't deserve that." Madeleine frowned. It probably wasn't what Buck wanted to see for a reaction, but *tant pis*. What did he expect? That she be overjoyed by this news? It was only because she loved him that she opted to hear him out. That she needed to pass her baby off as his was secondary.

"Don't be mad, *mon petit choux*," he cajoled, chucking her under the chin. "She thinks I died in that airplane crash over Alaska." Hearing himself say this out loud gave Buck pause. "So do my mother and father."

"That's cruel," Madeleine murmured. "Why would you want them to think that?"

"See this?" Buck shoved his maimed arm up close to her face. She recoiled just enough for Buck to pounce. "Precisely!" he shouted. "This is an abomination that put me in a psych ward for weeks. I wanted to die, not come back like this. What's worse is that while I was being a pathetic and ungrateful crybaby over the loss of half a limb, I had to deal with survivor's guilt. Why did I survive when all my buddies on that plane died? That doesn't make a guy feel good, ya know? I was so ashamed!" Buck's eyes filled with tears. "Can you possibly understand that?"

Madeleine nodded, then shook her head. "I want to, but how can I if I haven't walked in your shoes?" She reached across the space between them and laid her hand over his nub. Buck winced.

"I'm vain, Madeleine. I couldn't bear the idea of returning home to my family who place such enormous value on appearances. Claire was a celebrity model and was always preoccupied with how we as a couple presented ourselves to New York society. As for my mother? I'm ashamed to say she never could tolerate being near anyone who was handicapped. Besides, I really don't want anyone's pity!"

"Goodness."

Buck was heading into brooding territory. "Claire would have constantly harangued me with *I told you so* about enlisting."

"Seems to me you're not giving her much credit. How do you know for sure she'd do that?"

"That's pretty charitable of you to go to her defense." Buck looked rueful. "I don't s'pose I really do know how Claire would respond. We were married less than a year before I enlisted."

Madeleine shook her head. "You should know somebody in a year, I think."

"Well, I didn't or I don't." Buck thought for a second. "Maybe it's because I preferred to play tennis or go skiing rather than hanging around and talking."

"Or making love?" Madeleine tilted her head, ducked her chin, and looked coyly at Buck.

"Guilty as charged." Buck made eyes at her suggestively. "Anyway, my government sorta made the decision by asking me to serve undercover while everyone presumed me dead. According to them, it was the best opportunity for me to become somebody else without having to cover up my real identity. They could call me, Billy Campbell, dead and simply create a new guy from his ashes."

"That's deranged. If I were you, I'd feel a little taken advantage of."

"It's complicated, Madeleine. I needed to do somethin' big for my country, so I didn't mind. What I did in Alaska was not cutting it. Call it ego, I dunno. Plus I had to prove something to myself or my dad. That's my own insecurity, I guess. Bottom line? I allowed them to talk me into this crazy operation, and so here we are."

"You're in quite the pickle."

"I am indeed." Buck seemed relieved. "But I also got to meet you. and I want to spend the rest of my life with you. Not Claire."

Madeleine leaned in to kiss him. "What made you enlist at such a late date?"

"I tried right after Pearl Harbor, but, I couldn't pass the physical due to a slightly shorter leg. But when the Army gets desperate, the requirements are dramatically relaxed. They were willing to take just about anybody in '44."

"How come I think there's an even stronger reason?" Madeleine interjected, suspicious there was a catalyst for his trying again.

Buck looked at her startled. "You know me well."

"You're not hard to read," she countered affectionately.

"Claire lied to me."

"Was she already married, too?"

"Ouch! I guess I deserved that."

"You did. But it was mean of me, so I'm sorry."

"Just listen, okay?" Buck fingered Madeleine's braid. "She neglected to tell me before we were married that she couldn't have children. When I found out, I was crushed."

"Oh." Madeleine couldn't look Buck in the eye, her thoughts racing wildly through her mind. Now she was afraid. Claire's deceit was too close to her own subterfuge. Claire would never be able to give Buck a child. She, on the other hand, was pregnant and definitely could. But not his.

Buck interrupted the madhouse in Madeleine's brain. "You, my sweet, have given me the one thing I've always wanted. A child to love and call my own." Buck grasped the back of Madeleine's head and pulled her face close to his. Tracing her lips with his thumb, he breathed deeply, and then pressed his mouth hard against hers.

When Buck released her, Madeleine murmured, "I love you, Buck-whoever-you-are. And I'm so sorry for how much you have suffered."

Buck dug in his pocket and pulled out a small blue box. He flipped the lid open. Inside, an antique sapphire ring surrounded with ten diamonds glinted in the sunlight. "Madeleine de Beaulieu, will you marry me?"

Madeleine clasped her hands together and stared at the ring, its facets sparkling in a shaft of sunlight. "Are you sure?" she asked. "I mean, I'm not just some little toy you can play with while you're in France?"

"I've never been more sure of anything in my life," Buck replied as he swept Madeleine's plait behind her shoulder. "And in case you're wondering where I got this ring, I was able to purchase it in Paris at one of the many pawn shops that have popped up since the war."

"Well, I didn't think you stole it," Madeleine said smiling. "It's beautiful," she added.

"When I get home, I'll get a quick divorce and then send for you."

"You can do that quickly?"

"I might have to go to Las Vegas or Mexico, but it shouldn't be too difficult. Claire won't want to have anything to do with me once she finds out I faked my death. Shit, she might even go all the way to Mexico herself. And if I give her a generous settlement, she won't have any reason to object. I'll make sure of it."

"What if the baby comes before I can get to the States?"

Unconsciously, Madeleine massaged her midriff.

"Then I'll have you both come over sooner than later and put you up somewhere until everything is settled. How's that sound?"

Madeleine threw herself into Buck's arms.

"I'm putting this bauble on your finger, okay?"

Madeleine slowly extended her left hand, and as he slid the ring onto her ring finger, tears of joy slid down her cheeks. Or were they tears of relief?

Chapter Fifty-Five

Buck and Madeleine crept from their hiding place behind the headstone and began to move low and silent across the cemetery. The moon was ducking in and out as they made their way toward the hidden back door of the chapel. Whenever a cloud snuffed out the moonlight, they took a few more steps in the inky darkness. And whenever the moon's rays fell across their heads, they flattened themselves in the uncut grass.

"You shouldn't be here. Go home," Buck urged.

"Not a chance," Madeleine protested.

When the moon disappeared yet again, there were only twelve feet left to go and they both sprang for where they thought the entrance was located. It took a few tense moments to find the portal hiding behind the thick veil of vines because Buck had to feel for the telltale iron where otherwise there were rows upon rows of cold granite.

"Found it!" Buck breathed softly. With all the might his one arm could muster, he hauled the door open. In front of him lay a set of stone steps descending into an abyss of black. With his only hand, Buck braced himself against the wall, and swallowing back his apprehension, he listened with his ear cocked toward the crypt below. He waited for his eyes to adjust, but the darkness did not recede. Madeleine craned forward over Buck's shoulder to see into the murk. The night was at their backs, and before them, the dank crypt loomed. They huddled together at the top of the stairs, each feeling as though he or she were hanging in spooky abeyance.

Shaking off her jitters, Madeleine urged, " Let's go see. No one's down there."

Buck led the way, gravel stuck to the soles of their shoes crunching underfoot and obliging them to hesitate for fear of being heard. Afraid of whom, though? Père Gilles, long gone to bed? He was a harmless old cleric. Or the skeletal bones from centuries past lying in their catacombs? Maybe the ghosts of Sainte Haude and Saint Tanguy were watching them.

Step by painstaking step, Buck and Madeleine finally reached the bottom of the stairs. Buck, determining it was safe, pulled a candle from his back pocket, and clenching it between his teeth, lit the wick with a Zippo lighter. He held it aloft. The room was close, lined with wooden shelves on which a stash of tins and jugs were haphazardly stored. There were two benches, each against a wall, and on them bed pillows and rumpled blankets. It looked as though there were people who'd taken up residence in this cellar.

Beyond the jugs and jars atop the shelves, Madeleine caught sight of something just outside the candle's flame, Shapes of various widths and heights, stacked like shadows one against another, leaned against the wall. Their bulk loomed large. Suddenly, the candlelight jumped, agitated no doubt by a puff of wind from upstairs and outside. And in that brighter flash, Madeleine glimpsed the curve of a giant head. It was Adolf Hitler in bronze; a cold-blooded, cold-hearted and forbidding face no one would ever forget.

Madeleine screamed. Buck, who hadn't seen it, screamed too.

Suddenly, the floorboards above them in the narthex began to creak. Madeleine gasped and grabbed Buck's arm. They both held their breaths while their eyes traced footsteps hurriedly moving across the ceiling. The floor creaked again, and this time they could hear more than one person's strides, urgent and loud, coming down some wooden steps at the back of the crypt. From an unseen passage, Ernst and Klaus appeared.

Each man had a gun drawn. One Luger was aimed at Madeleine's face, the other at Buck, who immediately slid his own pistol from the holster at his ankle. He aimed it at Klaus. Madeleine brandished a letter opener she'd brought along at the last minute.

Buck was the first to speak. "What you gonna do, Ernst?" The two Germans looked scared, so Buck seeing an opportunity, went on the offensive. "You can torture us. You can kill us. But you won't live to see the new year."

Ernst rolled his eyes. "What do you know?"

"A lot. I'm very familiar with how your Nazi overlords operate."

"So?"

"They kill you, then ask questions after."

"That doesn't make sense," Klaus blurted.

"You're right, it doesn't. But that's how your SS like to do things." Buck kept his eyes trained on Klaus. "You can load up this junk and put it on a ship bound for God-knows-where, but you're dead when the job's done"

"We are good Nazi boys."

"Good Nazi boys whose days are numbered." Buck looked to Madeleine, his seeming composure inviting her to take a similar tack.

"He's absolutely right," she said. "If I were you, I'd save yourselves."

"Shut up!"

"Suit yourself, but I guarantee you the SS could not care less about a couple of nobody-delivery men," Madeleine said.

"You're just saying that. You know nothing."

"Think about it, Ernst," Buck jumped in. "You both know too much." Buck and Madeleine waited for that to sink in. "They aren't going to want you walking around with that big a secret to possibly tell. Let's say you're drunk or being bribed. What if you're caught by the French and they decide to torture you." Ernst and Klaus exchanged worried looks. "To your higher-ups, you're worth more to them if you're dead."

"It's what always happens to couriers," Claire threw in. *"Auf Wiedersehen!"*

Buck pressed the point. "Besides, there's no life for you back in Germany. Your cities are blown to smithereens. Your people are near to starvation, and if you like to live outside in the dead of winter . . .well, good luck!"

"So me und Klaus will stay here. Simple."

"Not a good idea," Buck said. "You stick around these parts, the French will make a public mockery of you. They'll shave your heads, rub your faces in shit, and piss on you."

Madeleine nodded her head vigorously. "He's not joking. I've seen them do it over in Ploudalmézeau."

"Why are you saying such terrible things?"

"Because it's happening. Not just to you men but your women, too. Anybody who collaborated with the Nazi regime is fodder for French retribution. Can you not understand that?"

Madeleine piled on. "It's a feeding frenzy right now. We're trying to help you." The presence of any German still hanging around was a miasma destined to the trash heap. It was a miracle that the Kersaint folk hadn't yet pounced on Ernst and Klaus.

Madeleine sensed the Nazi boys were weighing their options, their resolve weakening by hunger and thirst and having to hide in this dank and spooky crypt. An hour or so had passed, and all of them heard Klaus' stomach grumble. "If you think you can look forward to a Schnitzel and Kartoffel Salat when you run back to the Fatherland," Madeleine said, "think again."

And Buck, pleased with her brand of torment, scoffed, "You'll go back home where it'll be worse than after the first war. There'll be no jobs. Everybody will be hungry. You won't even think twice of ripping a piece of five-day-old bread from a starving child. You'll be sitting on a curb and begging like a dog."

"… and there won't be any handouts," Madeleine warned.

"Stop!" Ernst bellowed.

Klaus spoke. "They have a point, Ernst. What if going back isn't such a good idea?"

"*Dumme Esel*, where would we go?

"I told you we'd be killed at the end of this, but you wouldn't listen."

"Captor ambivalence is a captive's advantage," whispered Buck to Madeleine.

Suddenly, a flurry of steps could be heard coming down the steps. It sounded as though a couple of women were talking in whispers. "Shh!" one of them hushed the other.

Everyone's eyes swiveled in the direction of the voices. No one breathed.

Madeleine sat up straight. Presuming it was her mother on the other side of the door, she shouted. "They've got guns! Don't come any further."

"Are you all right?" Annabelle called.

"Oui, Maman." She scrubbed tears away from her face. "We're with Ernst and Klaus."

Suddenly, Ernst lunged for Madeleine, but Buck blocked him just in time.

"Help is on the way, darling."

"You see?" Buck pounced. "They know you're here. They'll be waiting at all the exits. If you kill us, you'll be hanged just outside this church. If you manage to get out of here alive, your *Kommandant* will track you down and shoot you anyway. Do you wanna take that chance?"

Madeleine looked at Buck with wonder. How was it he could think so fast in such a tense moment?

"Let us live, and I'll make sure you do too."

Ernst and Klaus bent their heads together. "How so?" Ernst asked.

"If you escort this art all the way to the United States with my men, in return the United States government will thank you and put you in a witness protection plan."

"*Was ist das*, a witness protection plan?" Ernst asked, finally lowering his gun and taking a seat on the bench. He looked exhausted.

"You'll be set free with new identities." He motioned to Madeleine to come sit beside him. "Sound good? The two of you can live in peace and quiet, no questions asked."

Ernst looked to Klaus, who was vigorously nodding his head.

"Right then." Buck drew Madeleine closer. "You hand over the art, the munitions, and all the gold—and America will give you a brand-new life. Wha'd'ya say?"

"Can we each have one gold bar to get us started with something in our pockets?"

"I think that can be arranged," Buck said with zero confidence.

"Then we'll wait for your men to make the arrangements and stay here tonight."

Keeping his gun trained on them, Buck said, "Put your weapons on the ground and step away." Once they complied, he nudged the pistols toward Madeleine with his foot. She picked them up.

"Go!" Ernst shouted. "Before I change my mind."

Buck and Madeleine practically fell over themselves to flee the crypt.

Once outside and panting hard, they stopped to catch their breaths.

"Man, I thought your mother would never come to the church."

"How did she know we were over here in the first place? You

told me to tell no one."

"Because I told her where we were going just before we left the house. You forget she's Résistance. I also said she should call for help if we weren't back within a coupla hours."

Claire

May-June 1945

Chapter Fifty-Six

Shortly after lunch, Red Cross Headquarters telephoned Claire. The austere voice of Harriet Allen rasped, "The Commanding General requests your attendance at dinner tonight."

Claire's back stiffened with suspicion. So many of the men around whom she worked were lonely. On any given day she was asked on a date by at least twenty soldiers. "Would it be rude of me to ask why?"

"It would, but I'll allow for your bad manners just this once." Claire pulled the receiver away from her ear and grimaced at it. "You've been personally selected, and I cannot say by whom because I do not know, to honor the Duke and Duchess of Windsor." Claire fell back against the wall, and for one brief moment considered declining the invitation.

As if reading her mind, Harriet barked, "This is not an invitation, Claire. This is a 'request,' which is as close to an order as you can get."

"Oh."

"Am I understood?"

"Yes, ma'am."

"Be ready curbside at six o'clock. Don't be late."

"Where will I be going?" Claire dared to ask.

Harriet snapped, "Antibes," and hung up.

The quaint marina of Antibes, nestled between Cannes and Nice on the Côte d'Azure was a burgeoning enclave of the very rich and famous. Quickly becoming renowned for two things, its multi-million dollar yachts and luxurious mansions, Antibes boasted a maze-like Old Town encased by sixteenth-century ramparts. Delightfully winding cobbled streets and shaded places ablaze with bougainvillea and fragrant jasmine afforded romantic views of the glistening Mediterranean Sea. The old Château Grimaldi had been bought by the local municipality in 1926 and restored for use as a museum and entertainment venue. It was here that the dinner reception was to take place.

Claire raced up to the third floor where she shared a suite of rooms with Betty, Frances and Carol. "I'm to dine with the Duke and Duchess of Windsor! Can you believe it?" Her roomies squealed their excitement, and thus the afternoon was spent in a haze of what-to-wear, how-to-do-my-hair, and which-shoes-to-put-on. Betty and Fran heated the bath water while Carol suggested a variety of coiffures. Claire ironed her little black dress, reserved for special occasions, and polished her nails a demure pink. By popular vote, three to one, it was determined Claire ought to wear her brand-new Italian-made suede pumps, even if they were a bit tight. Carol loaned her a gold poodle brooch and Frances gave her a pair of gold knots for her ears. Betty suggested she borrow her kid gloves, but Claire declined.

Before leaving, Claire said to her friends, "I can't thank you enough. You gals have been so terribly kind."

Carol mimicked, "You must have a *terribly* good time and we shall all be waiting up no matter how *terribly* late you are."

There were three other Red Cross women already standing at the curb when Claire came outside to wait for the car. She appraised each of them quickly: Sarah Wingert, the Club's R & R Director, was forty-ish with schoolmarm looks and a reticent manner; Claire's Program Director, a thirty-something chatterbox who was a pretty strawberry blonde; and Anne Horsley, whom she did not know, was a manly gal in military dress uniform. She announced with a pure upper-crust British accent that she was the attaché to the duke and duchess.

The four women were taken to the Château Grimaldi by chauffeur in a Rolls Royce. Sliding down the Promenade des Anglais, a glorious boulevard along the Riviera's most celebrated coastline in Nice, they picked up speed outside the city and headed west through the neighboring town of Juan-les-Pins. This was home to the area's first luxury hotel and casino hosting the likes of Charlie Chaplin, F. Scott Fitzgerald, and Marlene Dietrich. After a thirty-minute stretch of empty road and a lengthy discussion on the correct way to greet royalty, they finally came to a stop outside the château. Claire was a mess of nerves. The others seemed unperturbed. As soon as the four women alighted from the Rolls and joined the rest of the party already gathering in the castle courtyard, they were shocked to note they were the only women present.

A line of men quickly formed, and much to Claire's horror, it looked as though the women were going to have to run the gauntlet. Lt. General Clifford Lee, Commander of the Theatre Services Forces in the European Theatre of Operations (ETO), serving directly under General Eisenhower, was the first to greet her. Claire shook his hand, too shy to look at his face, her eyes instead riveted to his chest full of medals and ribbons. Next in the queue was Brigadier General Ratay, Commander of the Delta Base Section, whose growly voice reminded Claire of Commodore Campbell. After a few pleasantries, he ushered her toward the next fellow. This went on for ten more men, all aides and lower-ranking servicemen.

"Psst! What's a girl like you doing in a place like this?"

Claire couldn't restrain a gasp. There stood Scott, all professorial in his wrinkled button-down Brooks Brothers shirt, rumpled blue blazer, khaki slacks, and unpolished Weejuns, one of them missing its copper penny. Feeling heads turn in their direction, Claire resisted the temptation to straighten his collar or smooth his jacket. It would have appeared too familiar, wifely, even. Yet there he was, the unruly lock of hair falling in his eyes. He looked down at Claire with a shared secret hiding behind his lashes and a private smile so bright it was a jolt to her heart.

Claire gasped. "Heavens to Betsy! What are you doing here? Aren't you s'posed to be in Nuremberg?"

She realized too late that she'd sounded rude, but Scott, ever reading her right, joked, "It's swell to see you, too."

A bell jingled from the mezzanine above them and by the looks of the two liveried servants flanking the staircase, it was time to move upstairs toward the dining hall. As Claire and Scott began to climb the sweeping marble steps, Claire's name was called. It was the duchess, replete with her famous smile, string of pearls the size of turtle eggs and a figure as willowy as any Ford Agency model. Claire broke away from Scott and as she approached, the duchess extended her hand.

"My dear girl, how lovely to see you again. Please accept my condolences for the loss of your husband."

"Thank you," stammered Claire, perplexed by this familiarity. "You knew Billy, my husband?"

"The Simpsons and Campbells go way back, dearie. I was at the funeral. Slipped in at the very last moment hoping to go unnoticed. I wanted to pay my respects without a lot of kerfuffle."

Claire had no recollection of the duchess being in attendance, but then she had been in no shape to notice much of anything.

"I completely understand, Your Grace."

"Claire, I insist you call me Wallis." Edward VIII, abdicated King of England, came up alongside them. For the second time that day, Claire thought she'd faint. "Darling, this is Claire Campbell, the young lady whose husband's funeral I attended last winter when

I was in New York."

The duke, as slender as his wife yet looking a bit haggard, extended his hand and smiled graciously. "Yes, I do recall hearing my wife tell me about your husband's accident. Ghastly business, that. My deepest sympathies, my dear."

"Thank you, Your Grace." Claire curtsied and thinking she'd been dismissed when the duke addressed Anne, the attaché, she scurried up the steps to where Scott was waiting patiently on the landing. Seeing her frazzled, he quickly led her over to the balcony overlooking the Mediterranean. He flagged a waiter who was passing with a tray of champagne flutes and taking two, he proffered one, saying, "Down the hatch, sweetheart. Champagne is known to possess great medicinal properties."

Claire did as she was bid and sipped the sparkling wine. "The duchess was at Billy's memorial. Imagine that!"

"Small world!" Scott said cavalierly. "Come, we must find our seats."

They only got a few feet before the duke appeared. "So sorry, old chap, but I've come to escort this lovely widow in to dinner." Scott stepped aside with a small bow.

While the duke looked a little wild-eyed, he was, nevertheless, very charming. Linking Claire's arm across his, he indicated that her seat was at the far end of the room, so with great panache he guided her down the length of the twenty-foot refectory table to her chair. She immediately noticed the place card next to hers. Inscribed in gold calligraphy, it read HRH Edward, Duke of Windsor.

Noticing her surprise, the duke, bent over her shoulder and whispered, "There, there, my dear girl, I'm but a mere mortal. I promise I shan't bite."

Claire giggled self-consciously and sat down in the chair he held for her. Nervously, she smoothed the tablecloth with her two index fingers. *Speak to the person on your right through the first course,* she thought to herself, *and during the second, speak to the one on your left. That's all well and good,* she thought, *but what if one of my dinner companions just happens to have once been the king of England?*

Scott sat across from Claire and when he thought no one was looking, he threw her a wink every now and then. Most of the time, however, he was obliged to converse with the British attaché on his right. At one point Claire overheard the woman say to Scott, "There may not be any Germans left in Nice, but there are scads of Jewish refugees who need help getting out of France. Wouldn't Claire be perfect to handle that effort? After all, she knows all the official channels, the loopholes, and which visas to get and from where. She could really help us to get these poor people to Palestine. I'd be most grateful if you would put in a word for me."

It wasn't until much later when the group had gone to the casino in Juan-les-Pins and Scott was fox-trotting Claire around the dance floor that she learned the attaché wasn't who she said she was. She was actually a member of the SOE.

"Really? Does this have anything to do with you know-what?"

"Yes, and I've been dispatched to Brittany. Want to come?"

"I'd love to, but it takes weeks to secure a furlough."

"Really?" Scott asked all innocent in his demeanor. He stepped back and pulled a document from inside his jacket pocket. It was from Claire's Program Director. "We leave at zero-dark thirty," he said, brushing her nose with his forefinger. "In case you didn't know, that's military speak for just before dawn."

Chapter Fifty-Seven

It was four o'clock in the morning when Scott rushed Claire into his rented Peugeot Cabriolet.

"Why do I detect an element of urgency?"

"Because there is."

"What's wrong?"

"A telegram was waiting for me when we got back last night. Matters have escalated."

"Oh, how so?"

"My man in Brittany has just bagged his pigeon."

"Do you mean—?"

"Yes, but he's being held at gunpoint in a crypt below the Notre-Dame de Kersaint Chapel."

"Good heavens!" Before she could think it through, Claire asked a question to which she knew she'd not get an answer. "How do you know?"

"I'm not at liberty to disclose how I got that information, but I can tell you I fear for the girlfriend who's with him."

"Does this poor man have a name?"

"It's Buck. Buck Connor, but that's not his real name. The girl goes by Madeleine de Beaulieu."

"Gracious me!" Clare exclaimed. "How terrifying. Is this something you should be handling? I mean—."

"I'm trained for this sort of thing, though as you can imagine it's not my favorite circumstance. Originally, the plan was for me to join Buck after he secured the art. My job is to see that it gets out of Nazi hands. Buck was supposed to be the fella who held the Nazis hostage. Not the other way around."

Claire leaned back against the headrest and closed her eyes. After a few moments, she sat back up. "Damn if this war isn't over and a bully of a nation is finally reduced to dust, but its Nazi heart somehow still beats."

Scott cleared his throat, a habit he had when angry or upset. "I hate to admit it, but the determination of these Nazi pricks is impressive."

"Evil isn't supposed to survive." As soon as this statement escaped Claire's lips, she knew it was a callow one of the first order.

"Nothing makes sense anymore."

They drove in silence for a bit, the Mediterranean Sea glistening on their left, the hills of Provence rising to their right.

"You know, Hitler's dead, but there's still no marker erected for his grave. I bet there won't ever be a monument to Hitler."

"At the beginning of the war," Claire confessed, "I had no idea that that puny little nobody would become one of the most ruthless dictators of the twentieth century. If there were any memorial of him, he'd probably be glorified by those who were on his side. Best if his legacy is stricken from the record."

Scott, keeping his eyes on the road, shook his head. "Perhaps you're right in the tangible sense; that there should be no headstone or statue commemorating the bastard. But no one ought ever forget or not know about him in the history books. Humanity must always learn from its past."

"You're right, of course, but we don't seem to do a very good job of it, do we?" she said ruefully.

"I agree with you on that score. Nevertheless, no matter how gory the details, there are always lessons to be learned." Scott was in serious didactic mode. "It's been a shitty four years for us Americans."

Claire squeezed her eyes shut, wondering if she dared to be the first one to say the three little words that neither had yet dared to utter. "We found each other, though." She held her breath. "You know, in spite of everything." The *I-love-you* just wasn't ready to come out.

"In spite of it all. Yes indeed,"

It began to rain. The ta-dump, ta-dump of the windshield wipers was hypnotic enough that Claire found it difficult to keep her eyes open. The girls had kept her up until two in the morning, insisting she relay every detail of the evening with the Windsors.

"Nap. I'll wake you when we get close to Saint Tropez. You won't want to miss it." Grateful for a reprieve, Claire glanced over at Scott, whose gentle eyes were reflecting the city lights of Cannes. *Such a kind man*, she thought.

"You don't mind?"

Glancing at her eyes, which were already at half-mast, he chuckled. "See ya later, pretty lady."

When Claire woke up, Scott was frowning. "That's quite the scowl. What's wrong?" she asked.

"I was just thinking about Buck Connor and how so many of the SOE missions have ended in disaster. Operators who went missing all over France, Belgium, and Luxembourg . . . The Germans did everything they could to stop them, and they were brutal."

"How brutal?" Claire asked before she realized she didn't really want to know the gory details.

"Torture was a favorite of the SS: electrocution, ripping nails out, burning flesh by pouring acid over the prisoners, endless beatings, and waterboarding. The average life expectancy of a radio operator, for instance, was about six weeks."

"How utterly gruesome." Claire's next thought was an obvious one. "Has this Buck person been in France long?"

"I believe he arrived in France in late April." Scott checked the rearview mirror. "I'm afraid his time is up. He's already outlived the statistics."

"What's this Buck fellow like?"

"He's an amateur as far as a typical SOE agent goes. He's wasn't tasked with blowing up a bridge or infiltrating Nazi offices, so it's okay that he was lightly trained."

"I take it if he's in a crypt, he's found the art."

"It would appear so. I shouldn't be telling you any of this."

"Mum's the word," Claire said. "Is this the same fellow you met with in Paris? I never did ask you what he was like."

"Athletic build, blue eyes, and if you ask me, a bit of a Casanova."

"My husband was like that." Almost immediately, she regretted her words. It wouldn't be what Scott wanted to hear. "Dead husband," she corrected. "He had blistering blue eyes. And a lot of swagger."

"Do you still miss him?"

Claire struggled to provide an answer for Scott. Why was one ever drawn to someone? Why one man could be exhilarating and another have a calming effect was a mystery. She rubbed her neck and stretched it one way, then the other. *He wasn't the quiet and steady man you are*, Claire thought to herself, *the man who guides you home to where you feel safe from the vagaries the world throws at you.*

Scott kept his eyes on the road. "Are you stuck between your history with Billy and your feelings for me?"

"If I were truly honest, I'd have to say yes."

Without warning, Scott yanked the car over to the side of the road and turned off the engine. "I don't know how to compete with a dead man," he burst out.

"I'm not asking you to." Tears sprang to Claire's eyes. "All I can tell you is that I was naïve when I married Billy. With each day that has passed, I'm realizing he wasn't right for me—not for the long haul, anyway." She swallowed hard.

"When did you start becoming aware of that?"

"I don't know. Before I met you, if that's what you're looking for." She shook out her auburn waves, a nervous gesture she barely knew she did. "Look, I wanted the wrong things. Okay?"

"Like what?"

"I already told you."

"Convince me you don't still want those things, because I can't give you any of that. Not in a million years." He glared at Claire. "Even if I could afford it, I wouldn't want that life."

"It's not for me either." She thought for a moment. "Meeting a king being the exception, of course." Claire caught a glimpse out the car window of sailboats and yachts bobbing like corks on their moorings in what must have been Saint Tropez's famous Vieux Port, its old harbor. It reminded her of Amagansett. "As for my Campbell way of life, sure, I miss Isabel's Crêpes Suzette, satin sheets, or the pounding surf outside my window . . . but that doesn't compete at all with the kind of genuine camaraderie you and I share. I don't have to pretend with you. It's very comforting, and I—."

Their mouths met over the stick shift, and it seemed to Claire that Scott's kiss was almost desperate. Did he feel as though he were losing her? When he pulled away, he said, "Men are weak and stupid. Including me. We don't know how to love properly. Forgive me, Claire. I should never have doubted you."

"Fiddlesticks! You're neither weak nor stupid," Claire comforted. "I imagine it's very hard to resist comparing yourself with a woman's dead husband. After all, she didn't leave him in anger, as if *Good riddance, you're out of my hair.* She was widowed, left high and dry with no goodbyes."

"I guess that's what's in the back of my mind," Scott said. "I'm sorry. I've been totally selfish." He pressed her hand between his. "Life is like a book. Yours was abruptly cut short."

"Thank you, yes," Claire said, but then added, "A book has many chapters, though."

Claire and Scott found a table at one of the restaurants on the quay. They ordered ham sandwiches made on baguette with butter, Dijon mustard, and cornichons. Coca-Colas and an éclair to share for dessert rounded out the meal. Once they stretched their legs to digest by strolling along a few blocks of the noisy town, they headed back to their car.

Before turning the key in the ignition, Scott mused, "I don't know about you, but every time I gaze out at the sea—it doesn't matter if it's the nth time—it seems like a fresh miracle. The power of an ocean, its depth, its blueness as far as the eye can see. It's overwhelming every time."

"I agree."

"Kinda like falling in love, wouldn't you say?"

Claire reached for Scott's hand and squeezed it tight. "You're such a romantic, Dr. Jeffries."

The long road west and north around Marseille, up to Toulouse, through Nantes and Brest and eventually into the small village of Kersaint took them twelve long hours. With every mile that brought them closer to Brittany, their apprehension for Buck Connor's well-being grew.

Chapter Fifty-Eight

I t was eleven-thirty at night when Scott steered the Peugeot down the sandy lane on the north side of Kersaint. Their headlights sliced eerily through the fog and dark. The ruins of Château de Trémazan loomed, casting long and foreboding shadows. At the fountain in the center of town, Scott turned left and proceeded up the hill to a gravel driveway across the road from the castle. He shut off the ignition. Claire and Scott shared a glance but remained silent. Suddenly, the front door of the cottage was flung open and light from inside spilled into the front yard. Standing tall and almost imperial, Annabelle de Beaulieu's silhouette framed the entrance. She waved them into her home without calling out.

"I presume you're Professor Jeffries? What in God's name took you so long?" Annabelle practically pulled Scott into the house. She gave Claire a very slow up-and-down appraisal. "Who's this?"

"Forgive me," he said quickly. "Madame de Beaulieu, allow me to introduce you to Claire Campbell. She's my translator. She's fluent in French, so I bring her wherever I go." Both surprised and amused by the fib, Claire remained deadpan.

"Well, never mind the French. It's German we need to speak now. There are at least two of them in the church basement with my daughter and our man."

Scott's head jerked up. "Buck Connor?"

331

"Oh, come, now, Professor. Who do you s'pose I mean?" Scott was momentarily at a loss for words. "Well, yes, of course," he stammered.

"You presumed I was a man, *n'est-ce pas?*"

"Frankly, Madame, I did," he said, avoiding eye contact.

As if reading his thoughts, she said, "Don't fret, Professor. Had I not known all along that Buck was one of us, you might not be standing here right now."

Claire chimed in. "Shouldn't we, I mean, I assume they're still—."

"Alive?" Annabelle interrupted. "Yes, they are."

"How do you know, Madame?" asked Scott.

"Sophie, my housekeeper, and I went over to the church and heard two German voices, one of which was Ernst's I believe, and another who, according to SOE, is a Klaus Meili. My daughter heard us on the steps and yelled out to us that they were being held at gunpoint. But you know this already, as I told you on the telephone."

"I thought you were reporting it for someone else. Forgive me, Madame."

Claire couldn't believe Annabelle and Scott were having this conversation. Considering her daughter was being held hostage, this all seemed surreal. "If you'll forgive me, Madame, you seem terribly relaxed."

"Do I?" Annabelle smoothed a hand across her graying blonde head of hair. "It's probably because I know that Buck has hatched a rather ingenious plan." Annabelle actually seemed amused. "Anyway, last time we looked in, Buck was doing a splendid job of talking them into releasing the prop art into our hands."

Claire cleared her throat. "If you've made more than a few trips over there, why haven't you busted it up?"

"My dear," Annabelle said without hiding her condescension, "two old ladies have no business entering a quagmire such as this one. As I've already said, I believe our Mr. Connor is about to lay his hands on the missing art without incident."

"And it was time I take over anyway, is that correct?" Scott pulled an Enfield .38 from inside his waistband. Claire's eyes widened in surprise. She'd had no idea he was carrying a gun.

"You're armed?" Both Scott and Annabelle paid Claire no mind.

"I was informed you'd take receipt of that Nazi trash and see to it that it got on the tanker I requisitioned, which is now anchored in Brest. I've done my part all the way down to giving Buck my last sliver of soap. It's your turn now." Annabelle eyed Claire with suspicion. "As for the gold and munitions stashed up on the cliffs in San Samson's chapel, it's safely under lock and key."

"Shall we go over to the church?" Annabelle ushered them through the kitchen to the back door. As Claire passed the butcher block, Sophie handed her a meat cleaver. A chill ran down her spine.

"You should stay back, Claire," Scott cautioned.

"I've come this far; I might as well keep going," Claire said.

The little group circumvented the disheveled vegetable garden, crawled through an opening in a hedgerow of hawthorn, and single file they half-ran across the meadow to the cemetery behind the chapel.

Scott was the first to see a man and a woman stumble from the back of the church. They hesitated, appearing to be out of breath. As they began to race towards them, arms pumping, Scott braced for an attack. His pistol was drawn, but the girl with the long blond hair flew past him and into Annabelle's arms.

For the reunited Mr. And Mrs. Campbell, the world suddenly lurched to a halt on its axis. While whoops of joy, shouts and tears enlivened the night around them, Claire and Billy locked eyes in stunned disbelief.

In one delirious instant, Claire's muscle memory propelled her into Billy's arms. She cried his name and cupped his cheeks between her palms. She held him tight, stroked his hair and then leaning back and running her hands down his arms as if to convince herself he was really standing there and not a mirage, she came to a place where Billy's arm stopped short. She looked down at his sleeve. It hung flat and empty.

"Oh, God." It was Scott's soft voice off to the side which made Claire turn around. She saw anguish etched across his features. He had figured it out instantly.

Over Claire's shoulder, Billy's eyes met Madeleine's. Tears were running down her cheeks. She, too, had read the situation for what it was.

Claire was the first to break away. "How dare you!" she screamed. Billy spun away, mortified. "Shit!"

"Is that all you've got to say for yourself?" Claire screamed again. She looked at him with incredulity. "You faked your death? In God's name, why?"

"I can explain," Billy began, but Madeleine, who'd untangled herself from her mother's arms and come to stand next to her fiancé, interrupted the moment. It seemed as though she thought he needed defending. She slipped her hand onto the crook of Billy's elbow, and as Claire followed the possessive action with her eyes, she caught sight of the big sapphire on the fourth finger of Madeleine's left hand.

"Oh my God! Are you kidding me? You're engaged? How *could* you?"

"Lemme explain, will ya?" Billy scrubbed a hand through his hair. "It kind of stinks, you know, to have your body survive an airplane crash, minus an arm of course, and then have your government beg you to not only wrest a bunch of propaganda art from the Nazis before it can leave the continent, but in the process also tell your family you're dead." He removed Madeleine's hand from his arm and stepped away. "Don't for one minute think I was happy about any of it."

"Spare me," Claire snapped. "So typical of you to think only of yourself. Have you no concept of how I might have felt?" An emptiness opened inside her that was capable of swallowing the entire universe. "And your parents. What about them?"

"Would you please just give me a chance to . . ."

She spun around. "Get me out of here, Scott." But Scott was nowhere in sight.

"Professor Jeffries has gone to secure the art, *ma pauvre*," Annabelle said kindly. "Let me take you back to the house."

Not knowing where to turn, where she could crawl into a hole and hide, Claire accepted the invitation and followed the de Beaulieus and Sophie back to the cottage. The short trip across the meadow, through the hedgerow and into the garden, traipsing after these strangers felt ludicrous. Plus, these were people who were a part of Billy's new life. Nothing was more absurd than sitting across from Madeleine in the salon as Annabelle and Sophie fussed over a pot of tisane.

Claire stared at the walls beyond Madeleine's head, looked up at the ceiling and over to the fireplace. Finally, she cut the silence with false bravado. "Are you in love with him?"

Clearly caught off guard by so blunt a question and coming from the very woman who was still married to her fiancé, Madeleine grappled with an appropriate answer.

"You don't have to deny it," Claire said. "Knowing would simply help me to know what I should do."

Emboldened, Madeleine said, "Love seems like a strong word for someone I've only known for a couple of months." Madeleine said, "but yes, we're crazy about each other."

"So I see." Claire noticed the maternal gesture of Madeleine's hand on her belly but chased her observation away. "A coup de foudre. How typically French. And so terribly Billy."

"Excuse me?"

"I'm sorry, I'm prone to sarcasm. It's rarely helpful, I know." Claire looked around in desperation. She felt trapped. "Is there somewhere I might lie down?"

Annabelle approached with a tray. "You poor dear. It's been quite a shock. Come lie down in my room. I'll bring the tea."

Once the door was closed and she was alone, Claire, who had promised herself she wouldn't cry, did weep a river of tears.

Chapter Fifty-Nine

Claire felt the mattress sink beneath Scott's weight, tilting her toward him. He lifted her feet up onto his lap and now, as she sat up, he proffered her a cup of ersatz coffee. "Talk to me," he said.

An awkward silence rose between them. A tightness in Claire's chest, one she'd never felt before with Scott, throbbed. Throughout the night she'd lain awake, coming to terms with what she needed to do. Now, unexpectedly, she had to confront the one man she'd never had any intention of betraying. She stared past Scott, avoiding his kind gaze, the deep concern written all over his face.

"Look," she said, pointing. "A harvest moon is peeking from behind that cloud." Through the upstairs window of Annabelle's bedroom, they could see the moon's rays stretch across the Bay of Portsall, illuminating all the fishing boats. She looked sheepishly at Scott, obviously not knowing what to say.

And right on cue, as if Scott had read her mind, he said, "You must be utterly flabbergasted."

"That's an understatement." She pulled the covers to her chin. "I can't talk about him just yet. Not my feelings, anyway. Tell me what's happening with the prop art."

"Good enough," Scott replied, patting her knee. "The Finistère gendarmerie have placed the two German boys in temporary custody. They're under lock and key on the pretext of having been

337

arrested for stealing church art." Scott took a sip to wet his voice. "Once my men can get here, Ernst and Klaus will be released to travel with the Nazi propaganda back to the United States. They'll be under tight security every nautical mile."

"Goodness gracious!"

"Madame de Beaulieu commandeered a tanker a while ago in anticipation of our getting our hands on the art before it disappeared into Nazi hiding . . .

"Is this the ingenious plan Billy, I mean Buck, oh shoot, you know who I mean, hatched?"

"Yes, and it's a good one, because otherwise they're toast." Scott slid a finger across his neck. "The price we pay for their releasing the art to us is to give them amnesty back in the States."

"I hope they'll keep their mouths shut."

"We've sweetened the pot with a gold bar each."

"Is that wise?"

"Let's hope. Annabelle is doing the same for Père Gilles, although his silence is virtually guaranteed, given how badly he betrayed the people of Kersaint. He certainly won't want anyone to know what a traitor he is."

"No question they'd slaughter him if they found out." Claire placed her cup on the bedside table.

Both Claire and Scott were at a loss for words, neither one wanting to address the elephant in the room.

Finally, Claire spoke. "I'm not a widow."

"True statement," Scott replied.

"I have no right to be your girl."

"Before you show me the door, Claire, lemme please say my piece." Scott inched his way up the side of the bed to be closer. "The kinship we've developed, the tether of gravity between us, is no less powerful than that moon up there is to earth or earth is to the sun. You know that, don't you?" She marveled at how he could speak so eloquently of the love between them without using those three magical words.

"Well, what *I* was going to say," she replied, "is that we have formed an affinity I never imagined possible. While I know I have no right anymore to tell you that, there is nevertheless an undeniable chemistry between us. Our mutual respect makes my heart sing. So there!"

"What are you saying, Claire?"

"Oh, shoot! I don't know. My mind is in such a jumble." She took a deep breath. "What Billy's done is truly gut-wrenching." Scott tried to interrupt, but Claire stayed him. "All I know is that it will take time to blunt the pain of it. I can't promise you a future with me that won't include that wound."

"That's up to you, what you do with it." Scott reached across the space between them, his palm cradling Claire's cheek. "We all have heartache in our pasts." His soulful brown eyes reflected a tenderness Claire adored.

"It's been my habit to carry around a lot of it," she admitted. "With you, I had hoped not to do that anymore."

"Atta girl!"

Claire could tell Scott had another question on his lips, namely what she was going to tell Buck, but she waved him away before he could get it out.

"If you don't mind, I need to be alone to think." She shot him a watery smile. "Where can I find you later today?"

Madeleine

June 1945

Chapter Sixty

The early-morning sky was lit up in shades of tangerine. Wispy clouds kissed the horizon as the sun's rays stretched across the Channel. The sea was calm.

Not so Madeleine. She was on a mission to speak with Buck, and after going to his atelier at the hotel and finding him gone, she was at a loss to know where to look for him.

By pure chance, Madeleine caught sight of him through the trees. He was about to walk across the harbor to Portsall. It being low tide and the marina drained of its water, this was the best short-cut between Kersaint and its sister village.

"Buck!" she called. "Wait!" He spun around, and not moving toward her, as was his habit, he waited with arms akimbo for her to catch up with him.

"What is it?" he asked impatiently, looking over his shoulder.

"You look angry. Are you mad at me?"

"No, I am not mad at you." He dragged his fingers through his hair. "I'm just preoccupied, that's all."

"I have something I need to tell you," Madeleine said.

"Now's not a good time."

"Why?" Madeleine glanced past him and saw Claire entering the crêperie. "Oh, now I see." She knew her voice sounded accusing, but she couldn't help her tone. "You're meeting your wife for breakfast, aren't you?"

"It's not what you think."

"What am I supposed to think?" Madeleine demanded crossly.

"Look, I'm late. Can what you want to tell me wait?"

"I don't seem to have a choice, now do I?" Madeleine flung her lover a look of reproach, turned, and flounced off the beach.

Claire

June 1945

Chapter Sixty-One

Fat raindrops dimpled the sand while the seagulls huddled under the overturned fishing boats on the beach. Claire looked at Billy and wondered, *Did I ever really see you for what you are instead of what I wanted you to be?* The answer was no.

Seeing him now, facing her across the table at a crêperie in Portsall where they'd decided to meet in public in order to keep things on an even keel, Billy seemed unsteady. This was not the bon vivant Claire once knew. His formerly dark head of hair was streaked with gray. His tanned face was laced with lines across his brow and around his mouth. His blue eyes had turned to asphalt what with all the emotion. He extended a callused hand across the table, and judging by the way Billy looked, Claire knew what he was about to say.

Claire beat him to the punch. *Better to be the one asking for the divorce than being the one asked.* So, in a voice she thought might splinter, she said, "I don't think I can love you anymore."

"I wouldn't love me either." Billy stated flatly. Staring out the window, and without turning to face her, he added, "You deserve better."

Claire studied the man she had married, remembering how they used to be together. Her memories rushed in so furiously it hurt. It had been mostly a physical attraction which had connected them. Yet here he sat in his faded jeans and striped Breton tee, looking every bit the epitome of a *Gentleman's Quarterly* spread about vacationing on a Brittany beach, and she felt nothing but disdain. Not for him as much as for herself. How could she have been so foolish? When Claire bowed her head and covered her face with both hands, Billy scraped his chair back and strode around the table to comfort her. She refused to look up, and when her shoulders started to shake, Billy laid a light kiss on top of her head.

Pulling herself together and blinking through a blur of tears, Claire fumbled for the right words. "I can't think or breathe, I'm still so terribly stunned." Billy handed her his handkerchief. She blew her nose. "Tell me what happened to you in Alaska."

"When the plane hit, a bunch of us guys were playing cards." Billy paused, clearly uncomfortable with the memory. "I was tossed out like a rag doll, and almost immediately there was blackness." He scraped his hand across his face. "I can't be sure if that's because I was unconscious or because I was wedged in a crevasse where it was pitch dark.

"Apparently, on the way down my icy tomb, I broke a bunch of ribs, my collar bone, and had my arm ripped out of its socket." Billy waved his maimed arm.

"How ghastly," Claire uttered.

"My face was pretty banged up on the way down, too. The doctors said I must have ricocheted against the jagged, icy walls."

"How far down was the bottom?" Claire's eyes were as big as dinner plates.

"Oh, no, I only went twenty-five feet or so. What stopped me from going all the way to the bottom was getting wedged in an even narrower spot. My legs were dangling over an abyss that the army rescue team said was another forty feet or so."

"Good heavens!"

"Yeah, that damn wedge saved me, but it also almost killed me."

"How truly horrible." Claire didn't know what else to say. There were no words for such horror.

"When I woke up in an army hospital in Seattle, I didn't know my own name."

"The army told us there were three soldiers unaccounted for. Obviously, the army found you but didn't tell us. Do you have any idea why?"

"Well, hindsight being twenty-twenty, it's probably because they had ulterior motives for the three of us who managed to live."

"What happened to the other two guys?" Claire asked. "Did they become spies, too?"

"No clue," Billy said. "Honestly, I don't know."

Claire mulled that over and then said, "The army found your playing cards and pack of Benson & Hedges."

"Oh?"

"They found your cap, too." Claire couldn't keep her tears at bay. "I have it back home."

Instead of absorbing Claire's anguish with any empathy, Billy said, "I wanted to kill myself. It wasn't right that I made it outta there alive when almost everybody else died."

Claire reflexively reached for his hand and murmured, "No, don't say that."

Billy began to cry.

Claire waited patiently for his torment to ebb, the sight of his misery bringing fresh tears to her own eyes. She had never seen Billy like this. He was so miserable in his contrition that it pulled at her heartstrings, and for a teeny tiny moment, she wondered if she were judging him too harshly.

But then Claire sat up straighter, squared her shoulders, and forced herself to think logically. She was about to say Billy should do the same, when he blurted, "Madeleine's pregnant."

A long, uncomfortable ribbon of silence unspooled between them.

Claire glared at Billy. "Well, then, I guess that takes care of everything." She pushed back from the table, lifted her shoulder bag from the back of her chair and walked out of the restaurant. Standing with her arms crossed against her chest at the walled embankment of Portsall Harbor, she stared out to sea.

When he followed her, she persisted. "I'm more disappointed in me for wanting the wrong things than mad at you for not giving me what I wanted. When we married, what I thought I wanted was love and an intact family. I realize now I wanted an escape from my past and a promise of a rosy future. You were a vehicle to that end. For what it's worth, I did think I loved you. But I was in a rut waiting for life to happen to me instead of my making it happen."

"I don't know what to say," Billy replied.

"Well, I do! We are irreparably different from one another. You're brave. I'm a bit of a coward. Okay, a big coward. You are fit and strong. I don't have an athletic bone in my body. You won't read and I can't resist a book. You're a man of few words. I like to talk. A lot. Your politics are right of center. Mine lean left, although they may be swinging t'other way. You paint. I cannot draw to save my life. Shall I go on?"

"No, that's plenty."

Claire persisted anyway. "You grab at whatever life throws at you and deal with it spontaneously." Billy chuckled. "It's not funny! You drive me crazy how you live life by the seat of your pants." Claire began to pace back and forth. She looked for the man she once loved in the features of this new version of Billy. He was barely there.

"I crave contentment, predictability, two things you cannot provide. And you know what? It's not your fault you can't provide those things. Nor is it my fault I want them." She held up her hand when Billy looked as though he might interrupt. "You thrive on excitement and even danger. Don't try to deny it. Look at what's just happened?

Are you going to tell me that training with the SOE wasn't exciting? That taking on the task of intercepting that vile art didn't stroke your ego? Talking those Germans out of their mission to hide the Nazi art? Don't tell me you didn't enlist in this adventure to impress your father, either." She felt the shadow of recognition in a shift of his body language. "I'm willing to bet you even thought it pretty cool to take on another identity and walk somewhere in the middle of where you ought to be and where you wanted to be until someone came along who told you where that was. Like Madeleine!"

"That's not fair."

Claire spun around. "Maybe not, but you know I'm right." A squad of seagulls shrieked overhead, all of them diving for the same scrap. "When is Madeleine's baby due, anyway?"

Taken aback, Billy answered, "I don't know. Does it matter?"

Claire cocked her head to one side contemplating an unkind response, then shrugged. "I don't suppose it really does. After all, if it's a child you want . . ." Claire swallowed the rest of what she wanted to say.

"Wait, what does *that* mean?"

Not wishing to hurt Billy, Claire chose not to air her suspicions. She surveyed the man she had once loved and for whom she now felt nothing but pity. Billy was not only physically maimed but in love with a girl who was probably pregnant with another man's child. Let him discover the truth for himself.

"How are you planning on re-introducing yourself to Mumsie and the commodore?"

"Yikes! 'Re-introduce'?" Billy swung away and then back. "I haven't thought that far ahead."

"Of course you haven't," Claire said bitterly. "But I'd start, if I were you. Soon."

"What do you think is better? A phone call or just showing up in the library?"

"The latter plan would certainly give them both a heart attack."

"You're so good with words, will you help me?"

"No."

"Maybe a telegram," Billy mused.

"Absolutely not! Billy, for once in your life try to think of the impact your actions have on others."

"You're right."

"And marry the girl if she makes you happy. You are happy, no?" Billy nodded sheepishly. "Then you'll stay in France?"

"Probably."

Claire nodded. "I'll file for the divorce."

Under a darkening sky, the Channel outside the port pounded angry waves. Sea spray was shooting high in the air. Not too far off, a cargo ship steamed eastward, a cloud of seagulls surfing in its wake. Going westward, a container ship appeared to be on a collision course with the cargo ship. Foghorns rumbled as each warned the other to get out of the way.

"That out there is kind of like us," Claire said. Billy looked confused. "Never mind; I see symbolism everywhere. Being a reader, you know."

"I tend to be pretty literal."

"We were always at odds, Billy. You know that."

"I wish we hadn't been."

"Me too, but it's for the best that we move on." Claire wasn't sure how to end the conversation, particularly if she wanted to avoid making a scene.

Billy caught Claire's hand in his. "If you need anything, anything at all, don't hesitate to ask."

"That's big of you," Claire said.

"I mean it," he said. "And if my trust has already been turned over to you, I want you to keep it." Billy's eyes glittered with tears.

"The trust hasn't been settled yet. I'm not sure why it took so long, but that doesn't matter now." The bank and the lawyers had butted up against a snafu with the probate of Billy's will. No one had been able to figure out why. The commodore had stepped in to help and promised to have the estate settled by the time Claire came home from her Red Cross tour of duty. "Anyway, Billy, it's too much. You'll want it for your and Madeleine's future."

"No, it's the right thing to do."

"We'll see, but thank you." Claire said. She started to walk up the quay.

"Claire, wait!" Billy rushed to catch up with her. "Tell me one thing. How do we get back to the people we were before?"

"We don't," she replied.

"Why not?"

"Because we ought to focus on who we can become."

Billy put his hand to Claire's cheek. He traced her jawline with his fingertips. It was so tender a gesture, Claire feared she might burst into tears.

"You were always the better person, Claire. Intelligent, poised, and disciplined . . . I'm afraid you married down." Billy's words were startling. "You deserve someone far better than me, and I sure hope that one day you find him."

All too abruptly, Billy turned and walked away.

Claire watched his retreating back. "I already have," she said softly, "so thank you, Billy."

Madeleine

June 1945

Chapter Sixty-One

The setting sun spread gold and pink across the water. Madeleine sat with Annabelle on the cliffs above the English Channel while gulls and terns settled around them. They waited for Père Gilles, sure he'd come to Saint Samson after reading Annabelle's note.

With her pale-pink scarf draped over her slender shoulders and her knotted, blue-veined hands folded in her lap, Annabelle de Beaulieu wore an expression that was stern. It was a mien in sharp contrast to the serenity surrounding Saint Samson at dusk.

Père Gilles strode toward them, his long, black cassock billowing in his wake. Madeleine thought he looked sinister, with his sleeves fluttering like a raven's wings. In his mid-fifties, Gilles' face bore all the lines of someone much older. Someone, perhaps, who'd labored under a great deal of stress. Nonetheless, his gait indicated he was still strong. Or was it simply the posture of a man unafraid of an old woman and her silly daughter?

"Peace be with you, Madame de Beaulieu, Madeleine." Père Gilles murmured, stopping and making the sign of the cross.

"Codswallop!" Annabelle exclaimed loudly over the thundering tide below the cliffs.

"Pardon?" Père Gilles, Annabelle was surprised to note, seemed genuinely perplexed.

"I'll get straight to it." She stepped forward and jabbed his chest

357

with a gnarled index finger. "You've drunk the nationalist swill of the Third Reich. You are Milice, working for the traitorous Vichy government. How dare you ally yourself with the Nazis! And against us modest fellow villagers."

Père Gilles stumbled back, a look of indignation etched across his face. "Madame, I must protest."

Annabelle would brook no artifice. "How many confessions have you heard over the last five years?" Her breath caught in her throat. "And how many of those poor souls were the very ones the Gestapo dragged away at gunpoint two or three days later?"

"Madame, please . . ."

"You, Gilles, exposed them. For what? Stealing a loaf of bread? Moving about after curfew? Telling a joke about Hitler? Hiding a Jew?"

Père Gilles proceeded to whine an endless loop of denials. "Madame, you are badly mistaken... you might have me confused with someone else . . . in Ploudalmézeau, perhaps. The timing you speak of is surely coincidental."

Annabelle exhaled her disgust. "Gilles. That is your real name, *non*? Are you the keeper of Saint Samson Chapel?"

"Yes, Madame." His eyes slid over to the small granite structure no bigger than a one-car garage. "Why do you ask?"

"What do you keep in there?"

"Nothing, Madame. It's empty. Has been for years. Truly. I check on it every week when I take my walk. No one goes in there. All that's in there is sand. Maybe a few rats."

Methinks the priest doth protest too much, mused Annabelle as she removed a key from the folds of her skirt and inserted it into the lock. After she pushed it open with her hip and turned to face the priest, he wore a look of abject defeat. "Père Gilles, you are a liar and a traitor!"

The priest turned three sheets of pale. "Please, Madame, let me explain."

"Go ahead," she sneered. "I'm curious to hear how imaginative you are, although I fail to comprehend why a village priest has need for Nazi artillery and gold of this magnitude."

"I've been a fool, Madame." Annabelle nodded her head vigorously. "In the beginning, I believed in Herr Hitler's promise to restore Germany to its former greatness. The Versailles Treaty had cheated the Germans out of a decent quality of life . . ."

"Spare me the propaganda, Gilles. Let's not forget they were the attackers the first time." She shook her head. "Is there more?"

"By the time I figured out that my work was only helping to serve Hitler's lunacy, it was too late for me to withdraw. The Gestapo had their hooks in me."

"Is that why you've agreed to store that art presently sitting in your crypt at Notre Dame de Kersaint?"

"You know about that, too?" Gilles made the sign of the cross again, but this time it was for himself.

"I do. How do you suppose I got this key?" She waved it in front of his ashen face. "Your Nazi collaborators, Ernst and Klaus, handed it over."

Gilles looked confused and began to blather. "You must understand, I couldn't withdraw without raising suspicion. I couldn't let my family—I have three sisters and a widowed mother—be persecuted."

"You dare to speak of persecution? For shame!" Annabelle's throat was hoarse, but she continued to shout. "Traitor!"

A blizzard of gulls lifted up and flapped their wings angrily. Annabelle and the priest watched in unison as they took frightened flight over the Channel.

"I should turn you over to the Americans who are already in town. More are on their way, too. Or I can offer you my brand of absolution."

"Sounds like you have something to gain if I cooperate," the priest said. Annabelle wasn't about to tell him that the Americans wanted to keep the location of the propaganda art quiet.

"You have more to lose than I, so I don't think it wise that you play games with me," she warned.

"What are you proposing, Madame?"

"That you take two bars of that gold and disappear." Gilles' eyes lit up.

Annabelle went into the chapel, prepared to pry open one of the crates. "I see you've already helped yourself," she said, coming back outside with only one gold bar in her hand.

"Not me, Madame." He greedily thrust an open palm in front of her.

"Spare me," she scoffed, slamming a bar of gold bullion into his hand.

"May the Lord . . ."

"Oh, do shut up! Your blessings are utterly meaningless." She caught her scarf as the breeze threatened to snatch it away. "You know, Gilles, the greatest hardship a heart can bear is to endlessly wonder about one's own people." She swallowed hard and fought to curb her tears. "To think I trusted you! To realize none of us ever suspected you." She raised her gnarled fist.

The priest opened his mouth to speak and then shut it.

"Espèce de con!" Annabelle screamed.

"Come, Maman. Let's go home," Madeleine coaxed. She linked arms with her mother and led her across the wide expanse atop the cliffs. Neither woman spoke as they passed the smattering of sheep grazing in the tall grass. Nor did either remark upon the setting sun, dramatically large and round, as it made its slow descent into the sea.

"You have something you want to tell me, don't you." Annabelle's question was more a statement.

Madeleine chewed her bottom lip as she contemplated an answer.

Far off, a school of fish jumped, and in its wake concentric circles rippled outward. Madeleine watched until they were reabsorbed.

"I suppose I do," she finally conceded. While deliberately vague, Madeleine badly wanted to nestle within her mother's arms, lay her head on her shoulder and tell her about everything which had happened in Morocco. She was so tired of hiding her condition and her shame.

Annabelle offered no such embrace. "You're pregnant, aren't you?" Again, an assertion, not an inquiry. "Surely this baby isn't Buck's."

"It's not my fault, Maman." Madeleine reached for her mother, but she raised her hand to stop her from seeking any demonstrative consolation. Frustrated that there was to be no affection, no sympathy, Madeleine stomped her foot. "Aboud raped me."

"*Quel horreur!*" Annabelle stopped in her tracks. "I knew nothing good would come of that trip to Morocco. I should never have given my permission." Only after a few moments did Annabelle think to add, "Did he hurt you?"

"Yes, and . . ."

"Hush, not another word." Annabelle touched her daughter's lips with her fingertips. "I mean it. You will put this ugly business behind you right now. And you will marry Buck as soon as possible."

"For God's sake, Maman! He's already married."

Ignoring Madeleine, Annabelle persevered. "Nothing needs to be said about this fiasco in Morocco ever again. Not to me and certainly, not to Buck. Understood?" Madeleine nodded her acquiescence. "And you will marry him, *ma petite*. He's already asked me for your hand."

Chapter Sixty-Two

The storm was gaining strength and the tide was waning, so the currents flowed swiftly in the opposite direction. Buck held Madeleine tight until her tears subsided. "What's going on? Why are you crying?" he asked.

"Oh, I don't know," she sniveled. "You can dream something your whole life and when it actually comes true, it's terrifying."

"You should be happy," he consoled. "I'm free to marry."

"I was so afraid she'd want you back and that you'd want the same."

"Not a chance," Buck said. Waves had begun to slam onto Little Beach with loud booms. Once they flattened into quiet licks of foam, another surge waited offshore. The Channel spray was cold and salty, unseasonably so for June. "Come, let's get you and my son home before the storm."

"What makes you think it's a boy?"

"I just do."

Buck pulled her up and looped an arm around her waist. Together, they walked the sandy lane past the Château Trémazan and the still-abandoned vacation homes. Madeleine clung to him. She didn't let go until they were at her front door. Folding her hands over her belly, she looked into her lover's eyes. "*Je t'adorai jusqu'à la fin de mes jours.*"

"And I you, Madeleine. To the end of my days." He pressed

her close to his body. Salty breezes and the heady aroma of peonies wafted from the garden. "Come to my room after dinner tonight." He flashed his movie-star grin. "We'll make love and then you can tell me what you wanted to tell me earlier. Okay, darling?"

Madeleine froze like a fawn sensing a hunter hidden in his blind.

"Ma chère," he whispered, "What's wrong?" Madeleine shook her head vigorously enough to shake strands of her golden hair from its braid. "Tell me, sweetheart. What's upset you?"

Madeleine lifted her eyes to Buck, the tears ready to spill. His expression was so dear, she had to turn away.

Buck reached for her hand and clasped it against his heart. "I want to help," he said. "You can tell me anything. No matter what it is, I promise I won't get upset." She looked up sharply, as if to test the veracity of what he'd just said in his expression. "Don't you know by now how dear you are to me?"

Madeleine nodded, though her mind was racing. Despite what Annabelle had warned, there didn't seem to be any valid reason to hold back the truth. After all, this gloriously handsome man had pledged his heart to her. Didn't he deserve to know? Claire had misled him and look how she'd been tossed aside. Shouldn't she and Buck start their life together on an honest footing?

Buck tucked Madeleine's hair behind her ear and waited for her to speak. She remained silent. "God, you turn me on!" he declared, suddenly tugging her close to his taut body.

His kisses were hungry. While his hand traveled up and down her back, it eventually found its way under her dress. Buck clutched her bottom, his guttural groans urgent.

Madeleine, all too happy to postpone her confession by distracting Buck with her own desire, responded by pulling him around to the side of the house and wrapping her legs around his waist.

"I'll tell you later. Okay, *chéri?*"

Claire

June 1945

Chapter Sixty-Three

"In recognition and appreciation of the faithful and meritorious performance of humanitarian service overseas in the Second World War as a representative of the American Red Cross, Claire Fitzgerald Campbell is hereby recognized for her outstanding service."

"What in heavens?" Claire stood with her arms akimbo, a funny sight, she knew, given she was in her negligée.

Scott's golden brown eyes shone in the dusky light. "I guess I forgot to give you this." He held a piece of paper out to her. "It's your Red Cross certificate. Signed by President Truman, no less."

"You're kidding!" Claire squealed.

"Come, sit with me," Scott patted the sofa at the foot of his bed. Once again, they were staying at the Paris Ritz in the same two-bedroom suite. He swirled the ice cubes in his cocktail glass. She noticed him swallowing down a gulp of emotion. He seemed nervous.

"Would it be presumptuous of me to hope there's a future for us?" His hand was warm upon her lap. It was a genuine touch, not a greedy one, and it said *I love you* even if he had yet to utter the words themselves. Claire's eyes shone when he put down his drink and took both her hands in his.

"I love you, Claire," he said in deepest earnest. "In case you haven't noticed, I've been smitten since the moment I laid eyes on you." Claire's heart skipped a beat.

Scott bent his head and kissed her deeply. Kissing him back with a passion she'd never felt before, Claire surrendered herself completely.

Scott drew away and taking her face in both his hands, he said, "You're not going to play hard to get anymore, are you?"

"I was never playing hard to get." Claire brushed away the lock of hair which seemed to always fall across Scott's brow. "It's just that I was never a hundred percent sure Billy was dead. If he were still alive, it didn't seem right to be having an affair; especially if he was languishing in a muddy trench or worse, a POW camp." Claire looked into Scott's eyes. "I didn't want to betray him. More importantly, I didn't want to mislead you. You wouldn't have liked it had I started something I couldn't see through." She looked at her hands, which were knitted tightly in her lap. "I, too, have loved you from the moment you stood at the railing of our ship that first night. I just didn't dare admit it to myself."

There was a knock on the door. "*Entrez!*" Scott called. A girl from housekeeping stepped inside.

Scott smiled roguishly at Claire, his brown eyes with their amber flecks twinkling. "Shall I tell the maid to turn down both our beds?"

Claire dipped her chin, looked up at Scott, and said coquettishly. "Just yours, I think."

Afterword

"The Nazis were obsessed with controlling the visual." So says Cora Sol Goldstein, associate professor of political science at California State University, Long Beach. "They used art as propaganda. So it makes sense that in 1945 the Americans had to do something about all the Nazi iconography."

Pursuant to military regulations, "All collections of works of art relating or dedicated to the perpetuation of German Militarism or Nazism will be closed permanently and taken into custody." And so began a concerted effort to de-Nazify Germany and purge the country of its national socialism. Since Germany had contaminated almost an entire continent for over a decade, this goal was essential. Over nine thousand pieces of German propaganda art were brought to the United States. Over the years since then, all but 456 have been returned to Germany. Any images showing Nazi leaders, the Nazi symbol or rune known as the swastika, or overt propaganda have not been returned. Works bearing titles such as "Mass Hanging in a Public Park," "Jewish Prisoners from Ukraine," and "Drunken Russians in Infantry Attack" remain in the United States and are currently under lock and key at the Army's Museum Support Center at Fort Belvoir.

Author's Note & Acknowledgments

First and foremost, this is not a scholarly record of the events leading up to the requisitioning of Nazi Germany's propaganda art. To have assembled such a file would have required more research than was necessary for what primarily here is a love story. Also, the timing of events, as they are narrated, may not be accurate. All the locations, as they relate to the propaganda art, are completely fictitious with the exception of its discovery in the Merkers Mine at the end of the war.

I have huge respect for Rebecca Langley, my original editor. Your insights have been invaluable. Giving me such an honest appraisal of my erstwhile unstructured manuscript set me on the right path. Your encouragement has been everything I needed to give this book its wings.

Alpha reader Kurt Bierkan—husband, friend and helpmate—donated multiple readings to my project. I cannot thank you enough for your patience and devotion. Smooches!

As for Beta readers Sandra Warner, Maureen Taillon and Anna Marie Nelson, I cannot thank you enough for your time and input. Without your keen eyes and amazing attention to detail, this work would certainly have been incomplete.

And last but never least, many thanks to Carolyn Campbell, for teaching me how to create a scene, craft a dialogue, and develop a character. If it weren't for your instilling in me the value of the five senses—sight, sound, smell, taste, and touch— I would never have attempted to write a book, let alone three!

Finally, to my fans: thank you so very much for putting my work on your shelves or electronic readers. It's wonderful people like you who make me want to continue writing. I would love to hear how you enjoyed *In Spite Of It All*. So, please leave a review on the e-Book store where you purchased this novel. Reviews really do help the author.

Questions For Book Club Discussion

How realistic was the characterization? Would you want to meet any of the characters? Did you like them? Hate them?

Who was your favorite character? Least favorite?

If one or more of the characters made a choice which had moral implications, would you have made the same decision? Why or why not?

If you had to choose one lesson that the author was trying to teach us with this story, what would it be?

Which scene struck you the most?

How were the book's images symbolically significant? Do the images help to define the characters?

What did you think of the writing?

What did you think of the length and pace?

How is the relationship between Claire and Billy different from that of Madeleine and Buck?

Did the book end the way you expected?

What did you know about Nazi Propaganda art before you read *In Spite Of It All*? Was your knowledge and understanding of the subject enhanced?

What, if anything, set *In Spite Of It All* apart from others you've read in this World War II genre?

What other books have you read by this author? How do they compare?

What three phrases would you use to summarize this book?

If casting a movie version of *In Spite Of It All*, who would you cast for each character?

CPSIA information can be obtained
at www.ICGtesting.com
Printed in the USA
LVHW031704230122
709153LV00002B/212